Delaney's Ocracoke Cottage

Ethereal Wing BOOKS

Cover design by Diana Baxter.

www.DianaBaxterNovels.com

What readers are saying!

"Diana's Beach Heart Cottage Books captivated me with the first book! She incorporates beach romance and comedy. I'm not sure how she does it, but it works!"
Amy L.

"Beach Heart Cottage had me laughing! I felt as if I were there in the cottage with the characters. Page turners absolutely. Love her books!"
Celia B.

"Mosaic Mermaid left me speechless and in tears. Masterful plot, and I did not see the ending coming. Loved it and her characters come to life."
Debbie M.

"Diana's books leave me wanting more and spellbound. I have read all of them, from beach romance to mystery. She is magic with the pen! You Left Me Once is one of her best books."
Janine K

"I finished You Left Me Once. A true tempest of emotions. A tangled who done it. A great read." Nora P.

"Sapphire Moon was a mystery wrapped up in a romance in upstate New York. I highly recommend this book."
Sarah

Delaney's
Ocracoke Cottage

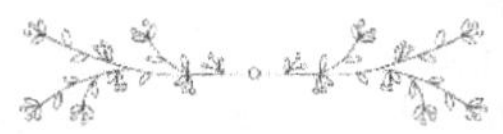

DIANA BAXTER

Listen—shhhh. In the gentle embrace of the night, with the Milky Way gazing down, the ocean waves whisper tender secrets of love. Schools of playful dolphins swim in a mystical dance under the brilliance of the moonlight, giving you a knowing sense that there is something magical on North Carolina's Ocracoke Island.

The velvety beaches reveal a deep truth as you sink your feet into the sand. You feel that this is a place where two hearts can come together as one at Delaney's Cottage.

I

Holding her Uncle Bo's vintage hammer in one hand and a few nails in the other, Delaney carefully descended the creaky wooden ladder. Gazing at the welcome sign she had painted and hung herself, she exclaimed with joy, "Yes!" It now proudly adorned the space above her beach cottage's front door. After tilting her head back and forth, she set the hammer and nails down on a small wicker table, then stepped back and squinted as she voiced her thoughts. "Do I need to put one more nail in on the left side? Nope, it looks perfect, and I welcome myself and all others to relax at the *Sea Gypsy*! A cottage that whispers love and patience." The air was growing dense with heat. Wiping her forehead, she picked up a glass of chilled lemon balm water and took a needed sip.

With wavy dark auburn hair, summer azure blue eyes, and fair skin, Delaney, a gifted woman in her mid-thirties, looked at the sign one more time with a radiating smile. As a self-employed textile designer and artist, she was taken aback when her Uncle Bo passed away three years ago, leaving her his beloved cottage on stunning Ocracoke Island in North Carolina.

After a long sip of the refreshing water and wearing a thankful gaze, she got comfortable in a vintage wicker chair on the deep front porch adorned with weathered vintage gingerbread fretwork that appeared as it did when she was a child. Out in the front yard, the painted white, hand-built arbor, surrounded by lively orange canas, deep cerise tea roses and a crushed shell walkway, called visitors to the bungalow styled cottage.

The painted white flower boxes were bursting with piles of vibrant flowers that spilled over the porch rails. Stuffed with fluffy throw blankets were two rustic woven baskets on either side of the front door that waited to comfort anyone who paid a visit on a chilly night. A few steps to the right hung a wooden porch swing and twin wicker chairs that had graced the space for many years, waiting to hear a visitor's whispers of love, loss, and life. She felt pride knowing this was hers and she could spend time there any time she wanted.

Uncle Bo's sister, Dottie, lived on North Carolina's Hatteras Island and was just a ferryboat ride away. Delaney paid many visits over to Hatteras Island to share laughter and Dottie's enigmatic stories of days gone by. Visits that would open her heart to love.

While on Hatteras, she not only spent time at Dottie's store but also visited the *Sea Glass Retreat,* where she met Dillan and Earl. Soon after, she hired them to renovate her cozy and vintage three-bedroom home, surrounded by a white picket fence. And yes, the place was rundown and a mess. It needed much TLC, and Delaney decided after her breakup with her fiancé that she would pour all her love into the cottage. An everlasting love that would never wound her. A place where her heart was safe, cuddled inside the comforting walls. Hosting modern conveniences, she brought her wonderful childhood memories. Growing up, she had many visits with her family to the beach cottage and fell in love with Ocracoke when she was in diapers!

The expansive yard, bordered by colorful oleanders, stretched from the back porch to the endless views of the Pamlico Sound and distant Portsmouth Island. Schools of playful dolphins frolicked offshore all year long. At night, the stars awakened along with the Milky Way as the water soothed one's heart as it lapped against the sandy shore, and on other nights the glowing full moon lit up the waters as it called one to dream.

This is heaven!

As she glanced at her phone, she noticed it was noon and her two best friends would soon be there for their summer vacation. After looking around, she voiced her thoughts. “There’s no time like the present to clean up the porch and myself!”

Not long after, her phone let her know she had a text she had been waiting for. Her friends were now minutes away. Delaney felt overwhelming joy since they had never been to Ocracoke, and she knew it would be memorable. Wearing her loose khaki shorts and pale pink tee shirt, she gave her best friends a wave as they pulled into the crushed seashell driveway. Wasting no time, she dashed across the front porch, down the three steps, and over to the convertible.

With their heads leaning back, Elisa and Margo inhaled the briny summer sea air before they got out to meet Delaney.

“You made it! Ecstatic is an understatement! It has been too long since we had a girl’s getaway!” Delaney cried out as her face blushed with the love she held for her best friends. Their shared history, from childhood to college, solidified their close relationship. A bond to be tested during their vacation.

“Delaney! This place is amazing! And the ferry ride here was beautiful, and we even saw dolphins!” Elisa gave Delaney a hug and stepped back and looked down to find a chubby calico cat rubbing against her leg. “Hello there, kitty.”

"Good to see both of you. Elisa, I love your hair long, and the color is amazing. Is it copper?"

Elisa smiled as she played with her hair. "Yes, Delaney, a toned-down copper, and I find it's growing on me."

"You look gorgeous!" The cat got on its hind legs and meowed at Delaney, who stooped down and patted the cat. "And that little girl is Lollie Cat, and I apparently am here as her mere servant. She is a stray, and I keep a bowl of food and water out. Sometimes she comes inside the cottage." She ran her hand over the cat's back and up its tail when Margo made her way over.

"Oh, my goodness, Delaney! Has it really been a year since we last saw each other?" Margo exclaimed, her arms wide open as she warmly embraced Delaney. Pulling back, she took hold of both Delaney's and Elisa's hands, her eyes darting around the cottage before returning to Delaney. "This cottage is absolutely stunning—even more beautiful than the photos and videos you've been sharing. It's truly a place that inspires creativity and design for your textiles!" After taking another glance at her surroundings, she added with excitement. "And look at that charming white picket fence! But you know, there's one thing that seems to be missing."

"What would that be?" Delaney, wearing a light smile, lifted her shoulders, knowing what was coming. Ignoring it was not an option because she had always dreamed of it.

"A lover!" Margo teased. "Come on, look at this place! It's so cliché, you know — the cozy vintage house, an arbor, a white picket fence, a Volvo in the driveway and a few kids running amok. You know, just like a scene out of a Hallmark movie."

Elisa added with an animated tease. "A light rain begins to fall as your brawny man swoops you up off your feet. He carries you inside the cottage, and you make love endlessly as the drizzle turns into a downpour tapping on the window as lightning and thunder roll in from the distance."

"Ha ha. That is quite a visual you have created. Someone has been in the car too long, and I'm convinced Elisa needs a lover or an erotica novel!" Delaney crossed her arms. She did not want to hear her ex's name, Hunter, mentioned. "That was once my dream life that became a nightmare, so can we leave it be?"

Elisa knew better and changed the subject. Why did she bring it up? That was foolish, and she knew better. "Agreed. Are there any single men here?" Clasping her hands, she looked up at the sky. "Please let there be someone."

"There are plenty of tourists! And no Hallmark romance movies or dating for me. Nope. You both know I'm done. I have the cottage, and my business, and that suits me just fine."

"Who can blame you, Delaney? After what that asshole, your ex-fiancé Hunter, did that cheating creep I would much rather have this place, a bicycle, and Lollie Cat!" Elisa said as she realized it was a sore subject, and it was best to keep her thoughts silent.

"How about we get your bags out of the car and inside the cottage!" Delaney suggested as she checked her phone. "It's afternoon, and welcome to Ocracoke wine time at my cottage."

"Wait a sec." Margo gestured towards the open one-car garage, then refocused on Delaney. "Is that a golf cart? Tell me it is."

Delaney nodded as she put her hands in her pockets and rocked from side to side. "Sure is! It was my uncle's, and I had it repaired and painted hot pink with my business logo on the hood. Vintage vibe fir sure, and I use it all the time to go around the island."

Elisa's face was wide with a smile as she went over to the golf cart and turned to Delaney. "Oh yeah! This is going to be one heck of an exciting girl's vacation, so bring it on." Swinging her arms, she made her way over to the garage and stopped. “A pink golf cart, three hot girls sum up to a terrific time.” She continued to walk over to it and pointed. “Bonus! I see it has a cooler built in it and seats four!”

“Yeah, my uncle loved his beer! And fishing. He had a boat we used to go out on, but what happened to it is anyone's guess.”

“I wish I had someone leave me a cottage like this and a golf cart!” Elisa threw her hands up into the air as she turned and walked over to the car. “Time to unload and get settled into my new beachy home.”

Delaney observed her friends while they marveled at the cottage, as they retrieved their bags from the car. Making their way onto the front porch, they came to a halt.

Margo let her bag fall onto the porch floorboards as her stare shifted to the wooden swing. “Is that?” She went over to it and gave it a soft push. “Seriously, this is all quintessential, and I love it! I cannot wait to sit out here at night and watch the stars.”

“Yes, Margo, it’s a special swing, and it holds a story for sure. Months ago, I found it in the back of the garage, behind a pile of folding tables. Surprisingly, it was in decent condition, so I did a little handiwork on it.” Delaney met Margo and brushed her hand over the back of the swing. “See the raised wooden heart in the center of the backrest?”

“Uh, huh?”

“My uncle built the swing and made the heart for his love, and you know me, I had to paint it pink!”

Margo chuckled. “Of course you did, and I love it!”

Delaney swayed like a young girl as her mind drifted. “I’ll never forget that special summer when I was visiting. Gosh, I had to be twelve years old, and the air was so thick with humidity. My uncle had bought one of those small plastic pools for his old hound panting dog named Treg, who sat in it all day. Treg’s thick tail thumped against the walls when he knew I had food! That old hound loved to hang out on this porch with my uncle. He sure was a smelly and drooling mess, but such a sweet dog."

Elisa breathed in a gentle, warm breeze while envisioning what it must have been like as her gaze swept over the property as she spoke. "I can only imagine those were truly wonderful times."

"Gosh, they were. I remember sitting on the swing when I was young, eating homemade strawberry ice cream as tall tales were told out here on the porch. That old dog's eyes watched me as it salivated and would take its paw and tap my leg," Delaney said as she pushed her hair behind her shoulder. "They were so in love."

Elisa narrowed her stare at the swing and back to Delaney. "Who was in love, you and the dog?"

"What? No silly. My uncle and his lady friend. He spoke of her as if she were the only woman in the world. And what a long story, but I know that this cottage was built with love." Delaney's smile found the swing as she spoke. "I may have made some changes, but you can feel the heartfelt love within the cottage walls. A love you will not find too often." She glanced across the street.

Elisa snickered. "Love? Try to find a decent guy these days. I went on a boring date, and this guy spent it on his phone, giggling at videos. Weirdo and I walked out! That was after a few drinks and a delicious meal. See ya! And girls, you can forget the dating sites. What a freak show!"

Margo interrupted the conversation. "Elisa, you and your dating drama. Maybe you will find a sexy surfer while on vacation and frolic in the waves."

"Hmmm … Where is this surfer?" She placed her hand over her brow as she looked around.

Margo directed her chin down the street. "Out there in the ocean. But first, how about you help me with this heavy bag?"

"Sure, and for your information, it's not drama, Margo. This is my life." Elisa's gaze landed on Margo's left ring finger. The square-cut diamond surrounded by rubies engagement ring was over the top bling. With a carefree attitude, she dismissed her worries, confident that her prince would eventually appear.

"I know, sorry. Finding your soulmate is no simple task." Margo forced a sympathetic smile, knowing her dating days were over since she was engaged to be married and have a winter wedding in Vermont. Margo, a soft-spoken and grounded person, was the head chef at a sought-after New York City restaurant. She was adamant about having her cook prepare some of her signature meals during their vacation. She was about to marry the son of the owner of the restaurant. They also owned several restaurant chains in Las Vegas and Chicago.

Elisa, with her bubbly personality, worked as an aspiring esthetician in a high-end, posh salon spa on Long Island, New York. After what she had heard from her hoity toity clients, she learned life can be short and crazy, so enjoy today.

Delaney was beyond thrilled that her friends were staying with her. Being that she was self-employed, owning a small business, working out of her home and living on Ocracoke, she felt her life was a vacation.

"Welcome to the *Sea Gypsy*!" Delaney cheered as she pointed at the newly installed sign above the front door.

Elisa let out a happy "wow" as they stepped inside the quaint cottage.

Margo removed her sunglasses. "Delaney, this is so adorable I feel like I'm inside the dollhouse we played with at your mom's house growing up."

"Wait, did you design this around that dollhouse?" Elisa made her way around the room, adding her approval. "You did. I feel like a ten-year-old, eating your mom's chocolate chip cookies in your bedroom and decorating the dollhouse."

Delaney twisted her hands together. "Terrific memories we have? In keeping with the past, I made my bungalow cottage a replica of the dollhouse! What do you think?"

"What do I think?" Margo ran her hands over the light gold wood and floral wallpapered walls. "No way. This is the pattern we used in the dollhouse! This is the wallpaper pattern that you painted on paper, and we glued it up in the dollhouse. I love it, and when can I move!" She praised as she marveled at the room.

"I recreated the design and had a company make the wallpaper!"

"Delaney, you are incredible. I did not know you could create your own wallpaper." Elisa's eyes roamed. "Where is that dollhouse? Did your mom toss it when she sold the house?"

"Glad you asked." With her index finger, she asked them to follow her to a doorway covered in sage green linen fabric. Delaney pushed the curtains aside. "Ta da! I had this little nook, and it fits perfectly!"

Margo stepped back, covering her mouth as she moved her attention to Elisa, who leaned in. "Look, it's *our* dollhouse!" She cried out and then peeked inside. "Gosh, the popsicle bed I made is still intact with the red felt bedspread. I burned my fingers on that darn glue gun making that bed. And there, side by side, are the plastic couple I took from my parent's wedding cake topper. My mom always wondered where they went! But look how cute they are. Geeze, they have been together in the same position in the popsicle bed for what, twenty-some-years ago. True love!"

Elisa had a puzzled expression on her face when she asked. "How? What? I thought your mom threw the dollhouse away or gave it to a thrift shop when she moved."

"Long story, but the short version is that I found it in a pile in the garage that was headed for the dumpster. Mom was getting ready to move to the retirement village in Florida, and she hired a crew to clean up the house to get it ready to sell. They mistakenly put it in the dumpster pile." Delaney reached inside the dollhouse to adjust a tiny painting on a bathroom wall and continued. "Here's a funny one. My dad, as you know, would toss his hands in the air and grumble as my mom insisted he give his stein beer mug collection to a thrift shop. He begged me to hide them, and I did."

Margo put her hair up in a clip. "That is your dad! He was always hiding stuff from your mom. He loved to flea market as I recall."

"Yes, he did, and I was his accomplice on many of his adventures. I have some of his *stuff* in boxes that he asked me to hold! I asked my mom not to empty my bedroom and allow me to go through it first. But when I got there, it was an empty shell, and the cleaning crew was vacuuming the carpet. She has such OCD with every room being tighty that in her frenzy to pack she must have forgotten to tell them to put the dollhouse aside, and the help never got the word."

Margo brushed her hand over Delaney's arm. "But the best news is you got there in time to find our dollhouse and rescue it. Your mom had to be overwhelmed with packing."

"She was frantic! She boxed up my art supplies and shipped them here. I can still hear her asking if I need new crayons, canvas, textiles, and paints. She was an amazing artist. I have her landscape oil paintings all over the cottage walls, which were also in the dumpster, and still unsure why they were in there, and I did not ask."

Elisa, with her hands over her heart, added. "I assume your mom had her reasons, and thankfully you saved them. And if not for your mom's encouragement in the arts and business world, you wouldn't be where you are now. She sprinkled you with ideas, and it shows. Your place is so filled with her love. It oozes out the moment you walk under the arbor."

Delaney felt a tear find cheek as she gave Elisa a hug. "Thank you." She wiped her tear away and asked. "What do you girls think of the dollhouse? It was in rough shape, kinda like this cottage was."

Margo reached for Delaney's and Elisa's hands. "We share the same sentiment as this dollhouse, which is packed with love and sweet memories!"

2

The afternoon sun was intense as it warmed Elisa while she walked down the backyard to the water. Removing her sandals and wiggling her toes, she let out an *ah* as her feet met the sandy bottom. She turned, placing her hand over her forehead, and called out to Delaney. "This is heaven, no buts about it, and you have a new roommate!" She called out as she ventured further into the water, splashing her feet around.

Delaney, with a bottle of wine and glasses in hand, responded as she made her way to her. "Deal, but first you better put on sunblock!" She sat down on one of the Adirondack chairs and joined Margo. "She never sits still, does she? Remember the winter in Vermont?"

"You mean when she talked us into cross-country skiing on those hilly, winding trails using Elisa's handwritten map and we got lost in the forest for five hours? Plus, we had never skied and fell umpteen times! My butt was so sore for several days. Worse, the sun was setting, and we had to use our phone flashlights to find our way back to the lodge."

"And you swore you heard wolves howling and were about to call 911, adding to that, we had no signal!" Margo shook her head. "Or was it a bear growling in the distance?"

Elisa cupped her hands over her mouth and called out. "They were werewolves!"

"Werewolves, it is!" Delaney yelled back.

With Elisa dancing by the shore, Delaney and Margo raised their wineglasses, cheering and clinking them together.

Moments later, Elisa turned around and aimed her finger toward the thicket on the side of the property as she headed toward Delaney.

"Are those kayaks over on the other side of the cottage by what appears to be a fence?"

Delaney craned her neck to look. "Yup, they need a good hosing, and you can use one of them. I think there are life vests in the shed, and I'm sure they need a good scrubbing. And, uh, on second thought, you had better check for leaks. I bet they have been there for a long time."

"A little duct tape can do miracles. And count me in!" Elisa slid into her sandals and wasted no time as she made a beeline for the kayaks, pushing back the tall grass as she did.

Delaney reminded her that there could be snakes.

Elisa, hearing the comment, stopped, looked around, and then lunged for the kayak.

Margo watched her friend struggle to get the kayak off the rack that was attached to a rickety fence. She reached in and with a second pull, adding a strained grunt, it fell off the fence. She stumbled back, tumbling onto her rear-end as the kayak landed on top of her.

Delaney set her wineglass on a side table and shouted. "Do I need to call 911?"

"We had better go and help her." Margo, in a panicked tone, got up from her chair and shouted. "Elisa! Are you okay?"

"I think so. Yup, all good." She called back as she pushed the kayak off her legs and got up to brush off her shorts. She found a plastic cord attached to the kayak and, with some struggle, she dragged it to the back deck. "Delaney," slightly breathless, she looked at her find and back to her friends. "Where is the hose?"

"Over there on the other side of the house behind the canas." Delaney shifted her attention to her friends' muddy and grass-stained legs. "You really are hell bent going kayaking?"

"You bet! This is my vacation. And there are a few other kayaks over there in the bushes if you lazy butts are interested in joining me." She looked around. "And, uh, what is a cana?"

Delaney directed Elisa's attention over to the lanky yellow and orange flowers. And with that, Elisa was off, pulling the grimy, algae ridden kayak behind her and yelling out that she needed to know where the duct tape is.

"In the garage, top shelf on the left by the golf cart."

Margo sat down and sipped her wine. "Elisa is a fireball. She is high-octane and needs an outlet. This trip is perfect for her to blow off steam."

"I noticed. What is going on?"

Margo inhaled and let it out. "Her new job at the salon is going terrifically. The owner asked her to be a partner since he is opening another salon and spa in Manhattan. She needs to decide by the end of the month."

"Seriously? That is a huge decision."

Margo sat back, crossing her legs. "Yes, but as a partner, he needs her to back it financially too. That is why she is acting this way. I feel for her. I mean, she is a top stylist and worked her way up. Now she can be part of something huge, but the money has her deep in thought. This man is talking franchises."

"She will figure it out, and if meant to be, it will come to fruition."

Margo shook her head. "I know. My David is interested in helping her. But with our wedding coming up, I'm nervous about it. The restaurants are thriving, and the money is flowing in, but as they say, never do business with family or friends."

Delaney sat back, inhaled, and let it out. “A significant decision for sure, and she will know how to proceed. Do you remember when that prominent designer approached me to work for his fashion house, expecting me to sell him my designs without any licensing agreements or royalties?”

“And you were over the moon with excitement.” Elisa put another pillow behind her head. “It then became clear that he intended to steal your designs, create imitations, and then get them licensed.”

“Yes, I was young, naïve and when I told my dad, being he was a journalist for the New York Center paper, he flipped out and told the guy he would do a story on him and his deceptive business. That creep was never heard from again. My dad made some calls and learned he had been shut down for many labor law and tax violations! Even after that, I had to get a lawyer to stop him from infringing on my designs that he kept. What a mess!”

Elisa rested her head back on the pillow. “And then legit people wanted your designs. Look where you are now!”

Delaney's lips curled into a smile. “Yes, and it was difficult. I know Elisa will make the correct decision.” Her gaze went to the side of the cottage. “How about we pull out the other kayaks, join Elisa and spend some time out of the water?”

“Yuck. Are there snakes over there?” Margo scrunched her face.

“We will find out. Come on! You are on vacation on Ocracoke!”

After a struggle, they hosed the muck off the kayaks and themselves.

“I need a shower before we kayak.”

Delaney observed Margo’s muddy legs and shorts. “That you do. How about we clean up, have something to eat, and then head out on the water?”

Elisa was trying on a life jacket. "Pee yew. I agree, and these could use a little cleanup too." She removed it and gave it a full blast with the hose. "I need more than water to clean these." She rubbed a dark stain on the back of the jacket. "They float, I hope!"

Delaney reached for the life jacket. "Just dirty. After lunch, I'll grab some cleaner."

Sitting out on the front porch, they enjoyed a few sandwiches and iced tea when an older woman from across the street waved and called out to Delaney. "I'm making fig jam and will bring ya a batch over later."

Delaney got up and walked down the front porch steps to the open gate of the arbor and crossed the street. She returned with a small basket covered with a blue linen napkin and placed it on a side table.

"Who was that? And whatever is in that basket sure smells yummy."

"That Elisa is my wonderful neighbor, Miss Opal Mae. I love her and call her Miss Opal. She bakes treats and gives them to me often, and her fig jam is yummy off the charts. The old fig trees are growing on her property." She held the basket to her nose. "Delectable. These are coconut chocolate chip cookies, and they are still warm."

Margo peeked into the basket and at Delaney. "A step back in time, and I absolutely love it. You certainly have it made here."

"Living here has been an adjustment for me, and yes, I think I have it made. It had not come without hard work." She pointed to the sign above the door. "*Sea Gypsy*" is what I named the cottage. A place where I can be free by the sea."

Elisa glanced at the sign. "It's so awesome, and I bet you painted it too!"

Delaney's finger met her chin as she struggled over the sign's alignment. “I did paint it!”

“Looks like your neighbor is heading over here.” Margo said as she looked across the street and at Delaney.

“Miss Opal likes to know who is visiting. I mentioned to her that my friends were here. She is being neighborly.” Delaney said as she made her way over to Miss Opal, and hand in hand they walked up onto the porch.

As she welcomed Margo and Elisa, the elderly woman with short gray hair, who was wearing an apron adorned with pears and grapes, offered a sweet smile. “Welcome to Ocracoke! I heard my Delaney is having company.” Miss Opal extended her hand to Delaney. “If ya need anything, please stop over. Tomorrow, I would like to invite you ladies over for supper. 6:00 pm sharp.” Her gaze shifted to Margo and Elisa. “Any friends of Delaney's are welcome at my home.”

“We would love to, Miss Opal. And this is Elisa and Margo. My best friends.” She then introduced Miss Opal.

“I see you girls got those old kayaks off the rickety back fence. They have been hanging around for a long time. If they could tell a story, they would.” She smiled at the group. “I had best be getting back home to finish my fig jam. They are ready to come out of their hot water bath. Bye, ladies.”

“Nice to meet you.” Elisa cheered.

Margo stood up. “It was a pleasure to meet you, Opal Mae, and the cookies you baked smell divine.”

“Enjoy them and please call me Miss Opal. Drop the Mae. I have no idea why my mother added Mae.”

Delaney wore an endearing smile at Miss Opal as helped her down the stairs and across the street. She returned and inhaled. “Those cookies make the porch smell so welcoming. Miss Opal is so sweet and keeps an eye on most of us here on the street. She grew up in that house and loves to bake. Help yourself to a cookie. She is going to want to know if you liked them, and I know she will bake more.”

"Her home is gorgeous." Elisa commented as she got up and helped herself to a cookie. "Is it a Victorian?"

"Yup, a scaled version of a Queen Ann. The inside is so quaint, reminding me of a dollhouse."

Margo finished crunching a few ice cubes and spoke. "What does she mean the kayaks could tell a tale? Kinda creepy. I mean, what happened?"

Delaney watched Miss Opal go inside her home and turned to her friends. "Rumors were that my Uncle Bo and Miss Opal had a fling way back when after her husband died. So that is what my mom told me. Uncle Bo never let her go. He died heartbroken. She too misses him. Sometimes we sip lemonade on her porch, and she reminisces about life back in the day. She has some of the best heartfelt tales, and many took place on my porch swing."

Elisa sat back, crossing her legs. "A fling, you say, in the kayaks and on the porch swing. Let me think about that. Kinky!"

3

After an hour of kayaking around Silver Lake, they paddled over to the beach at Springer's Point to take a break and drink some refreshing water. Elisa and Margo spent some time sea glass and shell hunting and were thrilled when Margo jumped up and down. She had found a piece of black sea glass. They then ventured onto the path near the beach only to discover it took them out to the road. Turning around, they chatted about love and life until they were back at the beach.

Sitting on the beach in a shady area, they cooled off. Delaney had to have some fun and regaled in telling the tale of Blackbeard and how English naval officer, Robert Maynard, beheaded him in November 1718 out in the Pamlico waters near shore. His headless body swam several times around the ship. So, the story goes! And at night, some claim to see him wandering the shore with a lantern in hand, searching for his head. She glanced at the black sea glass Margo had placed on her thigh. "Can I see that piece of glass?"

Margo gave a shrug and handed it over.

Delaney held it up to the sun and rotated it around a few times. She handed it back to Margo. "That is a rare find."

"Rare?" Margo pulled her sunglasses down her slender nose.

"According to legend, finding black sea glass means it originated from a pirate's rum bottle." Delaney's face lit up. "I have an idea. Why not turn it into a pendant for a necklace? It will make for captivating conversation?"

Margo gave a slow nod as she squinted at the glass. "Fabulous idea. Wait to tell my fiancé what I found!"

"Pirates, you say?" Superstitious Elisa was all ears as she focused out on the water and spoke in a low voice. "I think it's getting late. We should get back before Blackbeard wakes up." She stood up and brushed the sand off her bathing suit.

"Seriously? He is not going to rise out of the water and chase you with his lantern. Besides, by now it would be out of oil." Margo snorted as she rubbed her arms. There was a stillness in the muggy air as she paid her attention to Delaney. "My belly is talking! How about we head back and go out to dinner?"

"Ha ha you are a little unnerved, Margo?" Elisa snickered as she pushed her kayak into the water and got inside. "Come on, girls, how about we race!"

Delaney took one glance at Margo, and she dashed into her kayak. The wind was picking up, as was a powerful undercurrent. After struggling to paddle, they made their way to the sandy beach behind Delaney's cottage.

"My arms are killing me." Elisa moaned. "Ouch."

"Elisa, you need a margarita to take the pain away. I can taste the salty rim of the glass." Delaney suggested, then added a pucker.

"Agreed! We need to get cleaned up first." Margo said as she tugged her kayak onto the lawn. She wiped the sweat from the back of her neck. "This was a terrific workout. I go to the gym three times a week, wait tables, stand on my feet for hours at the restaurant, and this was a workout."

"That it is." Delaney felt her shoulders were sore and rubbed them. "I feel it, and it will be worse tomorrow, and that means a double margarita, and I know just the place!"

The women enjoyed dinner and drinks at a local restaurant and headed back to the cottage just as dusk arrived. A crescent moon was visible overhead as the sound of the water rhythmically lapped against the shore. Soft music played as candles flickered while they relaxed on the front porch and spoke of the past.

Margo was enjoying one of Miss Opal's cookies when Delaney appeared on the porch, holding a pitcher of fruity sangria.

"Oh boy, the margaritas are still toying with me, but hey, we are on vacation, and I never do this!" Elisa said as she picked up a glass. "Pour, and I'll regret this in the morning!"

Delaney happily filled everyone's glasses and sat down. "To us girls, may we never get old, and if we do, we will live together here at Delaney's place as the three sea gypsies!"

"Cheers!" Margo held up her glass.

"Hey, looks like Miss Opal has company." Elisa pointed with her chin.

Delaney, being protective of her neighbor, walked over to the edge of the porch and through the petunias in the flower boxes, observed a red sports car park in Miss Opal's driveway. "Hmm..." She saw Miss Opal step outside as a tall, dark-haired man got out of the car and gave her a hug. Hand in hand, they went inside.

"Guess she is not so old!" Elisa, having felt her cocktails kick in, said, adding a grin. "She is a *playyyyer!* And seduces men with her sweet cookies!"

"OMG! Stop that. She spent most of her life as a nurse. I bet he is a family friend. But I have never seen that car," Delaney tapped her glass. "We have a signal and I know she is okay."

"Signal?" Elisa asked just before she sipped her sangria.

"Being the nosy neighbor, aren't I?"

"No, Delaney, you are being a concerned friend. But tell me about the signal?" Elisa said as she watched Delaney.

"If one of us feels unsafe or is in an emergency, we flicker the front porch lights three times."

Elisa scrunched up her face. "Wow. Is this old school or what? We have cell phones."

"I know, but this is Miss Opal's idea. I go with the island flow, and she does not care for her cell phone. Plus, that is the signal she and my uncle used back in the day."

Margo gave a wide stretch as she spoke. "Cell phones or not, she can bake the most delicious cookie." She wasted no time biting into a second one.

Delaney did not want to pry, but in the two years she had been at the cottage, she had never seen Miss Opal entertain a man, and no less a young one. He must be a relative.

As the mosquitoes, known for sucking blood, became active, the women retreated into the cottage. Delaney stayed behind to clean up the front porch. She was blowing out the candles when she looked up at the sliver of the moon that appeared to smile at her. She felt certain that this was the right place for her at this point in her life. A place to create, dream and get her life in order after her fiancé broke it off. Letting her heart heal and the hectic life behind her, she could breathe.

Taking a needed inhale and letting it out, she could feel her uncle's presence. *He was overjoyed that she was fixing up the cottage, and she knew he was watching over her.* She could see his jolly, rosy, sunburned face as he held up a fish in one hand and a can of beer in the other.

As she looked at the porch swing, she pondered what it was like when he was in love with Miss Opal. What secrets had they shared on that swing? The secrets that Miss Opal has tucked into her heart. Maybe one day she will share them.

She said goodnight to her uncle and turned to head inside when the swing swayed.

"Huh." There was no breeze. She made her way to the swing and traced her hand over the pink painted heart and spoke in a soft voice. "One day I hope to sit on this swing next to the person who steals my heart." She gave it a push and went inside.

4

"Too many margaritas and sangria last night. Ugh, what was I thinking?" Elisa mumbled as she shuffled around the kitchen with one hand over her forehead and the other on her stomach. "Coffee. Where's the coffee and the pot?"

Delaney called out from upstairs. "In the Hoosier cabinet by the back door. Look at the upper shelf, and the coffeepot is on the enamel top under the door that slides up. It looks like an accordion."

"Accordion?" Elisa rubbed her sore temples, wishing Delaney was not so loud. "Ugh." First, she needed to find her purse and pop a Tylenol.

Margo strolled into the kitchen, cinching her robe, and faced Elisa. "I love you, but I gotta be honest. You look dreadful. Go chill out on the sofa while I make the coffee?"

Elisa squinted. Every word hurt her head. In agreement, she found the sofa and became comfortable.

The aroma of coffee filled the cottage as Margo handed over a full mug to Elisa, who wasted no time reaching for it.

"This is the medicine I needed. Thanks."

"I told you last night to drink lots of water and eat to absorb all the sangria!"

"Bla bla. I rarely drink. Now I know why. I feel horrible. There are little men banging drums in my head, and sumo wrestlers are in my stomach. Uh oh," she got up with her hand over her mouth and dashed to the bathroom downstairs.

Delaney came down the stairs and paid her attention to Margo. "Is she?"

Margo placed her mug on the coffee table. "Yup, she will feel better once she gets it out of her system. I warned to eat and drink water! Guess what?"

"What?" Delaney asked, looking over her shoulder as she went into the kitchen.

"Sweet Miss Opal across the street still has her handsome guest over there. I hope they saved some of those cookies for us!"

Delaney returned with her mug filled with carrot juice. "And they call me the nosy buddy!" She pushed aside the curtain, sipping her juice as her curious stare landed on the red car. "Hmmm. We had better mind our business." She sat on the sofa, tucking her legs under her rear end as she tapped her mug. "I have never seen a visitor spend the night. Should I go over and make sure she is okay?"

Margo craned her neck to look out the window. "Nope. Wait look! There she is, talking to the handsome stranger on her front porch!"

Delaney popped up and went to the front door and stepped onto the porch and called inside. "Psst—Margo, join me on the porch."

Margo let out an exaggerated yawn. "Sure."

They pretended to be trimming and dead heading a few of the flowers in the porch boxes as they kept an eye on the stranger, who kissed Miss Opal's cheek and then made his way to his car.

Delaney had to know what was going on. At a fast pace, she went down the stairs, along the stone path, to the arbor, and opened the gate.

Miss Opal waved at her as the red car was backing out onto the street

Delaney, waving at Miss Opal and not paying attention, was crossing the street when she tripped over something. She stumbled forward, landed on the back of the car, and screamed. Her mug went flying onto the roof of the car, crashing onto the street.

He slammed on the brakes.

Delaney, still dressed in her cotton pajamas, felt uncertain about her next step after stumbling backward. Her heart skipped a few beats for a moment. A quick glance down and then up reassured her that she was fine, as he was moving at a slow pace.

Margo watched, not sure what to do, while Delaney picked up a piece of the broken mug and went over to the driver, who was getting out of the car.

His face was as red as his car, and his panicked voice asked. "Miss, are you all right? Did I hit you?" His cerulean blue eyes met Delaney's. "I did not see or notice that you were behind me. So very sorry. Do I need to call 911?" His worried eyes trailed her legs to her feet and back up to her face. "I–uh, I was busy waving goodbye to my aunt." He turned to look at Opal's place and back to Delaney, rubbing his forehead. "What a way to start the day!"

Shaken, with her heart racing and embarrassed, she flashed a compulsory smile at the gorgeous creature with two-day stubble in front of her. "It was my fault. I was not paying attention in the bright morning sun, and it looks like the kids were making small wooden jumps for their bikes, and silly me, was not looking and tripped over this piece of wood." The carrot juice was dripping off the trunk and onto her slippers. She looked down and stepped back. "Let me run home and get paper towels to clean the mess I made on your car. I'm so sorry." She stooped down to pick up a few pieces of the mug and stood up, shaken, when she noticed Miss Opal was on her way over.

Miss Opal's voice, filled with fear as she met them. "What happened, Delaney? I thought I heard a scream, and I saw you trip and fall into the back of the car. Are you okay? Do I need to call 911 or take you into town to see the doctor?"

Delaney flashed an uncomfortable grin as she aimed her pointer finger at the wooden boards in the street. "I was coming over to see if you were all right. You are usually up early trimming the roses, and I was *not* paying attention."

Miss Opal glared at the boards scattered in the street and the small handmade bicycle jumps. "Those boys are at it again. Last week they were using boards with nails to see if they could avoid riding over them. I'll call their mother again!" Miss Opal, with her hands on her hips, was not happy as she paid attention to Delaney. "Thank the Lord you were not injured."

The handsome man listened and suggested that he would hose the car off at Aunt Opal's later, and once again did he need to call 911.

Delaney thought she heard him say, *aunt*. Wearing a confused expression, her stare slid over to Miss Opal. "I'm fine. No fussing, please."

"Honey, I meant to tell you I have a guest, since I know how you worry. This is my nephew, Justin, and Justin, this is Delaney, my wonderful neighbor. She lives across the street in Bo's old cottage. Delaney is his niece."

Delaney's surprised eyes looked up at Justin.

Miss Opal, still concerned that Delaney was hurt explained. "Justin is going to help me fix a few things over the summer. This old place needs some loving again, and since my husband passed away, I can no longer do it alone."

Justin, with raised eyebrows, faced Miss Opal and turned to Delaney. "Bo's old place? Well, it's nice to meet you, Delaney. Your Uncle Bo was a great man and taught me how to navigate the waters in his big old boat, and I caught my first red drum with him by my side as we fought to reel it in. I had to be about ten years old back then. Those were the best of times. Sorry to learn he passed a few years back." He directed his attention from Miss Opal to Delaney. "I can tell it has a woman's touch! The place looks fantastic."

Delaney did not hear a word he said as she fidgeted with her hair. All she could see was his face and chiseled jawline as he spoke. He was out of a romance novel, and a naughty one at that. Having no choice but to shake her head, getting back to reality, she sweetly said. "Yes. I am, uh huh," her face warmed as she realized what gobbledygook had just come out of her mouth? *Yes, I am, uh, huh?* She could feel the carrot juice seeping into her slippers.

He studied her and asked. "How about I buy you an iced tea?"

His appearance captivated Delaney, not to mention his physique. And here she was in her carrot juice-stained cotton nightgown. Once she realized how she looked, she covered herself just as Margo came over with a robe. "Juice — it was carrot juice. Yes. Okay. Juice." Once again, gobbledygook words found her.

"Here you go!" Margo eyed Delaney as she gave her the robe, wondering what was going on.

"Thanks, Margo, and this is Justin. He is Miss Opal's nephew." She pointed at his car. "And look what a mess I made. You know me, not paying attention." She gave an uneasy giggle, to Margo's confusion.

Margo could see Delaney was in some sort of daze, since she was one of the most organized-focused people she knew. Adding a soft smile, she inched forward. "Hi, I'm Margo, Delaney's best friend, and I'll be vacationing here at the cottage."

"Nice to meet you, ladies, and, uh, enjoy your vacation, and we better move out of the street. A car and two golf carts are heading this way. And, uh. Maybe I'll see you around." His boyish, sexy smile had Delaney wanting to head over to the local bookstore, *Books to be Red,* and grab a romance novel and pretend he was the main character. His red car would be a chariot to ecstasy. *Get a hold of yourself, Delaney.* She reminded herself as she cinched her robe and removed her soggy slippers.

Miss Opal wore an alarmed expression as she took Delaney's hand and asked once again. "Are you sure we do not need to head into town? I can call the clinic and get you in as an emergency."

Delaney shook her head as her eyes traveled down her legs and bare feet. "Nothing but some juice on my slippers. Thanks anyway. I'm so ashamed that I was not paying attention."

"Delaney,"

"Yes," she faced Justin as her heart was playing a fast game of ping-pong. Was it the encounter? The adrenaline — or was it something else?

He reached into his wallet and handed Delaney his business card. "Please call me if you need anything. I'm heading over to Hatteras today to see an old friend and be back tonight. If you need anything, I can get it while over on Hatteras. Perhaps some Band-Aids? New slippers?" His seductive eyes twinkled as he teased her.

Pursing her lips, she gave a slow nod as she took his card. Her heart jumped when the waiting car and golf cart beeped at them. She wasted no time and stepped back. "Thanks. All is good. No harm was done. Have fun over on Hatteras. And, uh—I have plenty of Band-Aids at home."

He flashed an alluring smile as he got into his car and drove off.

Elisa, with one hand over her forehead and the other on the stomach, walked onto the front porch. The strong rays of the sun made her feel worse, and she let out an exaggerated moan.

Margo excused herself and met Elisa to tell her what all the excitement was about. Elisa moaned again with one eye open and went back inside and found the sofa with Margo trailing behind.

Delaney spent a few minutes chatting with Miss Opal as she cut a few of her chubby blue hydrangeas and handed them to Delaney. "For you! And Justin is going to help me out. As you know, my place is not as young as me!" She said, adding a wink.

"Thanks! I'll put these in water now." With a radiant smile and flowers in hand, Delaney returned to her front porch. She placed the flowers on a side table and sat on the swing, tapping Justin's business card on her thigh as she spoke out load to herself. "That was bizarre! Let me see what this Justin is all about." She lifted the card and learned a little more about the man with a romance novel in his eyes.

5

Elisa was sitting on the back porch sipping ginger ale when Margo met her. "No kayaking today?" She laughed, amused by her friend's pale complexion. "Next time, drink a lot of water while you guzzle down those sangrias."

Elisa squeezed her face. "Ugh, must you remind me? I feel better, but wow, I do not drink, and I won't be doing that again." She held her hand over her stomach. "Now that I'm coherent, what was going on this morning with Delaney and that guy across the street?"

Margo took a quick look over her shoulder and back to Elisa. "Where is Delaney?"

"She went into town, to the market and a farm stand."

"I wish I knew that she was heading out to go shopping. I wanted to go. But my David called me to see how it was going." Her eyes found her engagement ring. "He misses me."

Elisa never cared for David and passed by the comment as she inhaled the briny air and let it out with an ah. "This place is so picturesque. Back to the subject at hand. What was going on across the street?" She rubbed her temples. "My head. Ouch."

Margo told her the details, leaving Elisa to question the encounter. How could he not see her? How could she not see him? Margo explained that faulty timing came into play, and, adding to that, a few kids had left boards in the street.

Elisa finished the last of her ginger ale and pulled her legs to her chest. "Boards in the street? And she never laid eyes on them? Even I saw them from the porch. I think it was a setup."

Margo gave a slight lift to her shoulders. "No doubt he is a hotty and Delaney's neighbor. Hmm, I think I need to move to Ocracoke!"

Elisa reached for Margo's left hand. "Uh hum. Your days of looking are over!"

Delaney returned soon after with bags of fresh produce and groceries. She put a bottle of wine on the kitchen counter just as Elisa was walking inside.

"Yuck. I'll pass on any alcohol for a few days." She peeked inside the bag. "Fresh peaches! My favorite."

Delaney spoke as she removed what was inside the bag. "I thought I would attempt a peach cobbler since the peaches are in season and so juicy."

Margo waltzed into the kitchen. "Did I hear peach cobbler? I would like to help make it. We serve some of the best desserts in New York City at our restaurant." She picked up a few peaches and inhaled their sweet aroma. "Sugary! These are plump, perfect."

Delaney stopped what she was doing, reached inside a cupboard and took out a Pyrex pie plate. "This was Uncle Bo's. Well, I think it was, and you may have the honor of being the first person to bake a pie in it since, I would guess, 1990!"

"Terrific, and what is the occasion?" Margo said as she took the pie plate.

"Glad you asked. We are invited across the street to enjoy dinner and engaging conversation with Miss Opal this evening. Did you forget when she invited us yesterday?"

Elisa tapped her cheek. "Now I recall. I have had a tough day! You know it's time to try that outdoor shower and wash my hair. That will help me feel better."

"The towels are in the linen closet in the upstairs hallway. And toss the towels on the clothesline on the side of the cottage when you are done." Delaney said as she put a quart of carrot juice in the fridge. "There are soaps and lotions in there!"

"Got it! I brought some of the expensive stuff from my salon."

"Thanks! The salty water dries my hair out." Delaney twisted her hair and looked at the ends. "See."

"Time to fix that. I brought my scissors!"

Delaney nodded. "Go take your shower!"

"Time to have beach hair, and I could not care less! My clients pay big bucks to get that look." Elisa fluffed up her hair as she headed for the stairs.

Margo, in a teasing tone, called out. "From the lips of one of New York's top hairstylists!"

Elisa was quick to return the comment. "Be careful. I brought my trimming scissors! Sleep with one eye open, my pretties!" She pretended her fingers were scissors, laughed, and then went upstairs.

Margo picked up a glass and filled it with ice and water. "I think a hangover has been good for our friend. She seems a little less stressed out."

"I agree." Delaney remarked as she finished putting away the remaining groceries.

Margo sat down and looked out the kitchen window and back at Delaney. "Okay, spill the beans. You purposely went outside this morning and be nosy, and maybe, just maybe, that bump into the sexy, mysterious nephew's car was on purpose? In your pajamas! OMG."

Delaney felt a flush warm her cheeks as she placed the empty shopping bags in the pantry and turned to face Margo.

"No way. If it were intentional, I would have brushed my hair and teeth, put on something cute with a summer vibe and a little lip gloss. And there was no way I would enjoy being run over."

Margo twisted her lips as she observed her friend moving around the kitchen and over to the sink, where she squeezed a sponge and started wiping down the countertops.

"I knew it! You are bouncing around!" Margo sat back, satisfied she was correct. "I bet you have binoculars and were spying all night on your neighbor and her guest. At least that is what I would do!" She tapped her index finger on the tabletop.

"You, Miss Smarty Pants, are wrong. And with that, it's almost 3:00, and we must be across the street at 6:00, so I suggest." She picked up the bag of peaches and handed it over to Margo. "You begin your New York peach cobbler while I prepare the cheese and crackers."

Margo got up, took the peaches and rattled off the list of ingredients as Delaney opened a box of crackers when her phone rang. "Huh, it's Dottie."

"Who?" Margo tilted her head as she reached for the butter in the fridge.

"I'll tell you later!" Delaney stepped onto the front porch and paced, keeping her eye on Miss Opal's place. Dottie was talking so loudly that she put her on speakerphone.

"Delaney, I sure am over the moon happy that you are here and close by. Well, a ferry trip to Hatteras. I sure miss your Uncle Bo. He was my oldest brother and best friend. He and my husband used to go out till all hours of the day fishing and telling tales. How about ya stop over real soon and pay a visit? I have a sale going on at the boutique and, heck, for ya it's a welcome gift. Whatever ya want. And I just got in some of the prettiest ruffled dresses you ever saw. Hold on."

Delaney sat down. She could hear voices in the background and Dottie hollering at what she believed was her husband and something about dirtying up her floors and stay away from the cash register. She knew Dottie well and usually had to hold back a chuckle, since she was one of a kind.

"I have returned, honey. I sure hope ya were not upset by my hollering at that man of mine. Once again, the old fart ain't paying attention, tripping over empty boxes."

Delaney looked up at the ceiling and back at her phone, concealing her laughter. "I would love to stop over and pay a visit to my Aunt Dottie."

"Oh, honey, I'll be texting ya in a day and what time is best. I bet you have been busy fixing up Bo's old place. I close my eyes and can see all the good times that were shared on that back porch overlooking the water. We danced until the sand crabs hid from the rising sun. That was back in the day when not too many paid a visit to the island. Quieter times, I assure you. Damn shame that he never married. He was a ladies' man for sure. He was always dapper in my mind — that was when he was not out fishing in his waders."

"I'm sure he was." Delaney said as she went inside and wandered over to a wall in the living room where a collage of framed family photos remained untouched. A fond smile found her heart as she eyed each one. Her gaze stopped at the black-and-white photo resting behind a driftwood frame that she had not noticed before. No way! On the back dock, Uncle Bo and Miss Opal were kissing. A dock that had floated away during a storm. She leaned in and got a better look. Yup, it was them!

"Honey, ya went silent. Are ya all right?" Dottie's tone was concerned. "Delaney?"

"Oh–oh gosh, I'm still here. You had me in a time warp daze of sorts, talking about the past." Delaney made her way out onto the back porch and gazed out to where the dock once sat. "How about I text you with a date and time? I have two friends visiting here. Would it be okay if they stopped in? I would love to take them to Hatteras for a day excursion."

"Golly, the more the merrier. But I cannot give them each a free ruffle dress. What I can do is give a discount on the sale items. Ya know it's a seasonal business and all. What I can give is advice on love, men, caring for feral cats and my old bugger of a husband."

Delaney rolled her eyes and could hear Dottie yell at her husband to shut the door. "Aunt Dottie, that is wonderful, and my friends will understand and enjoy meeting you and your shop."

"Wonderful. That is the best day for me. Oh, and ask Opal to join you girls. It's been too long since I have seen her cheery face." Dottie said.

Delaney strolled into the kitchen to find Margo deep in baking ingredients. "Let me ask my friends and I'll give you a call tomorrow."

"Goodbye, dear. I'll be waiting for your call." She ended the conversation.

Delaney went to put her phone down when Margo asked, "Who is that? And can you peel the peaches? I just parboiled them, and they are in the ice bath."

"Yup." Delaney took a peach out and peeled the skin. "To answer your *who is that?* She is my Aunt Dottie, who lives on Hatteras. She was my Uncle Bo's sister, and she invited us to her shop on Wednesday, and knowing Dottie, there will be a feast in her back-room kitchen area. Her coconut cream cake, she boasts about, is amazing, and she even met the president when he was campaigning down here, and he even took a piece of her cake with him."

Margo lifted her shoulders and had to ask. "Whoa, President Jameson was here?"

"No, on Hatteras. He was visiting a public relations woman who was here on vacation at her family's cottage. Dottie told me the president once had a fling with the PR person, and he came down here to win her love."

Margo's eyes widened. "Wow! I never heard that one."

"Yeah, he asked her to marry him on the night of the election, but rumor has it — and Dottie told me — that the woman ran off to Hatteras and fell in love with another man who lived had a cottage next to hers."

"I never saw that one on the news." Margo said as she reached for the sugar.

"No, it was on the hush. Dottie told me that the woman married the other man, and she recently had a baby! And they live on Hatteras."

Margo opened a drawer to reach for a spoon. "Sounds like a really twisted plot. It will be fun tonight at Miss Opal's. Maybe we can hear more island gossip. And if Dottie's cake is so good maybe she will share the recipe with me."

Elisa walked into the kitchen with a towel on her head, and one wrapped around her body. "What twisted plot? Share what recipe?"

6

Holding the peach cobbler in one hand, Delaney knocked on Miss Opal's front screen door.

In Elisa's hand was a cheese tray, and Margo had two bottles of wine in hers.

"Come on in, girls!" Miss Opal said as she made her way to the door and opened it. "Since when do you knock? My home is always open to you, Delaney." Her gaze shifted over Delaney's shoulder. "And your friends!" She stepped aside as they greeted Miss Opal as they entered the house.

Miss Opal led the way and stopped. "I smell something good." Her stare found the cobbler. "How about we put all of what ya girls brought over in the kitchen and settle in the living room for wine, appetizers, and girl talk?"

"Sounds terrific. And my friend," Delaney moved her chin to Margo, "Margo made the peach cobbler with fresh peaches from the farm stand. She owns one of the best restaurants in New York City."

"Well, now, how about that! It's an honor to have a celebrity chef paying me a visit, and I bet it tastes delicious. It sure has been a long while since I had a cobbler! I have vanilla ice cream too." Miss Opal's face softened as she led the girls into the kitchen. "Put it all over there on that table. Now go on and get comfortable on the sofa."

Delaney put the cobbler down as Elisa placed the cheese tray on the coffee table in the living room.

"Miss Opal, while I may be a pastry chef and not a celebrity, I truly appreciate your kind words."

"Now, now, Margo, no need to be modest. From the looks of your creation, you are a celeb in my world."

Margo felt her face warm. "Thank you for your kind words."

As they made their way into the living area, Delaney stopped. She surveyed the charming, quaint dining room adorned with vibrant cabbage rose wallpaper and painted pink beadboard that partially decorated the walls. "Miss Opal, I love your dining room, and the table setting you have done up is spectacular!"

Miss Opal stepped into the room with a tray of wineglasses. "Thank you, honey. It has been the same since my husband, Arnold, passed away fifteen years ago. We spent many a night in here enjoying whatever was the catch of the day." The wrinkles on her soft face seemed to fade when she spoke of him. Her voice lifted as her eyes flittered to Delaney.

"Miss Opal, let me get the wine."

"Thank you, Delaney, and you know where the ice and napkins are."

Elisa and Margo found themselves comfortable on the brown brocade sofa.

"Delaney tells me ya girls have never paid a visit to Ocracoke," Miss Opal mentioned as she placed the tray on a side table.

Elisa leaned forward and spoke in a soft tone. "No, we have not, and it's so scenic and quaint. So far, we have been kayaking and learned where Blackbeard was beheaded. And Margo found sea glass!"

Miss Opal clapped her hands and chuckled. "The tales of Blackbeard never get old." She placed a few cubes of cheese on a small plate and faced Elisa. "That was you fighting with that kayak tangled up in the vines! I saw ya out there and thought I was gonna have to call for help!"

Elisa burst into a fast laugh. "Yes, that was me, and I put up one heck of a fight and won!"

Margo was busy looking around at the vintage décor and had to ask. "How long have you lived in this home? I love the feeling in here as if I were back in time."

Delaney entered the room and placed the wine and glasses down. With some struggle, she removed the cork and poured the wine. "I heard Margo ask how long you have owned your place. I would also like to know as well if we are not being too personal."

"My dear, this house was built by my father in 1924. Embraced by love, it has withstood many a storm. After my husband's passing, I found myself torn between selling it and cherishing the memories." She lowered her eyes for a moment before looking up again, taking a deep breath as she reached for a wineglass. "My heart will forever reside here. This home was a gift from my father upon his death, and I transformed it into our sanctuary when I returned after marrying Arnold. I left my nursing career in Virginia behind. Life was delightful, one might say, until he passed away."

Elisa frowned. "So sorry to learn this."

"No need, honey, to be sorry. I was never alone since I had Bo across the street. It took him some time to find me in his heart after I left him for my Arnold."

Intrigued, Delaney held back a knowing smile since she had seen the photo of them lip-locked on the dock. Not wanting to push the subject, she asked if she was comfortable talking about Bo.

Miss Opal's face appeared youthful as she spoke. "Bo and I were teenagers in love. I would pack a lunch, and we would often sneak off and go down a sandy path not far away for a forbidden kiss and hold hands as we walked the shore for hours on end. He would give me the moon if he could. I left for nursing school in Virgínia and broke his heart after I married another man."

Delaney felt a tear settle on her eyelashes. Her Uncle Bo never spoke of his love for Miss Opal. The family knew him as a hard-working bachelor, and he had a love interest but never married.. She took Miss Opal's hand in hers. "Thank you for sharing."

"Oh, you girls are young and full of love and do not let life pass you by without one forbidden kiss!"

Margo finished her wine, then gazed at her engagement ring and spoke. "That is beautiful, Miss Opal."

"It was a beautiful love that we rekindled later in life after my husband passed away. I was Bo's caretaker until he took his last breath. His words still resonate with me."

Elisa had to ask. "Would you share them with us?"

Miss Opal got up and pointed out of the bay window. "The wooden swing on your front porch, Delaney, Bo made it for me. We would sit out there for hours, no matter what the weather. No words were to be spoken. What needed to be said was silent, resting in our hearts."

Elisa held back a gasp as she placed her hand over her chest. "Beautiful, Miss Opal."

Delaney's mother had occasionally mentioned the tale of the swing, and now Delaney was certain it was true. She leaned closer and inquired, "Miss Opal, I discovered the swing in the shed and restored it. I even painted the heart pink."

She turned and faced Delaney with her hands over her heart. "The wooden heart he added on the day he proposed to me. He painted it cotton candy pink."

"What?" Delaney nearly spat out her wine. "He proposed? And I used cotton candy pink paint!"

"Hello! Something smells delicious!" A voice called out from the kitchen. "Hello, Aunt Opal?"

Miss Opal called out. "We are in the living room!"

In stepped the handsome nephew, Justin. His smiling eyes circled the room and stopped at Delaney. "Hi, are you the pretty girl I nearly ran over this morning?"

"Uh—yea–no." Delaney felt her upper lip sweat as she put her wineglass on the coffee table.

"Hey, just teasing, Delaney, is it?" His broad shoulders and fit body had Delaney and her friends ogling. "And I hosed the carrot juice off my car at my buddy's place. I heard you were stopping over. This is an apology from me," he walked over and from behind his back he handed her a box of Band-Aids.

Delaney hesitated to take the box when Margo, in a saccharine voice, insisted she do so. She did.

"Justin, you are so sweet." Miss Opal said with cheer.

"Thanks," Delaney said, wanting nothing more than to hide behind the Victorian rocking chair as she felt her words would get tangled up. *Get a hold of yourself and stop it. He's just a man. Well, not just a man, he is one hell of a show-stopping man and Band-Aids?* Was he in Hollywood? No, why would he be here fixing up a cottage? Maybe he is on hiatus. Be cool and think of your words carefully. Finding a confident smile, she spoke in an easy-going tone. "Once again, so sorry. I was not paying attention." She held up the Band-Aids. "Thanks!"

"You know I'm the one who should apologize since I should have seen you. Oh, and I was going to get you a pair of new slippers, but I have no idea what to get." He said as he made his way to Miss Opal and kissed her soft cheek, and moved beside her, peeking into the kitchen. He inhaled and asked. "What smells so good?" He turned to Delaney, adding an alluring grin.

Tapping her wineglass, she turned her head toward the fireplace in the corner.

Elisa and Margo held back their comments, knowing Delaney was feeling uneasy. It was clear he was flirting.

"Justin, I made stuffed sole for supper. Delaney and her friends will have a place at my table. I thought you were going to stay on Hatteras til tomorrow at Buddy's place."

He ran his hands through his thick chestnut hair. "No, his wife was wrangling the five kids, dogs, and a litter of puppies. It was like a zoo over there. But he is going to stop by and look over Bo's old pickup. If that is good with you, and fingers crossed, we can get it running. I can use it to get materials for fixing up your place."

Miss Opal slid her arm into his. "Absolutely, have your friend look over the truck." She looked over her shoulder at her guests and back to Justin. "This is a girl's night."

Feeling uncomfortable in the estrogen dominating room, he needed air and replied. "No problem. I'm going over to the brewery and then grab some dinner at a restaurant."

Miss Opal's tone was of relief. "Thank ya for understanding. We girls have much romantic heart stuff to discuss."

"Whoa! —girly *romantic heart* talk is not my thing. You lovely ladies enjoy my aunt's cooking." Rubbing his belly, he turned to Miss Opal. "If there are dinner leftovers, I'm first in line."

"Of course, but I doubt there will be any. Now go on and git." Miss Opal, with a gentle push on his arm, directed him out.

He stopped and turned. "Ladies," his soothing cerulean blue eyes met Delaney's. "See you around, neighbor." With a sexy wink, he was gone.

"That boy is something else! I sure am blessed he is here to help. When Bo was alive, he and I used his pickup to go fishing. He left it here often since his garage was too small. It had been sitting idle, and Justin wants to get it running so he can pick up materials to fix my place." Miss Opal picked up her wineglass and sipped it. "I need to get our dinner out of the oven and onto the table. Excuse me, ladies." She left the room.

Mesmerized by his presence, leaving Elisa to daydream, Margo tapped her arm and whispered. "Yummy. But did you hear him say he isn't into romantic heart talk?"

"I know, but I can still fantasize." Elisa pulled her lips in and out. "I bet he is like the salt on a margarita. At first, it's bitter, but it goes down easy."

Margo continued to speak in a low voice. "Wow, I cannot believe you said that, and I thought you were never going to drink a margarita again?" She taunted as she elbowed Elisa.

"I like to give things another try!"

Delaney, in a questionable tone, added. "He must have had his heart broken. That is why he is single and not into girl talk. I did not see a ring on his finger, did either of you?"

Margo shook her head as she spoke in a low voice. "No ring or mark where one once was. Shush, Miss Opal will hear us."

Miss Opal stuck her head out of the dining room and announced that supper was ready and on the table. "Come on, girls, bring your wine and take a seat."

Elisa was blinking as she stood by a dining room chair.

"Pay no mind to the lights flickering. It ain't your eyes. They are on the list of repairs from my nephew. The house isn't walking with ghosts, just she be walking with age!" Miss Opal signaled the girls to sit down. "How about I light some candles? That may help with the flicker above."

"Sure!" Elisa said as she asked if Miss Opal needed help.

Delaney was walking behind Margo when she bumped into the door jamb. "Whoops!" She stepped aside and tapped it. "I did not see you."

Margo turned around. "Geeze Delaney, what's the deal with you bumping into things today? Need I ask! Does it involve a red car and a very exciting man with no ring on his left finger?"

7

Miss Opal placed her fork on the dessert dish and, with a satisfied smile, spoke to Margo. "Now, my mama made what I thought was the best peach cobbler in the state, but Margo, my dear, you can bake. I sure hope my mama up in heaven has not heard a word of what I said." She looked up, pressed her finger to her lips, and squeezed her face.

"You are too kind. And thank you so much. The recipe is from a woman who once lived in the apartment my family owned in the city. Known as stern Helga, she owned a German bakery in the space below. I was fortunate, and after she had gotten ill, she went to live with family and closed the bakery. She gave me her recipe card file box. The cards looked like chicken scratch written in German, and it took me years to decipher them into English. Then, all these internet tools came along to help me, and now I have an entire book of them. I bake one of her treasured recipes weekly. The guests love it."

"You never told me?" Delaney perked up as she placed her coffee cup on the saucer. "You should publish the recipes in a book."

"Me neither," Elisa added. "That cobbler is off the charts delicious."

Margo placed her napkin on the empty dessert dish. "No book. I would never betray Helga. I thought I told both of you that it was Helga who inspired me to become a pastry chef. When I was young, she often allowed me into the back kitchen where she worked. She was a tough woman, but had a gentle heart and loved to teach me. It was her workspace, and only a select few were permitted to watch her and, no less, learn her heirloom secrets."

"Margo, that is a wonderful story to be cherished, and I bet Miss Helga is dancing somewhere above, knowing you are sharing her recipes and continuing her legacy. If I were you, get that recipe book published." Miss Opal suggested while she relaxed, enjoying being in the company of such interesting young ladies and their fabulous stories. "This has been a wonderful evening, hasn't it?"

Delaney was wrestling with a yawn when the front door opened and in stepped Justin.

"Sorry. I hope that I'm not interrupting anything, am I?" He shut the door behind him, looking like a deer in the headlights. "Aunt Opal, ladies, I need to head to bed. Goodnight."

"So soon? It's only ten. Stay and join us, ladies." Delaney said as she sat back, crossing her legs. Was it the after-dinner brandy talking?

Margo's eyes popped open at Delaney's comment.

"That is a marvelous idea. Stay and chat. Your aunt must have some fun tales of you growing up." Elisa suggested with a twinkle in her eye, wondering what was in the brandy to get her to be so bold.

"Thanks, but I need to get to bed. And Aunt Opal, Buddy is stopping by tomorrow to work on the truck."

The room fell silent as all eyes were on Justin.

"Honey, what time will your friend be here?"

"Around eleven. It depends on the ferry schedule and the lines. Early, I'm sure, and I'll let you know." Justin walked up the narrow stairs and stopped halfway. Looking through the spindles, his eyes met Delaney's. "Night, ladies!" and with that, he continued adding a whistle.

They could hear a door shut and footsteps above.

Miss Opal got up and placed the empty dishes on a tray when Delaney stopped her. "We are your guests, and you have done plenty. Let me take these into the kitchen, and you sit and relax."

Hesitant, Miss Opal gave in. Having someone help her was humbling. She never wanted to be a burden, but at her age, she feared she would soon rely on others. She was more than grateful to have a neighbor like Delaney and her delightful friends visiting. With her hands folded in her lap, she said. "Thank you!"

"Of course." Delaney was more than happy to help. She was putting the dishes in the sink when she felt she was not alone. The creaky door to the back staircase opened. She turned around to find Justin a few feet away.

"Hi." He made his way to the fridge and reached in for a pitcher of ice water. "Can you believe it's 87 degrees at this time of night? A heatwave is starting tomorrow. I grew up in Raleigh and moved to the Chicago area, where it never gets this hot."

Avoiding eye contact, keeping her focus on emptying the tray into the sink, she agreed. "Yup, it's gonna be hot. A beach day for sure."

He poured a tall glass of water and drank it. "So, you are Bo's niece. That is amazing. I never knew he had a family. When I hung out here in the summers, he was often alone." He glanced into the living room and back at Delaney. "Well, until Aunt Opal's husband — well, you know."

Finding the courage to talk to him, her eyes met his. "Yes, my family, his sister, would spend many summers here since I was a toddler, and his cottage was always in my heart, and a dream come true when I found out that he left the cottage to me." She did not want to get into Bo and Opal's love affair. She was not ready to learn more, or was she?

Justin put his glass on the countertop and crossed his arms over his chest. "I have been coming down here since I was about ten. Funny we never met." He glanced around the kitchen and found the leftovers. "Aunt Opal makes the best stuffed sole."

Delaney was feeling calmer. She swore not to even look, no-less date, the male species for five years after her breakup. It had been year two of her commitment. She and her friends knew that it was impossible to go for five years. Being she was a dreamer who loved being in love. Since her last relationship ended, her heart went into her designs and the cottage. There was no time for a man in the present, and that wouldn't change.

"Delaney!" Miss Opal called out. "Are you all right in there?"

Drying her hands, she replied. "Yes, and bringing more coffee with me." She flashed an uncertain smile at Justin. "Have a nice night." She placed the dishtowel on the countertop and picked up the coffeepot. *Have a nice night! How lame* she said under her breath. She was a veteran with men, but Justin was intense and exuded male hormones from a few feet away, leaving her in a daze. With her face warm, she passed him.

He watched her and said, goodnight.

Elisa, once again wide eyed wondered what went on in the kitchen with Mr. Sexy.

Delaney placed the coffeepot on the dining room table. "I need to get caught up. What did I miss?"

Elisa poured a cup of coffee and sat back. "Miss Opal was telling us about Justin. And what a story she had been telling!"

Margo was silent. That was until her phone rang. "Excuse me, it's my fiancé." She went into the dining room.

Delaney suggested after the coffee they should let Miss Opal get some rest.

"Honey, I'm up most nights until the early morning working on my needlepoint. Having company and laughter in my home is a blessing."

Elisa let out a yawn. Her eyes teared up as she spoke. "I'm pooped. If you do not mind, I'm going to meander back to the cottage and go to bed."

Miss Opal folded her hands in her lap. "As long as you promise to stop by again for lunch one day this week."

Elisa nodded as she got up and went to give Miss Opal a slight hug. "Thank you for this lovely evening."

"Of course, young lady. Delaney told me that you are a fancy hairdresser in New York." She patted her hair, which was in a bun at the back of her head. "I do my hair these days."

Elisa took the hint and replied with a warm gesture. "How about one day this week I stop over and treat you to a new style?"

"Honey, that would be delightful!" Her aging blue eyes were watery. No one offered anything like that to Miss Opal. She was the giver, not the receiver. "I can pay ya."

Shaking her head and holding up her hands, Elisa said no.

"I'm so humbled. Today I had a fancy hairdresser, a pastry chef, and a fabric designer in my little Victorian home. This has been wonderful." She picked up a napkin and wiped her damp eyes.

Delaney got up and gave Miss Opal a kiss on her cheek. "And thank you for a lovely evening, and we can have a girls' spa day." She wondered if Justin would be around and had to ask. "If you need anything, let us know." Her eyes danced around the room, stopping at Miss Opal's. "Will Justin be here all summer?"

"Honey, he may be moving in after he fixes the place up. I'm getting too old to take care of it, and he is my only nephew. Time will tell. He and I discussed it, and he can work out of the house in the small bedroom upstairs. Part of his fixing the place up is for his lifestyle. He is working for himself in marketing and advertising. He had a larger firm and sold it." She spoke in a loud whisper. "Ladies, please never tell him I spilled the beans. He is very well off financially and has a kind heart that he mended after that gold-digging monster left him months ago. That was after the—" she let out a sigh. "It's not for me to tell you about his life. It was heartbreaking, I can assure you."

Elisa and Delaney glanced at each other and back at Miss Opal.

"No worry this is between us girls! Love you, Miss Opal, and good night." Delaney kissed her cheek again and let Margo know they were leaving.

"Bingo, a broken heart by a gold digger, but I wonder what happened before that. Whatever it was, it upset Miss Opal."

Delaney bit her bottom lip and then spoke. "How about we mind out business?"

"Agreed. But the awesome news is that he is going to be your neighbor. Shit, I want to move in with you."

Delaney reached for Elisa's hand and pulled her close. "Anytime, Elisa." She, too, was stunned to learn that Justin would be living across the street.

8

Delaney returned from a morning run as the sun rose. The day was going to be a swelter, and, keeping to her daily routine, she needed to get it done early. She went inside to get a glass of water and to brew a pot of coffee. Out on the front porch, she wiped the back of her neck with a small towel and sat down, taking her pulse when she noticed the morning mist was lifting as the rising sun found her face.

Her stare was across the street at Miss Opal's place. What she learned last night upset her. Was Miss Opal ill? Why is she having her nephew move in? Her home was not falling down. With too many uncertainties, she sat back and listened to the morning birds chirping when a hummingbird buzzed past her and returned. In mid-air, it faced her, then turned to enjoy the nectar of the petunias.

"Well, good morning, little one. Enjoy!" She got up, reached for a watering can and went to the side of the house to the hose spicket. She returned to water the flowers when she heard a car door shut. Trying not to be seen as overly curious, she hid behind the flower box, watching Justin leave the driveway and go up the street.

"Hmmm. I see he is an early bird." She finished watering the flowers and went inside to work on one of her drawings for a customer. Wanting to get it done before her friends got up and the day began; she sat behind her desk and took out her watercolor paints. Not long after she could see from the window, Justin had returned. As she returned her focus to her work, she heard a soft knock on the front screen door.

"Hello."

Delaney got up and, to her surprise, Justin standing there, holding a tray of coffee in one hand and a donut box in the other.

Delaney, wearing a tentative smile, spoke in a gentle voice. "Um—hello."

He paid his attention to Miss Opal's place and back at Delaney. "I wanted to thank you for keeping my aunt entertained last night."

"Please talk quietly. My friends are still sleeping. The porch is better, so we can talk."

"Got it."

She shut the front door and faced him.

"Here." He handed her the doughnuts and coffee. "These are for you and your friends. Thank you, since whatever you said last night has really given my aunt joy. I found her photo albums out on the dining room table, and I heard her singing last night."

Delaney put the doughnuts and coffee on a side table. "Thanks so much, but we did not do anything out of the ordinary. We had, as she calls a *girl's night.*" She placed her hands on her hips and looked past his shoulder at Miss Opal's house. "I'm glad to learn she is happy."

He squinted across the street and paid attention to Delaney. "Thanks again, and I want to apologize for nearly running you down."

"Please stop apologizing. It was my fault. No injures, and no damage done, and I'm glad that you hosed off the offending carrot juice." Delaney did not want to hear one more mention of her clumsy incident.

"No problem. And fingers crossed, my friend, that I can get Bo's old truck running so I can start fixing up the place. It was her *get around* vehicle, and she told me that it's been sitting in the garage for a long time. Not too long, I hope."

"I had no idea about the truck. I know she drives around on a golf cart, and when she goes off the island, her friend from church takes her. A few times I have taken her to the doctor's up in Virginia. We have even stayed overnight at a hotel since it's a long day for her. You know we had a few floods? I hope that did not damage the truck."

"So, I heard." Justin knew a little about Miss Opal's life on the island and wanted to make it easier for her as she aged.

Delaney walked to the edge of the porch, darting her eyes around to avoid him. She failed and turned to Justin. "Miss Opal's home is out of a magazine. It's lovely and romantic." She realized she had said *romantic*. Of all the words to say in front of the sexy man, as Elisa referred to him.

"For sure, it's a Queen Ann Victorian. They certainly do not build them like that anymore, with the turret and curved porches. And the bonus is I have met my new neighbor."

Nodding, Delaney added. "Welcome neighbor. I assume you will be busy fixing Miss Opal's place. It has such charm, and so much of her personality embedded in it. I hope you keep some of it intact?"

"Absolutely keeping the vintage vibe with updates. The truck needs to be running so we can get the materials here. Most of the work will be plumbing, wiring, and a new back porch for sure. You must have experienced the ghostly lighting in the dining room."

Delaney picked up the watering can and made her way to a flower box. "Yes, we experienced the strobe effect. It made it more memorable. Did you notice that the back gardens are overgrown? She told me after the last storm it flooded back there and most of her hard work left with the storm."

Justin looked up at the rising sun and went back to Delaney. "She told me that there was a fountain of a seahorse and a coy pond, but they are long gone and buried in the sand."

Delaney crafted a faint smile. "Dig them up and plan a restoration project?" *Why does he have to be so alluring? Go away! I have a five-year plan. Well, three years left. No matter. Go away before my plans fall apart.* Her thoughts were swirling, leaving her lightheaded. *Avoid saying anything foolish.*

He put his hands into the pockets of his shorts. "I may, but I'll need some help to dig out the fountain, landscape, and plant flowers." Viewing her flowers on the porch, he added. "I'm handy but far from a gardener." He held up his thumb. "No green thumb here."

Delaney knew what he was suggesting and shook her head as her stare found his thumb. "Surely you *will* find someone who is good at gardening. Ask around at Miss Opal's church." A warm breeze snaked its way onto the porch, brushing past her face. She pushed her hair back past her shoulders.

He took his hands out of his pockets and walked over to a flower box and dead-headed a petunia. "That is a super idea, but I may already know someone with a green thumb." His smile was killing her. How could he? How dare he be so intense? She wanted him to leave before he found her lips on his.

Turning away, she told him she had work to do and needed to get back to her new creation.

He asked what she did for a living.

She questioned why he was not leaving. And decided if she told him she was a textile designer and had to get back to work, he would leave.

"I have never met a textile designer. That sure is different."

"Yup, and I have a project I need to finish. I was about to work on it when you knocked."

He took the hint and went down the stairs to the walkway and stopped. "Delaney,"

"Yes."

"Enjoy the donuts!" With a minor wave, he stuffed his hands into his pockets and walked across the street.

Delaney felt as if she were holding her breath and let it out. She could breathe. What is his deal? How dare he not leave and want to chat? And worse, suggest she help him fix the gardens! Geeze men!

Elisa walked out onto the porch, expelling a loud yawn as she wrapped her arms around her waist. "Coffee and?" She noticed the coffee and donut box on the table. "Were you out running?"

"Yes, I usually go around eight and run three miles, but it's going to be a scorcher today." She was pulling dead flower heads from the marigolds and tossing them into the yard. "How about we go to the beach today? Get some sun and go swimming. I heard the water is eighty-two!"

"Unequivocally, that is a yes, and I, uh—well, I have been up for a bit and saw Mr. Sexy was here." Her gaze remained on the coffee cups and donuts. "And I heard he left these for us as a thank you?"

Delaney tensed her neck and was swift to wave her hands. "He is being kind and neighborly. No need to make a mountain out of a molehill. Did I just say that? I have become my mother!"

"Yes, you said it, Mom! Ha ha and be real. How many Mr. Sexy types stop over at dawn to leave a breakfast treat?

Think about this. How did he know you were out running? Who gets up this early? A man interested in Delaney, the five-year spinster. That is who." She teased as she opened the box of donuts. "He knows how to charm a woman's heart with sweets. Have you seen what he gave us?"

"No, and who cares. Just enjoy! And I'm not a spinster. I happen to be two years into my five-year plan." Delaney pursed her lips, not wanting to continue this silly conversation.

Elisa, always the antagonist, brought the donut box over and opened it, and shut it several times. "Look, the box is talking to you. *Delaney, try me. I live across the street.*" She kept the box open.

Delaney peeked into the box and broke into a chuckle. "Seriously, they have pink icing. I bet Miss Opal told him what to get."

Elisa reached in, took one, and then placed the box on a side table. She bit into it, letting out a satisfied moan. "Damn, this is delicious. Have one." She sat down and picked up a cup of cooled coffee. "I can imagine that his lips are as sweet as this icing."

"Stop it!" Delaney said, concealing her smile as she picked out a donut slathered in pink icing.

9

Margo was on the phone with her fiancé, David, discussing the lunch menu she had planned out while she was gone. All was going well until he dropped the bomb on her that two of the prep chefs had called out sick with the flu. The situation was difficult with David flipping out, and she was on the verge of returning home when Delaney intervened.

"Your fiancé is a big boy. He can handle this. There must be temp agencies with staff for restaurants. Wait, let me look something up." Delaney reached for her phone, and with a confident grin, handed it over to Margo. "Look at all the temp agencies for culinary help. Have David make some calls. You are on vacation and will not go back until I say so!"

Margo wasted no time and called David and solved the earth-shattering problem. She fanned her face and thanked Delaney for being so resourceful.

"No problem. So go get your bathing suit, sunblock, and your towel. We are heading to the beach."

"Are we taking the golf cart?"

"Not this time, Margo. We are going over to the first beach before the village to frolic in the ocean!"

Margo pulled her lips in and out and stopped as her scared eyes met Delaney's. She asked. "Are there sharks?"

Delaney held back an eye roll. "Yes, but not today. It's low tide, and we can walk along the shore and get our feet wet if that calms you. I bet there are all sorts of shells and sea glass!"

"Deal. And David told me he watched the movie Jaws last night and sent me screenshots of the man-eating shark. He told me to watch it on my phone."

Delaney had to bite her tongue, knowing all too well David was controlling and was not happy she took a girl's vacation. Why would he send her those screenshots? To get her home is the only reason. With continued reassurance from Delaney, she reminded Margo that there are lifeguards, and no one had seen a shark.

Margo forced a swift smile and went to get her beach bag when Elisa strolled into the room.

"Did I hear sharks were in the water?"

"No, and shush up." Delaney placed her finger over her lips.

Elisa looked around the room. "What's going on?"

Delaney told her about David, the photos, and how he was trying to lure her home by creating drama at the restaurant, and that sharks were going to get her.

Elisa whispered into Delaney's ear. "He's a pain in the ass! Maybe we can find her a new lover here on vacation and arrange something nonchalant. A none whiner type is preferred!"

Breaking into a slight chuckle, Delaney agreed. "He needs a pair and grow up. Time to head to the beach before it gets too hot, and the sand scorches our feet!"

They settled on the beach not long after. Delaney and Elisa spent time in the waves, laughing and floating around. The water was clear and warm! Margo spent her time walking along the shoreline, keeping only her feet in the water. Often, she would signal to the girls that they were too far out and to get back to shore. They would wave back and do so to keep her from panicking.

Once back under the umbrellas and settled into their chairs, Delaney opened the cooler and handed out ice water.

"Seriously, we are at the beach, and you bring iced water?"

"Elisa, look on the bottom of the cooler and you will find our beach chill out libations!" Delaney said as she toweled off her hair. "And I recall you said wouldn't drink again!"

"Yeah, yeah." She turned to find Margo was under her towel.

Elisa elbowed Delaney and pulled the towel off Margo.

"Hey! I was reading the local news underneath there."

"Were you watching Jaws?"

"No, thank you. But I just read on a local thread that there is a turtle boil, I think, here at ten a.m. one morning." She looked past them and pointed. "When I was taking my stroll, I saw signs and areas roped off for turtle nests."

"Boil? Ewe," Elisa squeaked as she rubbed sunblock on her arms. "They cook and eat turtles on the beach?"

Delaney put her towel on her chair and joined the conversation. "I know it sounds peculiar, but what it means is the baby turtles are hatching, and they need to evacuate the nest to find the remaining ones. Most head out to the ocean at night by following the moonlight. I watched a boil last summer and loved it. They even dug out empty eggshells. We got to feel them, and then a few babies were alive, and I got to see them. We can find out when and where it will be."

"As long as no one is boiling anything, we should go." Elisa said as she reached for a wine cooler. "Now, this is a vacation. Not a cloud in the sky, the water is calm and warm, and enjoying vacation with my besties!"

Later in the afternoon, they returned to the cottage and took turns using the outdoor shower.

Delaney, wrapped in her large beach towel and a smaller one covering her wet hair, was heading up to her bedroom when there was a knock on the front door.

"Who is it?"

"Just me, honey."

"Miss Opal, step on in." Delaney went to the front door.

She stepped inside with her oven mitts on and a casserole dish in her hands. "I see that you are not dressed. Let me put this on the kitchen counter and scoot on out. I baked a chicken and rice casserole with broccoli. I just got it out of the oven. A recipe I used to bake for your uncle Bo." Her sweet smile was contagious. "He never left a crumb."

"Thank you. That is so kind, but you do not have to cook for us."

"I do. I love being around you, young ladies. It brings my youth back to me and a smile to my heart. And being near you, Delaney, I feel Bo is beside me."

Delaney brushed her hand over Miss Opal's soft arm. "Then come on over and share dinner with us."

"Aunt Opal, where are you? I have the cake." Justin called out before he walked up the porch steps.

Delaney tightened her towel as she leaned forward to look toward the front door. "Crap!" She hid behind Miss Opal.

Miss Opal turned to Delaney. "Did you say something?"

She shook her head and then adjusted her towel.

"I had my hands full, and I hope you will not mind Justin is bringing over a buttercream cake I made this morning. Oh, honey, you are in your skivvies. Let me put this casserole in the kitchen and be on my way." She made her way, with Delaney trailing behind.

Margo came down the stairs and noticed Justin standing in the entryway, holding the tall cake. "Hi! You have your hands full. Let me take that from you."

He handed the cake over, adding a thank you, and asked where Miss Opal was.

"I bet they are in the kitchen. Follow me," Margo led the way in inhaling the thick, swirly icing. "This looks so yummy. Back in New York, I'm a pastry chef, and this may be better than anything I have ever made. Wait, did you bake this?"

"Heck no. Aunt Opal did and asked me to bring it over."

They entered the kitchen. Margo placed the cake down on the table and faced Miss Opal. "What a surprise to see your radiant smile, but look at what you have brought! Is that a chicken casserole on the countertop?" She could not help but notice Delaney wrapped in a beach towel hiding behind Miss Opal.

"Sure, and you girls deserve one of my home-cooked casseroles. I topped it with fried onion rings. If you'd like, I can give you the recipe. It was my grandmother's, and that was a long time ago. And the cake is my mile high butter cream with strawberries between the six vanilla layers. Make sure it goes in the fridge." She reminded Delaney in a loving tone. "I'll see you all later."

Delaney stole a glance at Justin and caught him checking her out. "Miss Opal will be sharing dinner with us tonight. Say six?" She made sure her towel was on snug.

"I sure will be here faster than a rabbit being chased by a hound dog." Miss Opal turned to leave and stopped. "Justin, thanks for helping me out. Oh, darn it, I forgot the tomato pudding. Justin can bring it over later."

He nodded and added. "Anytime. I'll be going to the back garage to open it up. Buddy will be over soon, and we are looking over the truck."

"Let me fetch them, and I sure hope you can get that truck running. Bye, girls, I'm looking forward to sharing dinner with ya all." Miss Opal's face flooded with joy as she took Justin's hand, and they left.

Margo watched them cross the street and smirked at Delaney. "Did he really need to bring a cake over? Or was it to spy on a cottage of women? And how convenient she forgot the tomato pudding."

"Miss Opal had her hands full." Delaney defended.

"What smells so good?" Elisa entered the room in her bathing suit.

"Our dinner and dessert. And Miss Opal prepared it and will dine with us."

"I see." She tapped her upper lip. "And what about the lonely, handsome nephew … will he attend? And there you were in nothing but a towel. Once again, he is spying on you!"

"No, he is not. And will you please stop it? No way am I interested in him or any other man at this time in my life. I enjoy being alone and working on designs."

Elisa lifted her shoulders as she went over to the cake. She ran her finger along the bottom icing and tasted it. "As sweet as those donuts." With a strut, she headed outside to take a shower.

10

The sun sent its morning smile across the ocean as it broke through the low, lavender clouds. A glorious sunlit day was in store on Ocracoke. Delaney returned from her morning run and enjoyed a glass of carrot juice on the front porch. Finding herself comfortable in a chair, she kept her eye on Miss Opal's place, wondering what Justin was up to. Tapping the juice glass, she sat back. Who is Justin? After all, she knew nothing about him, and he was going to be her new neighbor. A neighbor she could not avoid. A neighbor with a perfect view of her cottage.

A hummingbird zipped by the flower box before returning. It discovered the morning dew glistening on the honeysuckle that climbed the trellis beside the porch. With her gaze fixed on the delicate creature, she offered a gentle wave and spoke to it in a soft voice. “You are welcome to visit anytime!”

As if the hummingbird had heard her, it lifted and came within a foot of her face, and then flew off toward a live oak tree.

Margo stepped out onto the porch. “Morning! It’s gonna be a hot one again.” She let out a yawn, adding a sleepy stretch. “It’s so peaceful, and time to make coffee. I brought my press. Would you like a cup?”

"No thanks, but I know Elisa will. I thought we could take a ride in the golf cart into the village before lunch and get smoothies at Ocracoke Coffee Company."

"That sounds like fun. Can we check out a few stores too?"

Delaney gave a wide stretch and a slight yawn. "Absolutely, it's your vacation."

"Coffee time." She stepped inside and backed up. "I gotta ask you, is there any reason you are sitting out here facing Miss Opal's at seven in the morning?"

Delaney shook her head. "This is where I sit every morning after my run, so get those other thoughts of him out of your head."

"Uh huh, whatever you say, but that casserole and cake last night were off the charts delicious. I'm going to ask her if she will let me copy some of her recipes. I bet she has a folder full of them."

"Miss Opal did mention she would share them with you last night."

"Yes. She did. I may have a piece of cake for breakfast." She rubbed her stomach and continued inside.

Just before noon, Delaney backed the golf cart out of the shed.

Elisa was about to sit down when they heard a loud pop.

"What was that?" Margo jumped in her seat.

"Is Miss Opal's garage on fire?" Elisa narrowed her eyes, watching a plume of black smoke rise from across the street.

"We had better go make sure she is okay." Delaney, in a panicked tone, suggested.

As they were getting out of the golf cart, a rusted blue pickup truck was rolling out of Miss Opal's driveway, along with it were the remains of the smoke. A tall, muscular man was pushing it. Behind the wheel was Justin. It came to rest in front of the white picket fence, not without another brash pop. They watched as the man who was pushing it dashed over to the driver's door.

Elisa put her hand over her brow and watched. She turned to Delaney. "I assume that must be the truck Justin wants to fix. Look at that hot mess." Her gaze was fixed on the truck. "It has a flat tire in the back and, wow; it's in rough shape. I think the passenger door has random duct tape on it!"

Margo was fanning her face as she watched. "Boring! It's so hot. Can we head out and get our smoothies?"

"Yeah, sure." Delaney said, adding a slow nod, wondering why they were even trying since the truck looked more like a heap of scrap metal that washed in with the tide. She also did not know that her uncle's truck was sitting idle in Miss Opal's garage. She drove the golf cart down the street, pointing out some of her neighbor's cottages.

Enjoying their smoothies, Delaney took Elisa and Margo for a tour of the village. Margo wanted to shop around at various gift shops, whereas the alluring aromas coming from the restaurants captivated Elisa. After a delightful lunch, they went back to the cottage and voted that they would head down to the sandy beach in the backyard and chill out.

Elisa volunteered to make a tall pitcher of sangria and dashed into the cottage with Margo not far behind!

Delaney was parking the golf cart in the shed and headed into the garage for a beach chair when she heard a soft knock on the open door.

"Afternoon, neighbor."

There he was with no shirt, in his shorts, staring at her with his dazzling eyes. Delaney avoided his muscular washboard stomach as best she could. Shaking off the vision in front of her, she spoke as her eyes danced around to avoid him. "Hey Justin, what's up? I see you have gotten the truck out of the garage."

He looked over his shoulder and back at Delaney. "That we did. It's not as bad as it looks. My buddy is a seasoned mechanic and assures me we can get *Sally* up and running so I can start helping over there. Opal's place needs some serious updating."

She tilted her head. "Sally?"

"It's a nickname. Tall tales told to me by Aunt Opal, your Uncle Bo, named after an old hound dog he had when he was young. Apparently, she never left his side and loved to sleep in the truck! The dog was his first love. At least that is what he told my aunt."

Delaney found a soft smile. "Well, I sure hope I never have a truck named after me. And I promise never to mention to Miss Opal that *Sally* was his first love."

His piercing eyes wouldn't leave hers as he skimmed his fingers through his hair. "I think she knows who Sally truly was!" His gaze never left her as he brushed the sweat off the back of his neck. "There's no breeze, and it's exceedingly humid out. I may head over to the beach and take a swim."

"I heard the water is beautiful and calm. The weather people have said it's gonna be a rough ten days of this heat, so they say. Thank goodness for air conditioning."

There was silence until he broke it. "And the ocean." His stare moved to the golf cart. "I see you have a gas-powered golf cart. And it's pink."

Delaney glanced at it and back at him. "Yes. It's vintage for sure. It was my uncle's and was in dire shape. An oldie but a goodie that I painted to make it more me."

"You should give it a name."

She crossed her arms over her chest as she paid attention to the golf cart and back to the sexy apparition in front of her. "Maybe."

He stepped inside and looked toward the back of the garage and to Delaney. "I was wondering if you had a gas can I could borrow for a day? My friend did not bring one, and the can in Aunt Opal's garage is rusted out. I'll bring it back later today."

So, he did not come over to see me? Fine, since I'm on that absurd five-year plan. Who makes up such a plan? Life happens. She refocused. "Yes, there are two, and one is half full. Take whatever you need, and all I ask is that you return it with gas." She directed her chin to the left of the garage. "They are over there on the second shelf."

"Thanks so much. And once I get Sally running, how about I take you for a ride around the village?"

Did he just ask me out for a ride in the rust bucket? She wasted no time and answered. "I'd love it." *What did I say? Love it. Gosh no. I need to get out of here*. "Listen, my friends are waiting for me. I gotta run. And I hope you get all the hiccups out of Sally and get her running."

He passed her and stopped. "How about I come by later and we go for that ride, if ole Sally is to wake up?"

She could feel his energy as tingles rushed through her body. "Sure." Squeaked out as she added. "Sounds like you are Prince Charming, and instead of a kiss, a can of gas and a new tire will wake her up! Get it — the tire is a metaphor for a glass slipper." *What did I just say? A kiss to wake her up. A glass slipper? OMG, I need to run now!*

"That is very creative!" His irresistible lips curled into a smile when he suggested. "How about I hit the horn twice as a signal we are a go? That is if the horn works."

"Two toots of the horn." *Toots of the horn. Who says such a thing?* Delaney was wondering where she was getting her choice of words.

"Toots it is." With the gas can in hand, he gave a slight nod, said thanks again, made his way across the street and glanced over his shoulder, adding a wave of his hand.

Waiting until he was across the street, she fluttered her hand over her heated face and body as she watched him vanish behind the gate.

Elisa had been quietly standing by the side of the garage, eavesdropping, hearing everything. With a skip in her step, she wasted no time and dashed down to the beach to tell Margo.

Delaney was swinging her arms when she met her friends. She let out a sigh as she looked out over the water and at Elisa.

"Why are you looking at me like that, Elisa?"

"Delaney, it's how I look." She tilted her head back as she reached for a beach chair. "Did you lend Mr. Sexy a gas can?" She pouted and then giggled.

"Funny!" Delaney spoke, then sent a playful kiss soaring through the air.

Margo sat in her chair, not saying a word. Noticing Delaney had a twinkle in her eyes and flushed cheeks, she found it difficult to keep her mouth zipped.

"We sound like teenagers, and as far as what just happened in the garage is concerned, I was being neighborly. It's what we do here on Ocracoke." Delaney's tone was light as she made her way to the edge of the water. Her mind was swirling with Justin's invitation to take a ride in tooting rust bucket, Sally.

11

"Burgers are ready!" Margo called out as she placed them on the kitchen table. "Look at all this food we have. I'm going to have another fitting when I return to New York since there is no way my wedding gown will fit after this vacation."

Elisa picked up a plate and filled it with potato salad. "What's wrong with a few vacation pounds? It means you enjoyed yourself. Plus, these are veggie burgers, correct?"

"And organic ground chicken with my special secret ingredients!" Delaney said as her curious eyes focused out the kitchen window at Miss Opal's place.

Elisa waved at Delaney. "Margo made the best burgers. Come join us."

Delaney took a breath and turned around. "It smells divine." She went over to the fridge to get the pitcher of iced tea and called out. "The turtle boil is tomorrow at ten. It's so beautiful, especially when they find a few little babies." She poured herself a glass of iced tea.

Elisa said as she sat down and was about to bite into her burger. "Count me in!"

"Me too!" Margo said as she sat down. "How do we get there?"

Delaney explained that they would drive to Ramp 63 and then walk out to the beach. She glanced down at her watch and back at Margo. "Thanks for making dinner. You went overboard." She picked up a plate and glanced out the window

"What are we doing tonight?" Elisa asked Delaney as she reached for the iced tea.

"Not sure. There is a ghost tour, and it's a lot of fun."

"Nope!" Elisa wasted no time responding. "I came here to relax, not to be frightened."

Margo was fighting with the pepper grinder and won when she laughed. "I think that would be a blast. Maybe we will meet one or two available ghosts just for you, Elisa."

"You know what? I bet I could meet a really nice ghostly man, and I can hang out with him at the cemetery and talk about days gone by."

Margo shook her head as she placed the pepper grinder on the table. "Only you would enjoy a date with a ghost."

Delaney was about to sip her iced tea when she spoke up. "How about we chill out tonight and do the ghost tour tomorrow night?"

Elisa sucked in her cheeks and let them out, knowing Delaney had a date with Mr. Sexy and his truck. "Yeah, how about we go tomorrow night? I'm tired and in the mood for Netflix. My arms and shoulders are sunburned. Ouch so are the tips of my ears."

"I have aloe gel in the bathroom. Second drawer in the vanity. It will take the sting out and put sunblock on." Delaney suggested as she went over and cringed at Elisa's sunburn.

Margo fought a yawn. "I think that is a wonderful idea — that we chill out tonight. I want to wash my hair and watch a movie. Elisa, you pick the movie." She paid attention to Delaney. "Are you okay if we chill out?"

"Absolutely."

Elisa had to say something as her eyes met Delaney's. "What will you be doing this warm summer evening?"

Delaney had to be honest with her friends. After all, it would be rude to rush out the door after two toots and not tell them why and where. She placed her napkin on her lap. "Truth be told is that I was asked to go for a ride tonight."

Margo squeezed her face. "What kind of ride?"

"Justin across the street asked if I would go for a ride in the rust bucket of a truck if he got it started, and I said yes." She sat back, wearing a delightful smile. "How could I say no to my neighbor's nephew?" She tapped the side of her glass.

"Well, now, he wasted no time. He's a fast mover." Margo said as she pointed her finger. "Young lady, you be home by eleven, or you're grounded!"

"Yes, Mom."

Elisa dangled her fork under her chin. "I cannot even get a date to take me in a rust bucket. You have all the luck."

Margo had to add her two cents. "Delaney deserves to have some fun. Did you forget what that Hunter, the asshole, did to her?"

"I know. So sorry I said that. You deserve to be happy. And Justin may be what will help heal that heart of yours. I mean, you're not gonna run off at sunset and get married on the beach. Are you?"

Margo and Delaney's eyes met as they broke into amusement.

"Too late. He already asked me to marry him."

"Stop it." Elisa's eyes grew wide as she dropped her fork. "You are kidding. Correct?"

"Of course. We are going for a ride in his or Miss Opal's truck or, as I have learned, my Uncle Bo's old truck. It's no big deal. I look at it as a favor to Miss Opal. You're so gullible."

Elisa asked. "Wow, some favor."

"Just being neighborly to our new, lonely, hot, sexy neighbor!"

Margo lifted her glass and called out, cheers to the new neighbor.

♥

Delaney finished putting the last dinner dish away in the cupboard when she heard two toots of a horn. She tossed the dishtowel onto the kitchen counter and pushed her hair behind her ears as she made her way to the front door.

Margo and Elisa gave the thumbs up.

"Wait," Elisa called out from the sofa. "I want a full report, and you better be home by your curfew, or you're grounded!"

"Yes, Mom, and last I heard, curfew was sunrise." And with that, she was out the door. She stopped, and in silence, she counted to three.

The driver's side door moaned in pain as Justin opened it. He made his way under the arbor and up onto the porch. "My rusty chariot awakes!"

He was even more gorgeous with the sun setting behind him as he walked up onto the porch and met Delaney.

"It's not a prize, but Sally wants to get out and breathe in the Ocracoke air again. And as promised, Prince Charming has given her a new tire! Glass slippers would not be suitable."

A slight smile found Delaney as her heart fluttered.

Elisa and Margo, concealed behind the curtains, exchanged nudges as they watched Delaney go on her date, behaving much like teenagers.

Soft ocean breezes met Delaney as she pulled her lips in and out as Justin approached her.

"Follow me. Your rusty chariot awaits!" he chuckled as he pointed to the truck. "I put an air freshener in it too! I hope you like the scent of spring cherries."

"Yes–sure." A heated flush rushed her face as they walked out to the truck.

He opened the squeaky passenger-side door and gestured for her to get inside.

"Ouch, Sally needs some oil in her joints." Delaney joked in a soft voice. "And the side-view mirror just may need more duct tape."

"She needs more than oil and tape."

His voice melted her heart and calmed her soul as she settled into her seat.

He shut the door and made his way to the driver's side and got behind the wheel. "Where to miss?" he teased, adding. "I'll get you home before my chariot turns into a pumpkin."

"A pumpkin? Hmmm. Does this mean that if I lose my glass sandal, you will find it and return it to me?"

He gave an assured nod. "If it fits. I like your quick answers. I like you, Delaney, and happy we are neighbors." He turned the key in the ignition. The truck let out a pop and a puff of smoke. "Sally needs to learn some manners!"

Delaney settled into the aged seat with frayed and, in some spots, rotted fabric. "Sally also needs new seat covers and a little more air freshener."

He turned to her. "Sorry, he reached into the back and handed her a beach towel."

Her facial expressions spoke volumes.

"You can sit on the towel that was just washed!"

"Thanks." She wasted no time tucking in under her rear end. "Sally needs new foam padding and fabric for this bench seat."

He faced her, wearing a seductive smile. "I happen to know a textile designer who lives across the street."

Raising her eyebrows with a sunny smile, she asked. "You do?"

"I do! And how about we head into the village and get an ice cream, or would you prefer a drink?"

Delaney had never had a man ask her out for ice cream. Warmed, she wore a rosy grin. "Ice cream it is!"

Margo and Elisa were looking out of the front window and turned to each other.

"Let's find a movie." Margo suggested as she headed for the sofa.

"How about a romance?"

"How about one that takes place on Ocracoke, a hot single man, his old truck, and a textile designer?"

"Perfect! Time to make the caramel pecan popcorn!" Elisa cheered and wasted no time, as she made a beeline for the kitchen.

Justin parked in front of the ice cream shop and turned to Delaney. "They have delicious ice cream and frozen custard at this place. Have you been here before?"

"Once with Miss Opal."

"Now it will be twice." He hopped out of the truck just as Delaney was about to pull on the interior door handle, and it fell off in her hand. "Geeze sorry." She held it up.

"One more repair on the list. Allow me to open the door. I do not want it to fall off and hurt you."

"Wow, you are chivalrous and, uh," she looked at the handle. "The door seems intact, but the handle — well, that did not fare too well! And the window well, it's stuck halfway down."

"Boy of boy, what a terrible impression I have made." Justin grinned as he opened the door and found his hand strong and comforting in hers. She did not want to let go as her feet met the ground.

She offered him the handle and joked. "You may need this!"

"Thanks." He put the handle on the floor of the truck and shut the stiff door.

"The place is busy." Delaney said as she looked up on the porch. "The line is out the door."

"We can wait, but if you prefer to go somewhere else, Sally is more than happy to take us. But you may have to slide in and out on my side."

Delaney glanced at Sally and its faded blue paint peppered with rust, and the chrome bumper crisscrossed with duct tape, adding to that was the windshield that hosted spiderweb cracks. "You know, we can wait. I know it's worth it."

"Perfect. How about we find a place to sit up on the porch?"

"Sure," Delaney said, feeling light as soft, balmy summer breezes off Silver Lake found her. She went to move forward when she felt a hand in hers. She pulled away.

He put his hand beside him. "My hand wanted to feel yours. I won't do it again."

"Uh, well—"

"No problem. We just met, and we are only neighbors. I apologize if I was being forward."

Delaney shook her head. "Justin, you caught me by surprise. I like how it felt in mine. A neighborly handhold — how about that?"

With pursed lips, he looked from side to side and then back at her. "Would a kiss be too soon?"

"Yes!" She wanted to say no. Better yet, press her lips on his. Not now. Was it too soon? They toyed with teasing each other for days. What would one tiny peck on the lips do? A lot!

"Struck down, but heck, you are holding my hand."

She looked down until realizing his hand had found hers. Being preoccupied with where this new kiss would land, she forgot about their hands. Needing to change the uncomfortable subject, she pointed with her chin. "Look, the line is moving. That family of ten is leaving. I hope they have left some ice cream for us."

Justin observed the group adding. "I hope so! It appears they hit the chocolate section." They stepped inside. "What flavor do you like?"

"Plain vanilla bean."

"Sounds good. Sprinkles?"

"Na."

His hand felt comfortable. Extremely comfortable. She did not want to let go. Who was this guy? Why was this happening? Her mind was busy questioning herself when, the next thing she knew, Justin was handing her a waffle cone of vanilla ice cream.

They went outside and sat down in the Adirondack chairs. She reached out, and her hand sought his.

"I did not take you for a plain vanilla girl."

"Well now, I never thought you would be a pistachio type of man." She giggled on and off as she enjoyed her ice cream.

"Delaney, why did you decide to move here? I know your uncle left you the cottage, but a textile designer and you're so gorgeous. You have an aura about you, and I find it ethereal and mystical."

"Thanks," Delaney, unsure of what to say, wondered. *Ethereal mystical aura? That was certainly a new line if she had ever heard one.*

He cleared his throat as he continued. "But you are living here alone on Ocracoke makes me wonder if someone hurt you and this is where you are finding a place and time to heal."

Taken aback, Delaney wondered what Opal had told him. She felt her heart racing. How dare he ask such a question, yet he was on point? She moved there to heal, and now a stranger, a sexy stranger, opened her wounds. Maybe it was time to confront them and move forward. Forget the five year no dating plan. She already broke it!

"Justin, my previous life was complex." She bit into her cone as she sat back. "I love her. And I understand her place needs up keeping."

He looked out over the darkening sky and turned to Delaney. "I created a successful advertising firm up north that I sold two years ago and went solo. I also do consulting for them from time to time." He rubbed his forehead as his jaw clenched.

Delaney felt his mood and body language shift and hinted it was time to go.

He did not listen and continued as he looked up at the sky and then turned to Delaney. "I was dating someone before and after I sold the company. She was my head of accounts and was great at it. I credit her with helping me build my company. After I sold it to a rather large firm and made a fortune, the staff and I went out to celebrate." He took a deep inhale and looked down and back up at the violet clouds that were hovering above the setting sun. "The staff were happy to work for the new owners and better pay. My head of accounts is who I was dating." He stopped and got up to throw his napkin away.

"Listen, if you do not want to tell me, I get it."

He sat down. "She died that night. I was going to ask her to marry me." He dropped his strong shoulders as he turned to face Delaney. "I said too much. You certainly do not need to hear my sorrows. We are here to enjoy ice cream and take Sally out for some fresh air."

Delaney sank further into her chair. Her throat tightened as she fought to find soothing words. All she could say was that she was sorry.

He stood up and held out his hand. "How about we head back?"

"Sure, yes." Feeling unnerved and shaken, she got up, and they walked over to the truck.

It was a silent ride back to the cottage as he pulled into Opal's driveway and got out. "Let me get your door and walk you across the street."

He opened the door, and as Delaney turned to get out, their lips almost met as she pulled away. "To be honest, I wanted to kiss you on the porch of the ice cream place. But it's too soon."

Justin looked up at the dimming sky and went back to Delaney. "I felt the same. And what I told you is not for pity. I'm also here to heal my heart. I mentioned it, and I promise no more attempts to kiss you. We are just neighborly friends."

Delaney agreed, knowing they were both full of it!

In the lantern light of the porch, she could see his eyes water up. "You do not need to be sorry for anything. I had a wonderful time, and I would enjoy doing this again. Maybe next time I can try the pistachio flavor."

"Deal." With that, he helped her out of the truck and shut the door.

Elisa was looking out the front window. "Look Margo. I think they are holding hands!"

"Seriously," with a bowl of popcorn in hand, she got up off the sofa and darted to the window. "We look like spinsters watching our stepsister. Like Cinderella! Hurry, we had better go sit down before they see us."

They rushed back to the sofa, pretending to be engrossed in a movie.

Justin walked Delaney to her front door and let go of her hand. "I hope you had a nice time on our ice cream date."

Delaney, flooded with mixed emotions, looked past him toward Miss Opal's place. "Do you have any place to go tonight?"

"No."

"Follow me." She led him to the porch swing. "We can sit and talk — that is, if you want to. Or we can sway and listen to the cicadas and crickets just like Uncle Bo and Miss Opal did once upon a time."

12

It was a little past midnight when Justin went back to Miss Opal's. Delaney watched him go inside and the porch light go dark. Crossing her arms over her chest, she leaned against the pillar on the porch for a moment before entering the house. She turned on the kitchen light and then grabbed a glass from the cabinet. She turned around to find Elisa and Margo standing by the table.

"Yikes, you both scared me."

Elisa pulled out a chair and got comfortable. "How was your date? We want all and any details, cause we gotta know!" she rubbed her hands together. "Full version and no edits."

Margo let out a long yawn and then spoke. "Was it fun? Is he all that he appears to be?"

Delaney opened the fridge, reached for the water pitcher and spoke as she poured a glass of water. "It was nice. He's saccharine sweet and likes pistachio ice cream."

"It was nice. I mean, there must be more." Elisa tapped her nails on the tabletop. "You left here at seven and waltzed in after midnight, and all we get is he's sweet and like pistachio ice cream?"

"He is sweet, and we will see him tomorrow at the turtle boil. He is driving us in Sally the truck." She sipped her water and placed the glass down. "And how did you know when I got back?"

"I have psychic abilities, silly! I could not sleep and heard you come in." Elisa said, adding a yawn just before she rested her head on the kitchen table.

"What? We are going to the turtle boil in that rust bucket?" Margo squeezed her face. "You are joking?"

Delaney finished her water and placed her glass in the sink. "Nope, be ready at nine. Tomorrow is gonna be hot, so dress for it. Oh, and bring a towel to sit on since the seats in the truck are in tough shape. And the door handles fall off."

"How will we fit?" Elisa moaned. "Door handles?"

"Sally has a backseat. Small, but it will work. It's my bedtime, and I suggest you, nosy and concerned *mom's* also get some rest." Delaney brushed past Margo and stopped. "I had a pleasant time."

Margo, with a squirmed face, had to ask. "Sally, is this rusty truck correct?"

"Yup, and it's not so bad. Justin said that he needs someone to design new upholstery for Sally."

Elisa popped her head up. "How convenient. Tell me about the steamy time? Did your eager, salty lips find each other under the light of the Ocracoke moon?"

"If you only knew. Good night, ladies!" Adding a playful wink, she blew a kiss, made her way up to her bedroom and shut the door.

Just as the morning sun kissed Ocracoke, Delaney was out for her run. She found herself by the passenger ferry dock, looking out over Silver Lake. Her mind was on Justin and what he had told her on the swing. Her heart was waking up. His story was heartbreaking, and if anyone knew Delaney, they would tell you she loved to fix broken objects, people, and animals. Was Justin going to be her new project? Inhaling the morning sea air, she did a few stretches and continued her run back to her cottage.

"Good morning!" Delaney cheered as she walked into the kitchen to the aroma of pancakes. "Margo, you did not have to do this. But they sure hold an enticing aroma." She rubbed her stomach.

"I found blueberries in your freezer and had an urge to carb up with buttermilk pancakes for our big morning hike out to the turtle boil. I read that the walk to the nest is about a half-mile."

"It's so worth it. Coffee smells tempting, but I gave it up months ago. But lately, I crave it, so why not?"

Elisa dragged herself over to the coffeepot, poured a full cup, and cleared her throat. "Now tell us what happened last night? I'm desperate to live vicariously through you and Justin."

With her hands up in the air, Delaney shook her head. "What do you need to know? Nothing happened, if that is what you mean."

"No hot loving in the back bed of ole Sally under the Milky Way as the waves crashed to the shore, leaving you breathless yet yearning for more?"

"Gosh, no, Elisa, you have a dirty mind." Delaney scrunched up her face, although the thought of it gave her tingles.

Margo added as she sprinkled blueberries on the pancakes. "She does. I would like to take her to the bookstore in town later and get her a few juicy romance novels she can take to the beach. Maybe that will satisfy your lustful quench for a tryst."

Elisa sat down. "I'm in if you are buying! I would love to read a bodice ripping novel with a hot stud with rippled abs to take me away."

"And where will he take you?" Delaney asked as she blew a kiss in the air.

"Anyplace wants Delaney." Elisa caught the kiss.

There was a soft knock on the front door. Delaney looked out the kitchen window and smiled. "Miss Opal is here."

Standing in front of the screen door, Miss Opal had a basket in her hands. "Morning, Delaney." She lifted the basket. "I made an extra batch of those cookies your lovely friend, who owns the city restaurant, likes."

"Gosh, that is so nice." She opened the screen door. "Come inside. You are up early."

Miss Opal entered, and then Delaney took the basket. "Stay for blueberry pancakes."

"Honey, I'd love to, but today I need to get back to Justin and make an omelet to get his strength, cause as you know my place is gonna need muscle power! His favorite is ham and green peppers. He told me earlier that you are going to the turtle boil with him." She lifted her eyebrows and pursed her lips.

Delaney placed the basket on a side table. "Yes, we are *all* going."

Miss Opal folded her hands together, and she spoke in a soft tone. "Justin is a good boy and has had his share of heartbreaks." She leaned in. "I had best mind my business and manners."

Delaney did not want to make an issue of what she had learned from Justin and smiled.

"And if you ladies are free this week, your Uncle Bo's sister, Aunt Dottie over on Hatteras, invited us to her dress shop and a light brunch and is more than thrilled to see you."

"I spoke to her the other day, and she invited us to her shop. Should I give her a call? Wait. Let me ask my friends first." She faced the kitchen and asked. The response was a loud yes!

Miss Opal's face lit up as she reminded Delaney she would give Dottie a call. "I suggest we catch a nine-a.m. ferry to Hatteras. Will we all fit in your SUV?"

"Yes! It has seats in the far back."

Margo walked over to them. "Hello Miss Opal." Her nose found the basket. "Are those your yummy for the tummy cookies?" She lifted the green cloth napkin. "They are! Thank you."

"Honey, I'll give you my mama's recipe card only if you serve them in your New York restaurant and call them Tummy Yummies."

Margo's face lit up with joy as she spoke. "Absolutely! My soon-to-be husband and I are opening a bakery within the restaurant, and this will be our signature cookie. Thank you so much!" She approached Miss Opal and gently kissed her soft cheek. "I need to get back to making pancakes. Will you stay?"

"No, honey, I need to get home," Miss Opal said, adding a slight wave.

Wearing a joyful smile and a skip in her step, Margo left the room.

"Back to our trip to Hatteras, we will all fit in my SUV, and if not, Margo has her car too."

"Perfect!" Miss Opal clapped her hands together. "I best be on my way. Justin told me he took you out last night in Sally." She batted her eyes as she waited for a response.

"He did, and we went out for an ice cream. He is a perfect gentleman, and we had a lovely time."

Miss Opal's face illuminated as she took Delaney's hand in hers. "He needs a friend." And with that, she turned and left.

Delaney wondered what she meant by *He needs a friend*. Last night he said he had plenty of friends. She let out a weighty sigh as she picked up the basket of cookies and went into the kitchen just as Margo was doling out pancakes.

With a few laughs and concerned facial expressions from Margo, they settled into Sally's rustic seat and sat in awkward positions. Elisa was busy chatting about what life was like to be a single Long Island hairdresser, hinting about romance and ice cream. Margo elbowed her to clam up.

Delaney sat in the front seat, adding unsure smiles as Justin drove to the turtle boil, not saying a word. She wondered, was it her friends? Was it their conversation last night? Or maybe he was just being a man and not engaging in the female drama. Whatever it was, he changed as soon as they got out of the truck and walked down the sandy path.

Delaney was beside Justin as the sun and air let them know it was a steamy day ahead.

"Are you okay, Justin?"

"Yeah, why?"

Delaney lifted her shoulders as she put on her sunglasses and asked. "You have become quiet this morning."

He glanced back at Elisa and Margo and out to the ocean as he spoke. "Last night was great, and I gotta learn to keep my problems to myself. I did not want to burden you with my life."

Delaney stopped and took his hand in hers.

Elisa and Margo walked ahead, whispering to each other, glancing over their shoulders.

"It's okay, and I'm glad you told me what happened. It must have been terrible pain to deal with. If you let me. I want to be your friend. A sounding board."

He dropped his head as he pulled his hand away and pushed it into his pocket. "I must sound like a looser. You just met me, and I promise I'll leave you alone after today." He started to walk away when she told him to stop.

She strode over and faced him. "You know what you are doing? You're burdening yourself. If you want to pretend that I'm not across the street, I cannot stop you. If you want to play the ignore the neighbor nonsense, I can do that as well, but if you want a friend to talk to, I'm here anytime you want to open your heart." She turned around and went to catch up with her friends.

Justin watched her leave and wasted no time rushing up to her. "Delaney,"

She stopped and faced him. "What?"

His expression shifted from tense to relaxed. "I would like to be your friend. How about we start now?"

Delaney dug her toes into the sand as she looked up at him. "Friends, it is. But I thought our friendship began last night."

"It did." He let out a long exhale. "Can we shake on it?"

Behind the dunes, peeking through the sea oats, Elisa and Margo were watching.

"Deal." Delaney wasted no time and held her hand out.

His voice trailed off as their foreheads touched. No words needed to be said as the balmy sea mist surrounded them.

"Holy cow!" Elisa squeaked as she turned to Margo. "I'm not sure, but I think they kissed. I told you it would happen."

"It looks like they just pressed their foreheads together. We had better mind our business." Margo brushed the sand off her legs and looked toward the south. "Come on. I see a crowd gathering near the park rangers."

13

The girls stayed at the beach for the rest of the day after the turtle boil. Justin returned later in the day to pick them up. On the way back to the cottage, Margo kept her word to Elisa and asked Justin to stop at the bookstore where she picked up a few romance novels to keep Elisa busy.

Justin went over to get a coffee while Delaney and her friends spent time at the bookstore. He was eager to head home and work on Sally.

That night, out on the back porch, the girls enjoyed pizza for dinner and a pitcher of Long Island Iced Tea, compliments of Elisa.

Delaney sat back and looked out over the waters of the sound. "That was delicious pizza, and Elisa, how much gin is in our iced tea, or was it vodka?"

Elisa pinched her fingers. "A little of this and a little of that and can I feel it!"

Margo chuckled. "Slow down, Elisa. Remember that a few nights ago you felt dreadful the next morning."

"Yeah, I recall." She placed her napkin on her paper plate and paid her attention to Delaney. "Now that we are relaxed, what's up with you and Justin?"

"Nothing. We are neighborly pals." Delaney said in a quiet voice as she pulled the crust off her pizza. "You are such a busy buddy. And I want to make sure neither of you is upset that I went on a date and left you here. I mean, you are my guests."

Margo sipped her iced tea and then spoke. "No way! We love you and want to see you happy. There is plenty for us to do, or we do nothing. To be here on Ocracoke with you in your amazing cottage is a dream."

Delaney was relieved.

Elisa sat back, tapping her cheek. "Back to Justin. We saw you kiss! Now, if I recall, you have three more years left on your five-year plan of no dating." She held up three fingers and wiggled them.

Delaney felt her face warm up as her eyes circled the porch and back to her friends. "Put your fingers down. We did not kiss. It was a tender moment of *forehead touching*. I let him know he has me to talk to. He has had a tough time and is here to heal and help Miss Opal."

Elisa threw her hands up in the air. "Forehead touching or bumping? I would rather be bumping into something else!" The iced tea was kicking in when Margo suggested Elisa should start reading one of the naughty novels she purchased earlier.

Margo opened the pizza box and helped herself to another slice. "Why is Justin here to heal?" She picked the pepperoni off and placed it on her plate.

Delaney was biting her tongue. What he told her was personal. Should she tell them? In several days, they would be returning home, unlikely to see Justin again. What he told her, she found upsetting. After Hunter, her ex-fiancé, ran off with his friend's sister, she too had to heal. What Justin told her was that there was no match for her pain.

"If I tell you two, you must promise never to say a word. We are besties and know to keep secrets."

"That bad huh?" Margo asked as she reached for a napkin.

"Yeah, it's that bad."

"You do not have to tell us," Elisa said in a questionable tone. "But if it makes you feel better then go ahead."

"Justin is exceptionally kind. He possesses a wow in looks and is physically fit. Plus, he has a playful charm that I find appealing. And Elisa, please put down the three fingers! The five-year plan—what was I even thinking?"

Elisa sulked as she placed her hands in her lap.

"Two years ago, he was going to ask his girlfriend, who was also his head of accounts at his advertising firm, to marry him after he sold the company. They went out to celebrate with other co-workers and–." She stopped to sip her iced tea. "They had a fab time. His girlfriend, unknown to her, was going to find the ring on her pillow that night."

"This does not sound good." Elisa said as she rubbed her arms. "Go on."

"He waited up for her at his place, and she never showed up. It was almost dawn when a former coworker called to let him know she had been in an accident with another coworker, who was driving drunk. She was on her way home to grab a few things and was going to his place for the night."

"Oh, no," Margo said as she sat back, crossing her legs.

"Yup. She was alive, and the driver died at the scene of a head-on collision with another vehicle, and that driver survived."

Elisa reached over and rubbed Delaney's arm. "This is very sad. One minute they are on cloud nine celebrating, and the next fallen to earth."

"I know," Delaney continued in a distant voice. "His girlfriend was alive at the hospital. And he dashed over as they were pulling her off life support. She had succumbed to her catastrophic injuries. What made it more complicated was the huge lawsuit that ensued, which recently closed. It was not his fault since the former employee who caused the accident was just that, former, and driving his car. Not on company time. And that is why Justin is here. To heal."

The porch fell silent, only to be broken by a cicada in the oleander.

"Wow, talk about not judging a book by its cover. I would never have guessed he had such trauma and heartache. Now I want to go over and give him a warm hug," Elisa said, then let out a sigh. "So sorry I teased you. He needs a friend and a forehead bump from time to time." She said, trying to lighten the mood.

Margo rubbed her forearms. "What you told us gives me chills. Should we invite him over for dessert? Maybe we can all go for a walk or watch a funny movie."

Delaney's face radiated as she looked at her thoughtful friend. "You are always thinking of others. I bet he is tinkering with old, smelly Sally. Please do not mention any of what I told you. I want to keep him. I know Miss Opal mentioned he met someone after this that she called the gold digger, but he did not mention that."

"Gold digger. Wow! But what do you mean — lose him as a friend or more?"

Delaney tilted her head back and looked up at the ceiling and back to her friends. "He's a really nice guy, and I want to be there for him."

"Got it. How about we finish our pizza and cheer up? How about we head out for a ride around the village in that sexy golf cart?" Margo suggested as she stood up. "Better yet. How about we go on that ghost tour you told us about?"

"We have to do it!" Elisa cried out.

"Elisa, I thought you were afraid to go. But if you are in so am I! How about we go find old washed-up Blackbeard?"

"Delaney, I said ghost tour and no way am I looking for that guy or ghost!" Elisa shuddered.

As they were getting into the golf cart, Justin walked over to return the gas can. “Hey ladies. Just letting you know I had a fine time at the turtle boil. Thanks for asking me.”

Delaney’s eyes lit up as they met his, and she spoke. “We enjoyed it and especially our ride in Sally.”

He looked over the golf cart and lifted the gas can. “Here is the can, and thanks. What are you ladies up to? Behaving?” He glanced at Elisa.

Elisa wanted to cry as he spoke. Her heart ached for him. “We are going on a ghost tour. You want to join us? We have room on the golf cart.” She patted the seat next to her.

“Elisa, surely he would find that silly,” Delaney looked at him. “Would you?”

He placed the can on the ground. “Silly? Na. Interesting sure. Aunt Opal tells me that many souls wander around here. Even your Uncle Bo.”

“Stop!” Margo cried out. “Now I’m scared.”

“Just teasing.” He assured her, holding back a chuckle. “You ladies go have fun. I’m meeting someone at a restaurant. Delaney, I’ll put this in your garage and have fun!” He turned and walked to Miss Opal's place.

Delaney backed the golf cart out and drove down the street. “Elisa, I cannot believe you asked him.”

“Why not, Delaney?”

“Because—I don’t know why not.”

Margo held onto the dashboard and turned around to face Elisa, who was sitting in the back seat. “He makes my heart melt. But he said he was meeting someone. Hmmm, how about after our ghost walk we poke around and find out where he is and who this someone is?”

Delaney turned onto another street and stopped. “What are you two talking about? Leave him alone. He can do whatever he wants.”

Elisa leaned forward. "Come on. It will be a mini spy mission like we did growing up, looking in windows at night to see what that kid you liked was up to."

"What? I never did that."

"Liar!" Elisa clapped her hands. "We gotta go. The tour starts in ten minutes, then we look for Mr. Sexy and his dinner friend."

Delaney shook her head and let out a sigh as she turned the golf cart on.

The ghost tour took a little over an hour. Elisa wouldn't let go of Margo, who swore she saw a ghost here and there. Delaney was chuckling at her friends as they continued to look over their shoulders as the tour guide told tall tales, adding the beam of his flashlight under his chin.

Elisa let out a scream when a black cat raced across the street and sat on a tombstone. Its yellow eyes glowed in the flashlight beams as it let out a loud meow and ran off. Adding to that, in the distance a foghorn blew. The others in the tour group jumped, and a few huddled.

The tour guide knew he had an engaged, frightened group and added that the cat was not a cat but the spirit of an old sea captain who was looking to take a new wife with him to his grave. Naturally, Delaney held back her laughter at the tales. Elisa's fingers had a firm grip on Margo's shoulders.

When it was over, they giggled at how ridiculously they had acted. That was until the same black cat ran in front of the golf cart, sending them screaming.

"Delaney, I want to go home. No more ghosts, black cats, or the creepy wife seeking sea captain, and forget about finding Justin." Elisa was rubbing her arms. "This was fun, but how am I going to fall asleep?"

"I have some meditations you can listen to, and home we go!" Delaney said as she turned onto her street. "How about a Hallmark Christmas romance movie to lighten the mood?"

Elisa added her two cents. "Ah, Uncle Bo may wander into your room or watch the movie with us!"

"Stop it!" Margo cried out, holding her hands to her ears.

14

Delaney's morning run was met with a slight drizzle that soon lifted, allowing the summer sun to push the clouds aside to greet Ocracoke with another fabulous day.

Out on the front porch, Delaney was watering her flowers when a hummingbird stopped by to greet her. She stood still not to frighten the tiny creature as it circled her and stopped within inches of her face. Wasting no time, with the buzz of its wings, it headed over to the petunias for a morning drink.

"Wow, did I just see a hummingbird stare at you?"

Placing the watering can down, Delaney went over to Elisa. "It sure did, and this was not the first time that little creature has paid me a visit."

"Maybe you should get one of those hummingbird feeders with sugar water."

"Fab idea." Delaney sat down on the swing. "What do you want to do today?"

"Margo and I were thinking about trying to go stand-up paddleboarding. I picked up a brochure at one of the rental shops. We could have some fun, and I'm sure countless laughs."

Delaney agreed, and Elisa went inside to let Margo know.

Keeping an eye on Miss Opal's cottage was Delaney's newest occupation. She could watch them from behind her flower boxes anchored on the porch rails. How silly she thought to herself — that was until Miss Opal walked off her porch and Justin was backing Sally out of the driveway. She could see Justin getting out and Miss Opal running her hands over the side panels. She went to open the passenger-side door when Justin did it for her. With his hand in hers, she settled into the seat, and he shut the door.

"How sweet! He's taking her for a ride." She popped up when Justin called out a *hello* from across the street.

Embarrassed, he may have known she was spying on him, she gave an easygoing wave and called out. "Morning!"

Miss Opal spoke loudly from the half-rolled-down window. "Join us. We are taking the old gal out for a ride. Been many years since I sat on Sally's seats!"

"Thank you, but we are heading out to go paddle boarding."

Miss Opal put her hand to her ear and shook her head.

Delaney took the hint and went over to her. "Darn, my friends and I are going out in a little while. But have a fantastic time!"

Justin hopped onto the driver's side and leaned toward Miss Opal. "We have room in the back seat. And an extra beach towel."

How could she say no to that smile? Looking over her shoulder at her cottage and back to Miss Opal and the towel, she said. "Give me a second." She dashed to her place to let her friends know she would be back shortly.

Once she settled in the back seat, Justin started the truck up, and Sally bellowed her usual pop. He glanced in the rear-view mirror at Delaney, who wore a bright smile.

"The last time I was in this truck had to be, let me think." Miss Opal tapped her cheek. "Golly had to be before my husband died. I had packed a lunch. It was chicken salad with sweet pickles that Bo had grown and canned. What a day that was! Bo asked us to go fishing with him, and we were sure glad we did. A pinch of the south wind met us, then picked up, and the darkest of clouds came to pay a visit, and they were not coming in a kind manner. Deciding to hightail it back home, the darned fuel pump died, and we had to get Sally towed." Her face became softer as she resumed folding her hands in her lap. "Thankfully, we returned home before the heavens opened to a downpour. Bo fixed her up, but that was the last time I was in her." She ran her hands over the dashboard. "You look a little tarnished, and ya sure stink like ya had been sitting idle."

Justin agreed and added. "I'll have this truck shining and smelling like new sooner than later. My friend Buddy said it will not take much. He did, however, suggest we take it over to Hatteras since he has a garage and the tools to work on it."

Delaney sat back, enjoying it when Miss Opal shared the rest of her story of the past. "Miss Opal, that sounds like it was a wonderful day, rain and all."

"It sure was, and I have plenty of them to share. We had a wonderful fish dinner that night!" She turned to Justin. "That is fabulous news about your pal Buddy! Looking forward to seeing Sally shiny like a new penny. One thing I ask is that you keep her baby-blue paint. It was Bo's favorite color, and truth be told, I picked that color when he was thinking about buying her. My husband insisted Sally be green. Blue won in a poker game!" Turning her head from side to side, she chuckled.

"Sally's paint color was won in a poker game. I love it!" Delaney said as she eyed the interior and its decline.

"No worry, Aunt Opal, she will remain blue. I may keep some of the rust and original blue. First, I gotta see what Buddy says, and as soon as we can be roadworthy. I can start getting the smaller materials here and begin some projects at your place."

Delaney sat back as the breeze from the open window cooled her face.

"When do you want to take Sally over to Hatteras?" Miss Opal asked.

"As soon as I can get a ride back here. Buddy told me that it could take several days, if not a week, since his garage is full of other jobs. I can take the passenger ferry if need be to get home."

Delaney leaned forward and tapped Miss Opal's shoulder. "When are we going to see Aunt Dottie?"

"Honey, you are always thinking. Let me talk to her, and we can go over and bring Justin back with us. She did mention Wednesday."

"That works!" Delaney said as she sat back.

"Ladies, what are you talking about?" Justin slowed down at a stop sign. "Dottie?"

They explained who Dottie is and hatched a plan to take the truck to Hatteras and get Justin back to Ocracoke.

They returned, and Delaney met her friends, and off paddleboarding they ventured. As they attempted the newfound sport, laughter found them as they slipped and fell into the water. After a few hours, they knew it was time to call it quits and head back to the cottage.

Delaney stepped into the outside shower and let her hair dry in the sun out in the backyard down by the water. Relaxed in her Adirondack chair and sore from paddleboarding, she rested her head back and dozed off.

A tap on her shoulder startled her out of her peaceful nap. She jumped out of the chair when she heard a familiar voice say her name.

"What are you doing here!" Her heart pounded as she stepped back.

"A vacation to see my Delaney." He made his way in front of her. "Nice place you have here." Scanning the property and out to the waters of the sound, he paid attention back to Delaney. "Island life has certainly given you a glow. Or is that a leisurely life tan?"

Crossing her arms over her chest, she felt her body tense up and stomach tumble. "I asked you. Why are you here and I'm not *your* Delaney?"

He moved in closer. "Is that anyway to treat your ex-fiancé?"

A warm breeze tousled her hair as she curled her toes when calm words formed. "Hunter, I did *not* invite you, and you have some damn nerve showing up here after what has it been?"

He threw his hands up in the air. "It has been a long time, Delaney, and I came here to say that I'm sorry, and can we–"

"Whatever it is, no! I want you to get off my property." She slid past him and stopped. "Go back under the rock you crawled out of. I have a life here, and it's not with you and whatever her name is. You may recall the tramp you left me for." With heavy steps, she walked to the back porch and opened the screen door. "Go home!"

The door slammed behind her as she marched inside, taking deep breaths, wondering if she was dreaming. How did he know she was here? Better yet, why was he standing in her yard as if they were still a couple?

15

As Delaney circled her back porch, a storm of wild emotions brewed within her. She stopped and looked out the back window of the living room to see Hunter standing by the water. He needed to go! She felt sick to her stomach.

"Urg." She continued her pacing when the front door opened.

In stepped Elisa, wearing a radiant smile. "I love grocery shopping using a golf cart. We had a blast and got some awesome appetizers for tonight and a few bottles of wine." She wiggled her shoulders, adding. "And Justin said hello. We met him at the store. He is dreamy and gorgeous, and he has the whitest teeth!"

"White teeth? Wow, you need a date!" Margo said as she was closing the door behind her while Elisa made her way into the kitchen. "Go read one of those books!"

"Are you alright? You look flushed and upset." Margo asked with caution as she placed a shopping bag down. "Delaney?"

Sucking her cheeks in and tapping her foot, she pointed out the window.

Margo's heart sank as she walked over to the window and to Delaney. "I wondered who parked their SUV out front. I assumed it was a vacationer."

"Yup, it's him, and how the hell did he know I was living here?" She was shaking as she sat down, folding her arms. "How do I get him to leave?"

A thick lump formed in Margo's throat. She had a suspicion it was her fiancé who had opened his big mouth. He had told her several nights earlier that Hunter had stopped by at the restaurant, and that was when he most likely spilled the beans. He had to have slipped and said she was on Ocracoke with Delaney at her cottage.

She assumed it also wouldn't take much with the aid of Google to find Delaney. What was she going to do? Should she be honest and stress or ruin their friendship? It was not her fault.

"Delaney, allow me to go out and tell him to leave."

Delaney shook her head. "No, Margo, it's not your responsibility. I have to take care of it. I just need to breathe and get my act together." She sat down on the sofa and dropped her head into her hands.

Margo wore a nervous, flickering smile as she walked over to Delaney. "I can do it."

She looked up. "No. I got this."

Margo felt awful as she grabbed the rest of the groceries and met Elisa in the kitchen.

Margo spoke in a soft tone. "Elisa, Hunter is here."

"What? Where?" The two bottles of wine in Elisa's hands almost crashed to the floor.

"He's down by the water's edge."

"Why? That bastard." She walked over to the back door of the kitchen. "What is he doing here? I had better go check on Delaney. Does she know?"

"Yes, she knows." Margo wrung her hands together as she felt her heart pound. "My big mouth fiancé, David, must have told him."

Elisa spun around. "I'm totally confused?"

Margo explained Hunter's visit to the restaurant when Delaney walked into the kitchen and stopped. She rested her back against the wall. "Margo, this is not your fault. I heard every word. It was an innocent mistake. If Hunter had wanted to find me, he would have eventually. But we need to get him out of here."

"Call the sheriff." Elisa suggested as she unpacked a grocery bag.

Shaking her head, Delaney said, "There is no reason to call the sheriff. Hunter has only stopped by. He is not crazy or violent."

There was a knock on the front door. "Let me get it," Delaney said and then asked Elisa to keep a watchful eye on Hunter, who was lingering out by the water.

Walking over to the door, she took a deep inhale. She had forgotten Miss Opal was stopping over to borrow a pair of scissors for sewing.

"Hey, Delaney!"

"Oh, uh, hi Justin. I thought you were Miss Opal." She looked over his shoulder and back at him. "Guess not."

"My visit is to pick up scissors or shears. Aunt Opal said, her bunion is acting up, and she is unable to walk over." He felt uncomfortable even saying *bunion.* "I see you have company."

"Huh?"

"Yeah. The gray SUV parked by your garage."

Think quickly. "Uh, yeah. Elisa's friend is here visiting for the day."

"Cool, have fun. Hey, can you get the scissors or sewing shears? I need to run to catch the ferry over to Hatteras."

"Wait there." She dashed off and returned with them. "They are called sewing shears, or at least that is what Miss Opal calls them." She was jittery, messing with her hair as she kept her body between the door. "I gotta run."

He held the scissors up. "Thanks, and are you all right?" He studied her tense face.

"Yup! Just have a client on the phone. On hold. Sorry, I really must run."

"I got it, and Miss Opal wanted me to remind you that the visit to Hatteras to Dottie's is tomorrow, and I would appreciate it if you could give me a ride back to Ocracoke. I'm leaving tonight on the ferry to get over there and spend the night."

She tapped her forehead. "Absolutely. We will be in touch; I really must go. Bye." After closing the door and leaning against it, she dropped her head, inhaled, and let it out.

Margo walked over and rubbed Delaney's arm. "Please let me go out there and tell him to leave."

"Shit! Here he comes and is making a beeline for the back porch!" Elisa shrieked. "Delaney!"

Margo felt her face flush and stomach flip flopping as she went into the kitchen.

Hunter was not a monster. He was a terrific guy at one time. Delaney loved him as if there were no other man. They spent six years together, and he helped her grow her business. His mother was a well-known fashion designer in New York City and was her mentor. He was the type you'd find at the good guy's club. Was it the impending marriage to Delaney that scared him off? Whatever it was, the fact was that he ran off with another woman, crushing Delaney.

Why was he here now? He looked amazing. His voice, as much as she wanted to despise, had soothed her. But this is her life now, and there was no time for Hunter since at one time he had no time for Delaney.

16

Hunter made his way to the back screened-in porch and rang the ship's bell beside the door.

"Crap, what do we do?"

"We? Elisa, *he* is my problem. Let me handle it. Why is he here now?" Delaney rubbed her forehead as she inhaled and let it out. She didn't know whether to cry or scream.

Margo was twisting her lips and dashed off to text her fiancé and give him a piece of her mind.

Delaney needed to put on her big girl panties and deal with her past. The kitchen door closed behind her as her bare feet met the boards of the back porch. There he was, on the other side of the screened door. She must shake it off and remember how he hurt her. One, two, three, she silently said as she approached him and opened the door.

"Can we talk?"

"Hunter, not here. I have guests. How about was take a walk and talk?"

"Where?" His eyes searched the grounds and then back to Delaney.

"We can walk down to the edge of the sound in my backyard. Since the tide is low, we can walk along the shoreline. It's quiet there."

Hunter glanced back at the water before turning to Delaney. "Of course. Just so you know, I'm not here to play the villain. I came to see you."

"It would have been nice if you had texted me first to see if I wanted to see you." She quickly glanced at his ring finger, spotting a gold band.

Elisa was staring out the living room window and turned to Margo, who had just hung up her phone. "What do you think they are talking about?"

"I don't have a clue, but he has to go," Margo snapped as she tossed her phone onto the sofa. "I cannot believe that my big mouthed idiot of a future husband went and did this. Some men have half brains."

"No brains, and that is why this girl is single!" Elisa made light of it.

Delaney and Hunter discovered a spot along the shore where an ancient live oak tree had long since fallen. They settled on the smooth trunk, gazing out at the glistening waters of the sound. Hunter leaned in, picking up a shattered piece of a sand dollar. He rolled it between his fingers. "I did not come here to make you upset."

Delaney laughed to herself and then spoke. "Is that a joke? You are not here to upset me. You have no business being here. And I see you are wearing a wedding band? When did that happen?"

He was silent as he continued to roll the sand dollar until he tossed it into the water. "Last summer we eloped out in the Hamptons at my mom's house."

"Nice. Real nice." She stood up, and he asked her to sit down. She did.

"Delaney, I made a mistake not marrying you. Fear of being with someone as awesome as you blindsided me. We let things go that do not belong to us, then one day we wake up and want them back, realizing we made a terrible mistake." His lost eyes found their way to Delaney's.

"Hmm, sometimes they cannot find their way back, Hunter. They need to stay where they were, far away in safe surroundings." A chilling silence surrounded them as Delaney looked down at her bare feet.

"I guess, but hey, sometimes you can at least bump into them again."

"I'm happy for you." She lied as she fought to hold back tears. Her wounded heart was pulsing as she threw her hands in the air. "Fear of marrying me is crap. You wasted no time eloping with someone else. I gotta go, and so do you."

He stood up and pulled her into his arms. "I left her."

Delaney tugged back as her stare landed on his finger. "And the ring on your finger?"

"Yeah, I need to get rid of it." He twisted it around his finger until he removed it when she asked him to stop.

He did not listen, and his finger was free as he held the ring up to the sun and then tossed it as far as he could out into the water.

Delaney sprinted into the shallow water to find it.

"Leave it!" he called out as he dashed into the water, splashing as he made it over to her.

She was looking down, running her hands over the sand. "You keep your ring. I do not want it polluting the waters by my home."

He lifted her chin with his index finger. She offered no resistance, feeling the familiar, comforting warmth of his lips and the intensity of his body merge with hers.

She pushed him away and dropped her head as she spoke. "Please go. I cannot and will not do this. You need to find yourself again. I have been for a while. We once shared our hearts until you tore mine out." Her voice trailed off. She did not want him to see her tears. She moved away from him and at a fast pace walked along the shoreline towards her cottage.

He called out. "Delaney! But there is a reason I'm here."

"Go home, Hunter. Please, for the sake of my heart and yours, go home."

He watched her leave as the warm water lapped up against his lower legs.

She made her way to her cottage and slammed the back porch door, found a soft chair, and sat in it. Resting her head in her hands, she sobbed.

"Margo, should we go out there and say something?"

"No, Elisa, let her cry it out. Maybe this is what she needed. As far as Hunter is concerned, I'm going to wait out by his SUV and have a chat with him. He has to leave even if I must get my fiancé to get his ass down here and haul him off."

"Agreed. What a creep to have come all the way here to cause trouble. Delaney does not deserve this."

Lifting her head, Delaney wiped her nose as she sniffled. She could see Hunter walking past the porch toward the street. An epiphany hit her. She was not over him, and this was the final blow. How it hurt. Her body, mind, and soul ached.

Margo waited by the SUV when Hunter arrived. His pant legs were wet, and his hair ruffled. His edgy face and body language said it all.

He stopped at the driver's side of the SUV. "Go ahead, Margo, bitch me out. I should have come with a warning. But too late."

"Hunter, you should never have come here. Delaney has moved on with her life, and this was uncalled for. Did you think she would rush back into your waiting arms?"

Shoving his hands into his pant pockets, he tilted his head back and watched a seagull pass by.

"Well?"

He turned away, then looked up at Margo. "I came here to say goodbye."

"Huh?" Margo crossed her arms. "Your text a few years ago did that."

"No, I mean goodbye. I'm not well emotionally, and I need to spend some time in Europe. My wife left me months ago, and my mother died last year."

"Whoa, wait, wife? Your mother died? Oh my gosh. Sorry about your mother. Wait, a sec. You were married?" She tilted her head in confusion.

"Yes, the marriage was a joke. I was running from my feelings for Delaney. There is no explaining it, but it was a mistake I have lived with."

Margo felt her breath was being taken away as she asked. "Your mom passed away last year?"

"Yup, she did, and I came here to give this to Delaney and say goodbye." He opened the car door and reached inside. In his hand was a large manilla envelope.

"What is that?" Margo's curious eyes circled the envelope and went back to Hunter.

"My mom told me to give this to Delaney one year of the date of her death." He pressed it against his chest. "I believe she will appreciate it. My mom loved Delaney more than me. I broke her heart when I did not marry her."

Margo rubbed her forehead. "Wow. This is a lot to comprehend, that your mom passed away. I think you need to tell Delaney why you are truly here."

"Na, it's best I go. Give this to her." He glanced at the front porch as he handed the envelope to Margo. "I'm staying at the inn over by Silver Lake if she has questions." He gave a slight nod as he got into his SUV and handed her a printout of where he was staying, and drove off.

Margo turned to see that Delaney was standing on the front porch.

17

"What is that Hunter gave you?" Delaney kept staring at the envelope. "Is it a copy of his divorce? How rude!"

Margo shook her head as she walked onto the porch. "How about we have a seat on the swing?"

"Not good, huh?" Delaney said as her shoulders slumped. "Toss it. Better yet, tear it up."

They sat on the wooden swing.

"No, it's not what you think it is."

Elisa stepped out onto the porch. "What's going on? I was on the phone with my soon to be business partner. His ideas for the new salon are amazing." She noticed the somber looks on their faces, found a chair, and sat down. "Spill it. What happened?" She glanced out onto the driveway. "Looks like Hunter left." Paying her attention to Margo and then to Delaney, she pulled her lips in and out.

Margo held Delaney's hand. "Hunter is staying in the village."

"How long?" Delaney was more than anxious as she fidgeted on the swing.

Lifting her shoulders, Margo handed the envelope over. "Delaney, his mother passed away last year on this day. I'm surprised you didn't know."

Delaney felt her eyelashes tickle with tears. "My gosh, Madeline passed away. No one told me. She was like a mother to me." She looked up at the ceiling and back at her friends as she placed her hands over her heart. "Is that why he came here to tell me? A little late? Now I feel terrible." Looking down at the envelope, she asked in a low voice. "Should I even open it?"

Margo got off the swing. Her eyes met Delaney's. "You should open it since it's from Hunter's mother. I do not know what's in it. But he said he came here to hand this to you as per his mother's request. Apparently, she wanted you to have this a year to the date of her passing."

Elisa got up and asked if Delaney wanted her to read it.

Delaney squeezed her eyes shut, then opened them, she said. "I got this. I think."

Margo met Elisa and took her hand. "I think we should go inside and allow Delaney her privacy."

Together, they stepped into the cottage, leaving Delaney alone on the swing.

She unclasped the envelope and revealed the two-page letter inside. As she read the inked words, warm tears streamed down her cheeks, landing on the envelope. In that moment, she could sense Madeline's presence as the document transported her back to a cherished time. It was a beautiful period when she would sit in the New York workroom studio that Hunter's mother deeply valued. Like a parched sponge, she absorbed every bit of knowledge from this incredibly talented woman. Madeline's creations graced the runways of the most esteemed fashion shows and were featured in many high-end boutiques. For a while, her patented jeans and sparkling hip sweatshirts flew off the shelves on a TV home shopping network, selling out every time.

Madeline was a creative, encouraging woman who left heartfelt words in ink. She inspired Delaney to be who she is. A textile designer who was working on her own line. After the breakup between Hunter and Delaney, it was too straining for Delaney to spend time with his mother. There were times when they shared ideas via texts, but that was the extent of it. As time drifted, so did their relationship.

She wiped away her tears as a warm smile lit up her spirit. His mother had bid her a heartfelt farewell, leaving behind not only a touching message but also a collection of drawings, fabrics, trimmings, and designs amassed from her fashion house. All Delaney needed to do was dial the attorney's number listed on the document, travel to New York, sign a few papers, and everything would become hers.

Doting Margo could not help herself. She came outside to see if Delaney was all right. Elisa was not far behind her.

"I know you are both curious, and first off, I find this to be a lot." She sniffled.

Elisa got closer. "You do not look fine with those red eyes."

"Here you go, a nice refreshing glass of iced tea with that lemon balm I picked from your garden." Margo placed the glass on a side table.

"Thanks, and I know you two are more curious than a cat, so have a seat. Hunter did what his mother asked, and that was out of respect for her. He came all the way down here since she wanted him to hand it over in person. Maybe it was in hopes that we could reconnect." Delaney worked her way into a dim smile. "That will never happen."

Elisa was picking at one of her manicured nails. "Are you going to tell us what is in the envelope?"

"As my two besties, yes. Madeline T. Labrok has left me with her drawings and textile designs she had put away and never worked with. From what I read, after the estate had settled, it was then I was to receive this. I'll have to make a trip to New York to sign documents, and then they will send me the keys to the storage units."

"Wow! That is terrific news! She was a premier designer, and I wonder why she never left it to Hunter or any of her employees. She had to have a person she trusted."

Delaney delayed her answer as she looked over at Miss Opal's place. "I bet she feared Hunter would sell it off. Or maybe she never trusted her team."

Elisa crossed her arms over her chest. "Can you imagine what she must have left you? The trust she had in you. I mean, is she asking you to take over the company?"

Margo cleared her throat before she spoke up. "Do you think that the new owner wants rights to what she left you? It *is* New York and the competitive fashion industry."

Delaney tapped her cheek. "I'm going to call the attorney now and get the details. The last thing I need is to inherit something that I have to fight over." She got up. "Come on, girls, we have a call to make!"

"We?"

"Yes, Elisa, we!"

18

The call to the attorney was short and informative. There was no need for Delaney to head up to New York. She did, however, need a notary to sign the documents. Once signed, the keys to the storage units would be sent to Delaney.

Delaney hung up, relieved she did not need to make a road trip, which she was not in the mood for, preferring the quietness of Ocracoke to the crowds and horns of New York City. She wondered what Madeline had left her. Her mind was active with what she was about to have transported to her cottage.

Not long after the phone call, they decided on heading over to the beach to avoid Hunter since he was still in the village.

As they were getting into Delaney's car, Justin made his way over. "Hi ladies! Gorgeous this afternoon. Are you all heading out to the beach?" His eyes twinkled in the sun. "Opal wanted me to thank you for the scissors or shears, and here they are!" He pulled them out from behind his back.

"Great, can you put them up on the porch? We have a date with the ocean." Delaney said as she slid on her sunglasses to hide her red eyes.

"You got it. Have a beachy time, and if you need a tent, I found one in the shed over at Opal's. It may need a cleaning, but looks kinda cool."

Elisa had to ask. "Does it have mouse holes or musty?"

Justin had to think about it and then answered. "Not sure, but later I can take it out after I get Sally backed out and into the driveway."

Margo thanked him.

"Our trip to Hatteras is tomorrow. Are you leaving tonight?" Delaney asked as she put her hair in a ponytail.

He gave a wide stretch. "Yup, I gotta take a late ferry over. Are you sure you want to give me a lift back here? I can always take the passenger ferry and grab a bike or walk back here to the Opals."

"Of course we are giving you a ride back here! The more, the merrier. You get the spend a few hours with us girls and that *girly talk*." Delaney winked, adding a chuckle and a twist of her ponytail.

"You can have all the girly talk you want since I have amazing new earbuds, so I won't hear a thing!"

They all gave a slight laugh.

"Chat later and put the scissor up on the porch on the swing."

"Will do, Delaney, and have a fantastic time. Surf is up, and the sand is hot." He leaned in and whispered. "Tan lines?"

Taken by surprise, Delaney shook her head as her face flushed redder than Opal's roses as she said. "See you later!" She backed out as he stepped aside and gave a wave.

"OMG, did he just?" Elisa said with a tease.

"He did!" Margo added. "I think he has one thing on his manly mind, and that is your tan lines!"

"You two have to tame those sexy thoughts or fantasies." Delaney giggled to herself. Heck, he can see her tan lines, and today she will spend more time in the sun! She turned the old FM radio up, and with the warm summer breezes finding them, they drove off.

Justin, wearing a subtle smile, approached Delaney's porch just as a gray Range Rover arrived in front of her cottage. He turned to see a man step out, not in beach attire, but dressed for a preppy golf outing. With his pink gingham button-down shirt, tan khaki shorts, and faded dress loafers, Justin couldn't help but wonder about this unfamiliar figure. Had he just walked out of a GQ magazine shoot? Justin observed him as he strolled up the walkway.

"Hi, are you lost? On vacation?" Justin called out.

The man stopped. Their eyes met. "No, are you?"

"I live across the street."

The man continued and stopped at the bottom of the stairs. He looked up at the cottage and pointed at the sign above the door and said in a dry tone. "*Sea Gypsy*. Of course she would name this shack that."

Justin looked over his shoulder and back at the stranger. "That is the name of the cottage. Wait, are you talking about the owner?" He walked over to Hunter.

"Yeah. What are you doing here? From the looks of it, there is not much you will find in this place if you are looking to rob her."

"Rob her?" Justin snapped back as he turned around.

The stranger pushed his mirrored sunglasses up over his thick, dark hair. "It's difficult for me to accept that she chose to live in this beach shack. This feels like a gypsy hideaway. Some people never truly mature."

Not liking Hunter's tone, he wasted no time replying in a sharp voice. "The owner is a friend. And you?"

"Hunter Labrok and Delaney, the owner of this place, is my ex-finance." His voice, filled with arrogance, babbled on. "Is she home?"

"Ah," Justin was unsure if this man was here for a good reason or was it something else. Was he even who he said he was? He engaged in conversation. "No, she is not here, but I can tell her you stopped by." Curious, he ran his fingers through his hair and asked. "Are you staying here on Ocracoke?"

"Yeah, at an inn over by the water." Hunter turned to leave. "Tell her that I'll stop by later. She knows why, and I gotta ask you something. Are you her beach boyfriend or just an unemployed neighbor who hangs out on her porch?"

Justin felt his fists clench and loosen as he replied. "A neighbor returning something." He wanted so badly to punch Hunter in the nose. Not wanting to stir the pot, he loosened his fists. "I gotta get back to working on my truck."

"Hey, listen, I'm not looking for trouble. Just a messenger and wanted to make sure Delaney got the packet I left with her friend, Margo. You know the hot one of the trio. Too bad she wears an engagement ring."

Justin faced him. "Enjoy Ocracoke." Shaking his head and feeling his fists clench, he walked across the street to Opals wondering why Hunter was there. A package? An ex-fiancé? He must shake it off as he made his way over to Sally.

Hunter was in no hurry to leave, as he found himself comfortable on one of the front porch chairs.

Keeping a close eye on Hunter, he texted Delaney.

Justin texted: *Hope you are having fun in the waves. You have a guest on your porch. Thought you should know, he is sitting on the swing.*

There was no response. He waited a few minutes and texted again.

Justin texted: *A heads up. You have a guest here. A guy named Hunter is on your porch. More to follow.*

Still waiting for a response, he went back to working on Sally and got the truck ready for the trip to Hatteras.

Elisa was reaching for her towel when she heard Delaney's phone ding. "You have a text from Mr. Curious about your tan lines!" She laughed out loud. "We heard what he said since he stinks at whispering, and you need to let him know to keep his naughtiness for your ears only."

Drying her hair, Delaney looked down at her phone. She put her towel on her beach chair and picked it up. "Just a few texts from Justin. Shit!"

"What?" Margo asked as she slid her coverup over her head.

Delaney held her phone up. "Guess who is at my cottage, sitting on the porch?"

Justin took a photo of the SUV and sent it along with a new text voicing his concern over Hunter.

"Yikes," Margo cried out. "He needs to go away. Why is he at your place? You got the envelope and spoke to the attorney."

Elisa added with alarm. "Did you lock the cottage doors?"

"I did not. Crap, I hope he is not going inside."

"Call Justin right now."

"Why, Margo?"

"Delaney, do you want to walk inside and find him sitting on your sofa wearing that stupid grin?" Margo's tone hinted with mockery said. "He is a lost puppy looking for a nipple."

"That is the vilest description that is now stuck in my head." Elisa placed her hand over her mouth as she dramatically gagged.

"Margo, that is nasty." Delaney wrinkled her nose as she put her sun hat on. "Please refrain from those remarks!"

Elisa teased her, adding. "He needs a nipple!"

Margo seized to chuckle at the comment and continued. "It's how I see him, Delaney. He's divorced and fishing to see if you will come back with open arms. Nope. He must go home. Besides, I refuse to let him ruin our vacation."

Elisa was applying layers of sunblock to her arms. "Margo is correct. Give Justin a call to watch him."

Delaney, gazing over the ocean, inhaled and let out as she reflected on her past with him. "Let me ask Justin to keep a close eye on him." She picked up her phone and dialed.

"Hey, Delaney, are you having a fun time?"

"I was until I got your texts. Listen, it's a long story. But you could do me a favor?"

"Sure. Do you want me to punch *him* in the nose? I have a good right hook."

Delaney burst into laughter. "Yes!"

"I'll go over there now." Justin said as he got inside Sally and put his phone on speaker.

"No——no, I was joking. Gosh, no, he will have his team of lawyers at your door. Trust me, stay away."

"That bad, huh? FYI, I can see him now, and he is on his phone and looks like he is texting. He did a little pacing, but that is about it. Wait a sec, he's peeking in a window."

Just then, Delaney saw Hunter's texts.

"He stopped and is sitting down again. I think, and he has one attitude."

"That he does, and thanks for looking over at my place. We will be back in a little while. Wait, you said he has an attitude? Did he talk to you?" Delaney was biting her pinky nail when Margo stopped her.

"Yup, I was returning the scissors, and he showed up. He said a few things to me. I guess he does not like your sign above the door. Something about your being a gypsy will never change. And oh yeah, he told me his name is Hunter Labrok, as if I was supposed to know who he is. What a snob!"

Feeling her stomach hit her feet and race back up, she told Justin to ignore him, and she would deal with him when she returned home.

Justin, although curious, did not want to get involved in whatever Delaney and Hunter had and went back to working on Sally. When given the opportunity, he would steal a glance to see what Hunter was up to.

"You must not let him upset you and turn our day at the beach into your past. Let him sit there in his crap. He must have nothing else to do. So how about we take a beach walk and look for some shells?" Margo suggested as she put on her floppy straw beach hat. "Again, I'm so sorry my blabbermouth fiancé told him where you are. Men!"

"I agree a walk will do us and you some good. And with the tide going out, the sandbars are calling us!" Elisa reached for Delaney and gave her a hug. "We are not, do you hear me, not going back to your place with him sitting there. He is akin to a hungry mosquito searching for something to feed on; if it doesn't find what it needs, it will simply disappear. Otherwise, a massive fly swatter can tackle the issue!"

Delaney contemplated her situation. Would she choose to return if he stayed too long? Perhaps she would confront him, only to find herself enveloped in his arms, reconciling as though they were characters in a dark romance novel. What was wrong with her? She needed to shake off those thoughts. *He is a jerk!* He hurt her and had the audacity to run away with someone else mere months before their wedding. And worse, get married not long after to another woman. Yet, he is undeniably charming, and his mother was once her mentor. But she passed away. Why cling to him when he has no solid ground to stand on? His heart is as cold as ice, and how could he invade her life like a rogue wave crashing onto the shore, dragging her into a tumultuous sea of despair? He should return to where he belongs—under a rock. She was utterly heartbroken.

"Did you say something?" Elisa asked as she slid on her sunglasses.

Shaking her head, Delaney smiled. "Nope. And let's go for our beach stroll!"

Justin started up Sally just as the girls returned. He gave a wave and pointed to the SUV parked in from of Delaney's cottage. She returned with a nod as she pulled into her driveway when Elisa reminded her to remain calm.

"I know." Delaney sighed as she got out and reached for her beach bag.

Justin made his way over and spoke in a low voice. "Hi, you all look like you got some sun!"

"Yupper! And look at this shell I found. It's what did the surfer guy on the beach say it was?" Margo held it up.

"A helmet shell is what he said." Elisa said as she reached for her towel.

"Cool, I have not seen one of those is years. Terrific find." Justin said as she handed it over to him, and he studied it. "It's solid and not defects. A keeper!" he handed it back and turned to Delaney. "Your friend, I think he took a nap!"

"Ugh, he is not my friend. He is a pain in my ass." She removed her sunglasses and squinted up onto her porch. "I need to take care of this problem." She walked past Justin when he called out.

"I wanted to let you know that I'm leaving for Hatteras soon. Sally and I have a date with a garage at my friend's house."

She stopped and faced him. "I hope he can fix old Sally and not worry. We will get you back here tomorrow! Have fun."

"I'll text later. Listen, if you need me, call." He looked around and back at Delaney. His voice was sincere as he asked if she was okay. Was Hunter a threat?

She could feel her heart racing, overwhelmed by a whirlwind of emotions. For the moment, she held back her excitement and calmly reassured him that everything was fine, promising to see him the next day. With that, Justin crossed the street.

19

Hunter's smirk met Delaney as she walked up onto the porch. "Well, now, look what the sea dragged in? Is it the sea gypsy?"

"Hunter, go home. You are not welcome here. I received the information I needed from your mother's lawyers, and thanks. Too bad you never told me that your mother had passed away. You are a real class act."

Elisa and Margo stood behind her.

"I see the Three Stooges of New York have taken over Ocracoke." He sat back and stretched. "Nice place you have. Cute island. It's not like my place in the Hamptons, but it serves as a nice staff cottage. It could use a little work, but hey, to each his own." He yawned, knowing he had bruised her heart with every word. "I wanted to tell you that I'm leaving tomorrow."

"Why do I need to know this? You can leave now." Delaney placed her beach bag on a side chair. He was always good at painful stabs at how she preferred to live.

Elisa tapped her shoulder. "We are heading inside. If you need us, call out."

"Bye, Elisa. It was *good* to see you. And Margo, tell your soon to be better half that I'll stop by the restaurant. I want to thank him. I could have Googled all about Delaney, but hey I like spectacular meals and conversation."

Margo gave him the stink eye as she marched into the cottage.

"You are a pompous ass. Go home!" Elisa declared, standing behind Margo.

Hunter gave her a passive wave of his hand and then paid attention to Delaney. "Nice friends." He looked at his Cartier watch. "I wanted to say goodbye and see if you were interested in sharing dinner with me? One last hurrah and a thanks since I suggested to my mother years ago to leave some of her talent with you."

She found it impossible to trust anything he said. There was no doubt he had made no suggestions to his mother. He possessed an extraordinary talent for deceiving those around him to fulfill his own desires. As a true narcissist, she chose to dismiss his words, believing none of what he said. There was absolutely no way he had offered any advice to his mother. His ability to tell lies in pursuit of his goals was remarkable. She disregarded his statement, saying, "No dinner. You need to return to your life, and I must return to mine. Your mother was very generous to leave me what she did, and I'm forever grateful to her."

Hunter got up out of the chair and walked up to Delaney. He traced the outline of her face with his index finger as he spoke. "She was a generous person. I hope what she left you is something you can make use of. I sold her company to another fashion house and, to be honest, they would pay handsomely for what you will have in your possession."

Delaney pushed his hand away. "I'm not interested. I respected your mother and will fulfill her wishes with my talent." She turned to pick up her bag. "Goodbye, Hunter." And with that, she went inside.

He hung around for a short time and eventually headed out to his SUV and drove off.

From behind the curtains, Elisa announced he was gone and they could breathe.

"He is staying in the village at an inn. At least that is what he told me," Margo frowned. "I'm going to take a shower outside. And Delaney, I think he got the message and will be gone for good." She picked up a towel and went outside.

With crossed arms, Delaney maintained her gaze out the window when she saw Miss Opal walking across the street. Wasting no time, she met her on the porch.

"Hello Delaney. Just checking in to make sure we are heading over to Hatteras tomorrow morning. Justin is on his way over there now. I sure hope old Sally doesn't buck and start up on the ferry."

Delaney, wearing a welcoming smile, assured her that Sally would get Justin safely to Hatteras.

Elisa walked up behind Delaney. "Hi Miss Opal!"

"Hello young lady, and please accept my apology. I forgot your name. You know it's a sunny day if I can remember my name!"

"No problem. I'm Elisa, and we are going to have a hair spa soon. You let me know!"

Miss Opal's face brightened as she adjusted the bun in her hair. "You know I believe it is time to rid the gray hair. How do you think auburn would look on me?" She moved her head from side to side. "I once had dark hair, and that was a long time ago."

"Marvelous! Auburn it will be."

Delaney turned to Elisa. "Where are you getting the color and supplies?"

"Online darling! We can have it here in no time and let the spa day begin." Elisa clapped her hands. "I think some highlights will look fab."

Miss Opal gave her a soft hug. "My heart is so happy to have young ladies so full of energy around me, being I'm seventy-six years old."

"You look fabulous." Elisa praised her as she glanced at her watch. "Time to gather my stuff and take a shower. See you tomorrow for our trip to Hatteras." She went inside.

Miss Opal waited until Elisa was out of sight and leaned into Delaney's ear. "I saw that young man hanging around your place. I know Justin had a few words with him. He also said he was your ex-fiancé?" She lifted one eyebrow. "He sure was acting like he's too big for his britches. Being more important than Justin with his fancy car."

Delaney approached a window box and began fussing and dead heading several flowers while speaking in a soft tone. "Yes, that is the one I told you about, and he thinks he is a big shot. He came here to give me something from his mother, who passed away last year." She tossed the flower heads off the porch. "He is gone, and life marches on."

"Oh, honey," Miss Opal met her. "Listen, you do not have to say another word. I can see your feelings written all over your pretty face."

Delaney felt relieved as she sat down on the swing. "What we had was complicated and over. I received wonderful news from his mother's attorney, which was a total surprise. She was my mentor and inspired em to become a textile designer. His mother was a well-known fashion designer in New York."

"From the sudden light in those eyes of yours, it was pleasant news that he brought?"

Delaney gave a slow yes.

"How about we talk about tomorrow? Dottie said she is expecting us around noon. She is closing the store for an hour to share food and stories."

Delaney was swaying on the swing. "I cannot wait to see her again. She sure is one to tell wild tales."

"That she is. A ball of fire, your Uncle Bo would say. Hard to believe she is Bo's sister." A soft laugh escaped her. "Your Uncle Bo used to say Dottie is like whiskey in a teacup. She appears delicate on the outside but is strong and perhaps a touch wild on the inside."

Delaney burst into laughter at the remark and reminded Miss Opal they would be leaving at nine in the morning.

20

Delaney stepped out of the car just before noon and opened the passenger side door for Miss Opal.

"Nice to be back on Hatteras, and what a glorious day it is." Miss Opal said as she scanned her surroundings. "This place looks pretty darned good!" she had a ray of sunshine on her face. "I can stretch my legs, and glad to be out of the car."

Before Elisa and Margo got out of the car, Dottie's boisterous voice met them.

"Well now! Look what Ocracoke has brought me on this fine day!" Dottie's arms were wide open as she rushed to Miss Opal. "I sure am glad to see you." She pulled her close, stepped back and turned to Delaney. "You sure get prettier with age. My brother would be so happy to see his niece all grown up. And your mama must be so proud. I hear you are a fancy textile designer. I sure would love to see what cha got. Maybe you could design some dresses for my shop."

"That could be a, possibly. I have-not designed nautical, but I can look into it."

Dottie's eyes were as wide as a full moon as she raised her hands to the ceiling. "I would surely love that! Back to you, how's the cottage coming along? Been plenty of years since I stepped foot in there."

Delaney kissed Dottie on the cheek and stepped back. "The cottage is marvelous and filled with such memories, and I swear I can feel love oozing out of the walls. I'm blessed to be the new owner."

"Now, honey, you gotta fill that place up with little ones sooner than later. Nothing like the laughter of those chatting angels waking up the walls."

Delaney flashed a fragile smile and replied. "One day, Dottie."

Miss Opal gave her a soft wink, knowing all too well how pushy Dottie can be.

Elisa and Margo stood beside the car wearing awkward smiles when Delaney introduced them.

Dottie held her hands over her chest. "Welcome to Hatteras and my shop. I apologize for taking Delaney from you, ladies! Come on inside, cause it sure is hot out here. I have a new air conditioner, and I cranked it, and I swear the darned thing is blowing snowballs."

Margo let out a soft chuckle. *Blowing snowballs.*

Dottie's husband passed by them, mumbling something under his breath.

"Ladies, pay no mind to my old husband shuffling around. Darn lights over my ruffle dress selection have gone dark. No telling what is going on, and I sure hope he can figure it out. He spent an hour just finding his toolbox." Dottie reached for Miss Opal's and Delaney's hands. "Come on now, we have much to chat about and plenty of food to eat." She looked over at Elisa and Margo. "Girls, follow us!"

Elisa could tell she was going to enjoy her afternoon with Dottie.

Once inside, Dottie led them to the back room where she had set up a small buffet.

"This is lovely, Dottie, and you did not need to do this!"

"Delaney, you are my niece, and I sure wanted to fill your belly with my home cooked food. You are looking a little thin."

"Thank you." She could feel her belly growl. "I run a lot."

"Lord, no way could I run. You would find me flat on my belly." She asked with her eyebrows raised. "Besides, what are you running from?"

"Gosh, no, I'm not running from anything. When I run, I create." She lied, knowing she was running from her past.

Dottie patted Delaney's hand. "I understand, honey."

"Thank you for inviting us to your store, Dottie. Your place is beautiful." Elisa said as her eyes circled the space.

"That reminds me. Girls, grab your lemonade." Dottie said. Using her index finger, she led the group out onto the showroom floor and over to the left side. "Looks like my husband got half the lights working. Delaney, you pick out whatever you want in the ruffle dress selection. They sure are pretty on a young lady like yourself." Her busy eyes volleyed over to Elisa and Margo. "How can I give to one and not her friends? You girls go on and pick out a dress too, and there's plenty in the sale section." She turned around and noticed Miss Opal looking at the slippers. "You go and find a pair you like."

"That is too generous. We will gladly pay." Margo said as she thumbed through the silly dresses.

"Nonsense. Honey, the lavender one with the large octopuses would look so pretty against your skin."

Margo found herself speechless as Dottie pulled out the hideous dress with violet and yellow pompom trim.

A bell chimed, letting Dottie know there was a guest. She looked over the racks and called out to her husband, "You forgot to lock up and put up the closed sign!" She handed the dress to Margo.

"Ya didn't tell me!" he yelled. "Do it yourself instead of yapping at me. Where da'ya put my darned hammer, woman?"

Dottie shook her head and shouted back. "I ain't got no idea and I sure ain't gonna fetch it for ya." She whispered to the women. "I would like to tell him where to put it! That man piddle paddles around like a one-legged turtle." She rubbed her chest. "Good Lord he gives me heartburn. You girls go on and get yourselves a dress, and I'll scat the shoppers away. This is our girl's afternoon." She walked off only to let out a loud. "Caroline!"

Miss Opal was busy trying on cozy slippers when Dottie returned.

"Ladies, look who popped in for a visit! It's Caroline and her husband, Dillan! And their delightful baby, Seraphina! They are welcome here anytime. Seraphina, you are growing so fast and prettier than a summer peach with those rosy cheeks, ginger hair, and sapphire eyes. Ain't this baby a precious doll? This little one turned one just the other day. Let me tell you, she had one heck of a party over at her great grandma Dorea's cottage last week."

Caroline blushed as Seraphina waved her hands and wiggled her feet at Dottie. "We had to stop in and thank you for the lovely tiny ruffle dress you gave Seraphina for her first birthday."

Dottie clapped her hands together. Her face was beaming with pride when she said, "I made it myself!"

Dillan ran his hand over his daughter's hair and spoke to Dottie. "Our little one loves the ruffles!"

Dottie reached for Seraphina's little hand. "You sure are loved you little mermaid. Ya sure she ain't growing a mermaid's tail!" She started laughing and then became serious. "Just teasing."

Caroline's eyes widened, wondering why she had said that. After all, it's her family who, in secret under a full moon, celebrate the mysterious return of the mermaid of Hatteras. Her eyes met Dottie's. "This little girl is so loved." She kissed her daughter's chubby cheek.

"I sure am glad you like her gift, and you are welcome! I have my niece here visiting and her friends along with a long-time friend of mine, Opal Mae." She introduced them. "They are from over on Ocracoke. I hear the ferry ride is taking a long time."

Miss Opal agreed. "Too long!"

"Nice to meet you all." Caroline said as she swayed with Seraphina on her hip.

"Hi Dillan," Delaney greeted him and spoke to her friends. "He did the work on my cottage with his dad, Earl, before I moved in. It was in rough shape."

Dillan nodded as he spoke. "The cottage was in dire need of repair. It has good bones, and I sure hope you are happy."

"Happy? I love it!"

"And thanks for the antique fishing tackle box. My dad uses it all the time."

"You are welcome, Dillan. That was my Uncle Bo's, and I had no use for it. I know your dad liked to cast his line into the sound waters in my backyard around lunchtime."

Miss Opal entered the conversation. "It sure was Bo's favorite tackle box. He and my husband would go out all day fishing. I could not have asked for a better neighbor." She pulled Delaney close and kissed her cheek. "You are the best."

Caroline could not help but notice the ruffled dresses and had to speak up. "Dottie has the most magnificent dresses, and I'm sure if you girls are looking for a man, those dresses will do it!"

Dillan concealed his smile, knowing all too well the secret about the ruffled dresses and how they lure men!

"We want to say thank you and are heading back to the Sea Glass Retreat. I have to prep appetizers this afternoon and tomorrow since we have a bridal party arriving. Much to do." Seraphina was pulling Caroline's hair. "She is bored, and it's time Daddy took her. Also, if you all would like to stop by the Sea Glass Retreat later and enjoy some appetizers — and that means you too, Dottie."

"Well now, honey, I may take you up on that."

"Bye now!" Caroline said as she handed Seraphina over to Dillan.

Dillan added as Seraphina wiggled in his arms. "Delaney, if you need anything else at your cottage, let my dad know. I recall the tin roof on your back porch was not in the best of shape."

"Sure will, and the roof is holding up. Maybe a winter project. It was nice meeting you, Caroline and Seraphina."

Dillan took Seraphina's hand and waved. "Bye!"

The threesome headed out.

Once the door shut, Dottie wasted no time locking it and rushed back to the women. She took a glance over her shoulder and back to the group, then spoke as if she were on a clandestine mission. "You know who that was?" Her eyes were wild.

"No, who?" Elisa said as she put a dress back on the rack.

"Girls, let us go enjoy some food, and I'll tell you all about Caroline and the president."

Intrigued, Delaney asked. "You mean the Caroline I heard about who had dated President Jameson?"

"Yupper. And talk has it they were fire and water! But she put his fire out."

"Lordy, Dottie loves her gossip!" Miss Opal, wearing her new slippers, said as she turned her head from side to side. "Go on, tell the story, and girls, it's a doozie!"

Dottie rubbed her hands together as she began. "Caroline's grandmother, Grams Dorea, was not fond of the president, and she spilled the beans to me over iced tea last year. Caroline was his public relations gal when he was a senator campaigning. They had dated years before. He had family ties with her daddy, another senator who also made a run for office years back." She tapped her forehead and continued. "Jameson wanted to marry Caroline, but she said no and ran off during the night he won the election. Rumor had it she drove down here on that windy night to meet Dillan." She put her hands on her chest. "So romantic. I heard she fell into his arms as the bitter north wind blew. It was love." The excitement on her face dimmed as she continued. "I still like to imagine Caroline as our First Lady, but I know her, and she'd be one unhappy woman."

"Wow!" Margo said with excitement in her eyes. "Is this true? He is married now."

"Yes, we have a new first lady, and it sure is true, young lady!" Dottie cried out as she reached for a glass of lemonade. "She fell in love with sweetheart Dillan on a vacation here on the island, and what a wedding they had on the beach. I need to back up. I met the president when he was on the campaign trail. One night he was here on Hatteras, sharing supper with us at Caroline's grandmother's place, known as *Beach Heart Cottage*. He just loves my raspberry coconut cake. He even sent me a wonderful thank you note."

"What?" Margo squeaked out. "Cake? Supper at a cottage?"

"Be right back!" Dottie dashed behind the register and reached up for a framed letter and returned to the women. "Look here! He sent it to me after he won the election. I cannot believe he remembered me." She ran her finger over the glass. "It has the presidential seal and all. Caroline said that the signature is his! I jumped up as if I were standing on hot coals the day I got this by a courier. The local paper even did a story about me and my cake!" Her heartfelt smile found the intrigued women.

Miss Opal asked to hold the frame. "Dottie, I recall this, and I'm so proud of you." She turned to Margo. "Maybe Dottie would share her cake recipe with you?"

Taken by surprise, Margo smiled at Miss Opal.

"Margo owns a fancy restaurant in New York City, and I have given her some of my recipes. Some were my mama's."

"Well, isn't that something, Miss Opal," Dottie faced Margo. "If I share it, will you call it Dottie's presidential cake?"

Amazed by this new discussion, Margo said she would have to talk to her husband to be and loved the idea.

Elisa whispered. "That is fantastic. Go for it."

Dottie's face lit up as she rambled on about the cake and the night at the Beach Heart Cottage.

Miss Opal handed the frame to Delaney, who showed it to her friends and congratulated Dottie.

Elisa asked if Dottie would share more of the night at the Beach Heart Cottage.

"I would love to, honey. That was one heck of a shindig at the cottage. And there's more." She went on for several minutes as she eyed her eager guests. "I gotta share something that I have been holding on to. Now, no sparking any fires by telling anyone."

The women, entranced with Dottie along with her tall tales, eagerly nodded.

Dottie patted down her hair, looked out the window, and back at the wide-eyed women. "I have heard that the women at the Sea Glass Retreat, the sister cottage of Beach Heart, believe a sea siren from the 1800s is on a quest for her lost sailor. At night, she sings only beneath a specific full moon, while dolphins frolic around her in a playful dance at dawn. Should you come across a black whelk shell washed ashore, it signifies her search for wisdom among the stars to locate him. If you hold the shell to your ear, you can hear the enchanting melody of the siren's song as she calls out to him."

She pulled her lips in and out and then continued as the group leaned in. "But you must return the shell, since her song could lure you into the sea, never to be seen again." Sucking in her cheeks, she stood straight with wide eyes.

Elisa's ready gaze met Dottie's. "Really, a mermaid. Tell me more!" She rubbed her chilled arms. "I love fables. Gosh, Dottie, I love your stories."

Dottie's face twisted as she leaned in toward Elisa and spoke. "Honey, this is no fable." Her eyes darted around the room. "It's as real as I'm looking at you. I heard of a man who had fallen in love with the siren song in the shell and was never seen again." She turned and winked at Miss Opal, who knew all along it was a farfetched tale. Or was it?

Delaney placed her napkin on the table. "Seriously?"

"Yup, why, Goshen Wallace vanished after he had found the black whelk during low tide, and as the sun rose, only his shoes washed ashore. God rest his soul." She clasped her hands and looked up and back to the women as she shook her head. "Well now, ladies, we are here to enjoy our food and company."

Elisa nudged Margo, who nudged Delaney.

As they enjoyed food and laughter, Dottie's husband walked in. "There's a young fella out front who says he is looking for a Delaney." His stare met Dottie's. "Ya ain't sharing those tales of the mermaid and old Goshen again, are ya? They say those weren't even his shoes."

"Hush up and go find ya hammer!" she waved him away. "And answer the door! And they were his shoes, a size 10 with a wide width." She called out.

He squinted at her as he marched off, mumbling inaudible words.

Delaney shrugged, then realized it must be Justin. "Geez, so sorry, Dottie. Miss Opal's nephew is here on Hatteras getting a truck repaired, and we are his ride home."

Miss Opal spoke up. "Guess he made it!" she whispered into Dottie's ear. "He has a schoolboy crush on Delaney."

"Well, now, bring him in! We could use a young man paying a visit. You know Caroline met Dillan at my store, and you see what happened. First came love, then marriage, then the baby carriage!" She made herself laugh.

"I sure would like to see them as a couple." Miss Opal said as Elisa overheard.

"How about we reel that young man in here?" She paid attention to Delaney. "I have fishing gear on the other side of the store. You think he may show interest?"

Delaney raised her eyebrows as she shook her head. "I have no clue."

"Young lady, it's time *we* found out. You gotta show interest in a man's hobby to hook em then reel em in." She pretended to cast a fishing line and handed Delaney the invisible fishing pole.

Her comments and actions left Delaney with her mouth open as she held the imaginary fishing pole.

Elisa faced Margo, and they burst into silent laughter.

Dottie yelled out to her husband once again to open the front door. He returned with the hammer in hand, giving Dottie the stink eye as he led Delaney to the door.

Opal's face softened as she spoke. "Justin is a lovely young man and is staying with me to help fix my place up." She leaned in. "And you never heard it from me, but he can be shy and such a gentleman. And he talks about Delaney at the supper table." Her dreamy eyes twinkled. "Reminds me of Bo back in the day."

Margo came close to spitting out her lemonade as she elbowed Elisa.

Dottie's eyebrows lifted as she spoke. "Now we had best get Delaney the prettiest ruffled dress on the rack. You know, a few ruffles and a little cleavage are all it takes!"

21

Delaney led Justin over to the women by the dresses. His body language spoke volumes. He was uncomfortable biting the inside of his lip, and he shoved his hands into the pockets of his shorts.

"Well, now, this is what a girl's day is all about." He said as his eyes met the women then the food. "Looks like fun."

Miss Opal took Justin's hand. "I would like to introduce you to Dottie. She is Delaney's Uncle Bo's sister and, obviously, her aunt. And a dear friend to me."

"Nice to meet you, Dottie."

"Oh, honey, this is a pleasure to meet such a handsome young man who is gonna help over at Miss Opal's place. A true blessing. If I were a young gal, I would snatch you up in a New York minute." She snapped her fingers.

His face turned crimson when Dottie's husband came to the rescue. "Don't ya go worrying 'bout what my wife says. She ain't been to New York City but once to see a lit-up Christmas tree. Come on, boy, we can have something to eat. My Dottie may be one cackling hen, but she sure is one heck of a cook." He turned around and spoke. "Dottie, it's best ya ain't tell anymore of tall fish tales about mermaids, whelk shells, and those gracious ladies at the retreat up the road, are ya?"

She crossed her arms over her stomach, and with a tilt of her head, challenged him. "And what if I am?"

Her husband threw his hands up in the air.

Unsure, Justin raised his shoulders, more than willing to join Dottie's husband.

Dottie could not help herself when she reached for Delaney's hand and pulled her close. "Now, young lady, you got yourself one heck of a catch in that fella. Go for it! You ain't needing bait. I saw how he looked at you. You already got him hooked now reel him in. Go on and ask him on a date."

Delaney forced a smile as her friends turned the other way to giggle at how bold Dottie was.

She responded in a low voice. "I like Justin—but."

Miss Opal, seeing how uneasy Delaney was by Dottie's outspokenness, came to her rescue in a kind voice.

"I'm going to share a secret, and that is Justin likes you too. Whatever you do with that is up to you. Is that correct, Dottie?" She lifted her eyebrows. "Dottie?"

"Sure is. I was not playing matchmaker, and if I sounded that way, I'm so sorry. How about you girls continue to shop, and we can join the men to enjoy my coconut cake!"

A few hours later, they were heading back to Ocracoke. Parked at the ferry dock and cramped in the back seat, Justin could not wait to get out and walk around. Unfortunately, it would be close to a two-hour wait at the dock since a ferry broke down.

Justin, feeling restless with all the women talking, got out to walk around and stretch his legs. He found a bench over at the docks and sat back with his face up to the sun.

"Do you mind if I sit down next to you?"

He opened his eyes and looked up to find Delaney and patted the bench.

"Thanks." She checked her phone. "It has been an hour. I hope the ferry arrives soon. Miss Opal is tired."

Justin checked his watch. "I hope so. And I gotta tell you, Dottie is something else. That woman does not stop with gossip and chatter, does she? I learned more about her neighbors, her love life, the one-eyed man with a cane up the street, and stray cats than necessary." Justin said as he stared out at the water. "My ears hurt. Her poor husband must live in another cottage." He laughed inward recalling how Dottie's husband referred to her as a *cackling hen*.

Delaney cracked a smile as she pointed. "FYI, your ears are turning red!"

"Stop it. Are they?" he reached for his ears. "They feel hot."

"Told you so!" Delaney teased, tilting her head slightly. "What are your plans for tonight?" She was surprised by what she had said. Was this the Dottie effect—speaking freely? In her mind, she could almost hear Dottie urging her to *"reel him in"* as if he were just a fish!

He waited a moment to reply. "I was gonna head out for dinner and meet up with my buddy."

Delaney was tapping her upper lip, swaying side to side. "My friends want to chill out and watch something on Netflix, and I was thinking maybe I could meet you for a drink? Or come over and we can hang out down by the sound. I could get the old fire pit working."

Justin looked down and back up over the water. "You know what? That sounds like fun." His dreamy eyes met hers. "How about at sunset we have a drink at one of the restaurants and then we can head back here for a private fire pit party?"

Delaney's heart raced with excitement. It had worked! All she needed to do was ask! She had a date with Justin! Now, she just had to share the news with her friends. Suddenly, she heard a horn honking and turned to glance over her shoulder!

"Wow, looks like we are boarding the ferry, and we better hurry since they are letting the cars on now."

Wasting no time, they dashed to the car, and within minutes they drove onto the ferry to head back to Ocracoke.

The late afternoon ferry ride was eventful as dolphins swam and played near the ferry. Some of them dove into the wide wake while a few raced beside it. Elisa and Margo were busy snapping photos and videos while Delaney and Justin stood side by side in silence, also watching the dolphins show off.

"This is heaven." Justin said as he turned to face Delaney.

Pushing back stray strands of hair from her face, she focused on the ripples on the water in silence.

Justin skimmed his hand over her arm. "Are you all right? Is it something I said?"

"No——no. Just admiring all the beauty and the heavenliness. Is that a word?"

"Now it is!" he grinned

"Sometimes I feel I live in a dream, not only living here and working out of my cottage."

"Whew, I thought it was something I said. And, uh, I'm looking forward to tonight. And yeah, and you have it made. I do not miss the city, the noise, the crowds. I have only been on Ocracoke a week or more and feel such peace."

She bumped against his hip. "I hear ya. I have been creating more than I ever have."

Justin tensed his jaw and released it as he tapped his index finger on the rail. "Delaney, is your ex here for a while? Sorry if I sound like I'm prying. We are neighbors, and I want to make sure you are okay."

She tipped her head back as she gripped the rail and then faced him. "Hunter came here to give me something from his mother. She passed away last year and left me something, or should I say *things*."

"He came all the way here?"

"Yup. She made it a request in her will. I know, weird, but she and I were very close. She taught me how to design textiles and the business. My experiences were wonderful, and if not for her, I would *not* be where I am now. And Uncle Bo!"

He nodded. "Cool." His mind was immersed as to why Hunter had to hand deliver the packet. Did he make it up to see Delaney? He shook himself out of his thoughts. After all, they are friendly neighbors.

"I call Uncle Bo and his mother my guardian angels." She inhaled the sea mist and let it out. "His mother left me her stash of designs she kept locked up."

Justin lifted his eyebrows. Not knowing much about the textile business, he had to ask. "Was she well-known?"

"Was she? Yes, she was. Women's fashion and home linens. Her clothing line is known as *Maddy L*. She started out hosting trunk shows."

"Trunk shows?"

Delaney explained to Justin what it was, and that was how she met Hunter.

"Miss Opal knows who she was. After she passed away, Hunter sold her business, as she requested, to the Jammie Spark Company."

"I have heard that name. Hunter must have done well?"

"Who knows or cares? All I know is soon I'll have in my possession many designs tucked away!"

Justin was inches from her lips as his eyes sought hers. "Wow, this is awesome, and a celebration is in order tonight! How about I bring champagne to the fire pit soiree!"

Wearing a shy smile, Delaney was glad she had let him know the truth about Hunter's visit. There was no need to keep it a secret.

"Delaney!" Margo called out as she weaved around cars and SUVs and stopped in front of them.

"Where is Elisa?" Delaney glanced over a few cars.

"She is flirting with a guy here on vacation. A family reunion or something."

Delaney's eyes lit up. "She is something else. Where is he?"

"Over there. He's wearing a blue tee shirt and tan shorts. Try to look in front of that box truck." Margo bopped her head around as she pointed. "I overhead them, and he and his family are staying at their cottage on Ocracoke."

"I see a romance at an Ocracoke cottage." Delaney winked at Margo.

"Maybe!" Margo said as her eyes flashed to Justin and then to Delaney.

Justin turned away, wondering if he would be having a romance at Delaney's cottage.

22

Elisa and her newfound friend exchanged numbers before she got back into the SUV and Delaney drove off the ferry.

"Do tell? Who is the mystery man?" Margo teased as she fanned her face. "Delaney, please turn up the air conditioner."

"Yup." She did so.

"His name is Sam. And he said that his parents' cottage is near your place, Delaney. Maybe I can borrow the golf cart tomorrow and go for a drive?"

"And go for a casual drive to stalk Sam?" Delaney said as she broke into a wide smile.

"Yes! That is what I plan on doing!"

"Honey, you do not know this man. Better you meet him at a restaurant." Miss Opal said as she held her shopping bag on her lap.

Justin added his two cents. "Aunt Opal is correct. Instead of stalking him, we should see what we can find out on Google."

Elisa slumped her shoulders. "He looks normal. His family seemed normal. They even had a dog with them."

Delaney giggled. "You know you really should not judge a book by its cover."

"You are all a bunch of killjoys." Elisa took out her phone, looked at his number and held it up. "I'll investigate him later and give all of you a full report!"

"You do that! We can convene at midnight and decide if you can meet up with him." Delaney said as she looked in the rear-view mirror only to find Justin's sexy smile gazing back at her.

Not long after, they pulled up to Delaney's cottage and got out, adding yawns and stretches.

"Delaney, I'll text you later. Let me get Aunt Opal home." Justin said as he reached for her purse and shopping bag.

Miss Opal kissed all the girls' cheeks and thanked them for an exceptional day on Hatteras. She and Justin headed across the street and home.

Margo was on her way to the front of the house while Delaney and Elisa were grabbing shopping bags from the back of the SUV when she stopped and walked backwards to Delaney. She turned around and tapped Delaney on the shoulder.

With her hands full, she faced Margo. "What? Can you close the hatch?"

"Shush…"

Delaney fixed her gaze on Margo. "Shush?"

"Yes, and please keep calm, but Hunter is asleep on one of your chairs on the front porch."

She dropped the shopping bags at her feet. "No." Her body shivered as she wasted no time staring over at the porch.

Margo stooped down to pick up the bags. "Yes, but where is his vehicle?" She looked around.

Elisa pointed at the golf cart that was near the shed. "That is how that creep. What do we do?"

"We? No, this is my problem." She marched up onto the porch. "Hunter! Wake up."

Startled, he shot up from his slouched position. "What time is it?" He opened and closed his eyes several times.

With her hands on her hips and in a direct tone, she told him it was time for him to go back to New York.

He let out a yawn as he looked around the porch. "I thought I was dreaming. This place isn't so bad. I find it to be a cozy cottage."

She advanced toward him. "Did you hear me?"

"Yup." He gave a wide stretch and let his arms fall to his side. "I wanted to say goodbye and see if you would have a drink with me before I head out. My flight from Virginia leaves early in the morning. What do you say? For old times' sake, and thank you to my mom. She left you with what I believe is a small fortune in drawings and fabrics."

Delaney felt guilty. But why? He loved to play her like a fine-tuned violin, finding the perfect strings.

Crossing her arms, she stared him in the eye. "I thank you for bringing me the information, and your mom, and there is no way I need a drink."

He got up out of the chair and let out a loud yawn, noticing Elisa and Margo standing at the bottom of the stairs. "I see you brought your girls with you!"

"Hey Delaney!"

She spun around to see Justin crossing her street. Her heart was pounding, and face flushed.

He held up a shopping bag as he approached the girls and stopped. "Uh, you accidentally gave Aunt Opal your bag. I'll leave it here."

Elisa whispered. "No problem. Let me take it. Hey, go punch that creep in his snobby nose."

"Huh?" He stared at Hunter, who then turned his gaze toward Delaney.

Hunter snickered. "Your beach boy is here with your shopping bag. Surfer lingerie?"

Delaney walked over and grabbed him by the elbow. "Enough of the games. Go back to your life in New York."

"Geeze you are not the Delaney I once loved. Did I say once?"

Justin's fists clenched as he walked up the stairs and to Delaney. "You heard her. Time for you to go."

"This is supposed to be a friendly island. So much for the travel guides." Hunter said, feeling ambushed and uncomfortable. He knew he had pushed the wrong buttons, and the last thing he wanted was a physical altercation.

Elisa spoke through her teeth to Margo. "I wish Justin would punch his nose. What is it? His third nose job."

"I think it is."

"Adios! And Delaney, congratulations on the small fortune my mother gave you." He patted his hands over his heart as he slid past Justin in a cocky strut and down the stairs. He brushed past Elisa and Margo as he went over to the golf cart and drove off.

Delaney turned to Justin, flushed with embarrassment. She could not stop thanking and apologizing.

"This is what good neighbors do. We stick up for each other." He kept a watchful eye on Hunter.

Elisa walked up to the porch and into the cottage with Margo not far behind.

Justin was a little puzzled, trying to figure out why Hunter was bothering Delaney. Did she still have a piece of her heart with him and he with hers?

He ran his hands through his hair, paying his attention across the street. "Listen, I need to head back to Aunt Opal's and look for my texts later." With his head down, he left her alone.

Pulling her lips in and out, she watched him cross the street. Her silent thoughts ran untamed. Her past has interrupted her peaceful life. The only joy she found in that moment was that Hunter was leaving in the morning. Letting out a slight moan, she tossed her head back and went inside.

Opal was holding a bowl of green beans she had picked up at the farmer's market on Hatteras. She sat down at the kitchen table and asked Justin to sit with her.

She patted the tabletop. "Honey, I can see in your eyes that your heart is finding Delaney."

Justin pulled out a chair and sat down. "That obvious, huh?"

"Bo had that same moonlit look when he had come over asking for cream or sugar that I knew he must have stockpiled since he asked every other day. Or he had a serious sugar addiction!" Caught in a nostalgic moment, her face glowed as she continued. "I shared those feelings too, then one day I invited him in for a cup of coffee. Come to find out that he never used cream or sugar!" She wore a reminiscent smile as she snapped a few beans. "When your uncle passed away, I believed I would never experience love again. Surely after the loss of your girlfriend, you felt the same way. However, the reality is that our hearts naturally seek to be filled with love once more. It's simply part of being human." With her index finger and fondness, she tapped the gold heart-shaped locket resting against her chest. "I carry Bo in my heart. He is in this locket, a gift he gave me on our second anniversary, shortly before he departed to be with the Lord."

His eyes found the locket. "I understand, and I'm sorry he left you so soon."

"Honey, it's the way of the Lord. He was here for me when I needed him. I see Bo in Delaney's face and mannerisms. Her wit, and the way she curls her lips when she smiles, and her soft eyes. That is why I keep her close." She picked up a handful of beans and handed them Justin.

Justin could not believe what he was hearing. He felt as if she were reading his mind as he reached for a bean. "I like Delaney. A lot. She's smart, funny, and talented."

"That she is and single too!" She reached over and touched his hand. "My heart tells me you do not want her to slip away. I know you are here to heal and help me out, but you are young and have so much ahead of you. Do not let one heartbreak hinder you." She pulled her hand back.

"I know Aunt Opal. I needed to hear this!"

She summoned him with her crooked finger. "And if anything, never let that snobby ex of hers get your heart in a tither. He is nothing to her but a bag of wind. I may be an elder, but I can tell by her voice and body language that she is done with him. She told me why he came here, and we will leave it at that."

23

Justin hopped on Delaney's golf cart, and they headed over to a restaurant to enjoy a few drinks and watch the sunset over the water. They shared laughs on the way to avoid any conversation about Hunter. That was until she passed by the inn he was staying. There sat his rental car. A gray Range Rover with a Virginia license plate. She memorized the plate number, knowing that if she saw it in the village, she would avoid it.

"Delaney, watch out!"

She swerved off the road when Justin grabbed the steering wheel as her foot hit the brake just before she careened into a fence and a couple walking their dog.

They jerked forward.

"Sorry! I was not paying attention." She flashed a bashful wave at the couple as their dog barked.

They let her know she had better keep her eyes on the road.

Justin apologized to the couple. He knew why she went off the road, since he saw the Range Rover as well. She got back on the road, and he suggested they have an enjoyable time and go home a different way.

Over at Delaney's cottage, Elisa and Margo were on the back porch petting the stray cat, Lollie, that they let in after her constant meowing. After finishing a can of tuna fish, the cat quieted down and cleaned her paws.

Margo was petting Lollie and asked Elisa. "Are you gonna call that guy you met on the ferry? He is cute."

"Maybe. He has my number too, and I bet they are getting settled into their place. Truth is, I'm having too much fun here with all the Delaney drama!" She pushed a bowl of water toward the cat. "Here you go, little Lollie. Wash down your dinner." She sat back and sipped her iced tea. "I think Justin and Delaney are perfect for each other. Did you see the way she wiggles when he is around and talks so sweet, twirling her hair like a teenager with a crush?"

Margo was staring out at the water as she answered. "Yes, as if he is going to ask her to the prom!"

They burst into laughter.

Elisa twisted her lips and then spoke. "Hunter is curious since Delaney has something from his mother, and he will taunt her."

Margo lifted her shoulders as she sat back. "You know, I bet he wants whatever it is she inherited from his mother. Somehow I got the feeling that's what he wants. That greed riddled asshole wants more money. And to be honest, I'm still annoyed at my fiancé for telling him we were here. Blabber mouth. I told him that I have decided to stay here another week because of the hassle that he caused."

Elisa shook her head from side to side. "He is a man, and they say stupid things blindly." She turned to Margo. "Wait a sec. Are you serious? You can stay another week?"

"Yes, he hired temp prep chefs and a few pastry chefs on internship, and they are working out great. I must ask Delaney first, but you have to as well since I drove us here!"

Twisting her lips, Elisa was deep in thought, wondering if she could pull off another week. A phone call would answer that.

Margo finished her glass of wine and looked at her phone. "I nearly forgot. Miss Opal asked me to stop over tonight."

"Why?"

"She is giving me some of her recipe cards so I can test them for the restaurant."

"That reminds me, I owe her a hair spa day! Do you mind if I go with you? She is the sweetest woman and is about to have auburn hair!"

Margo played with the cat's tail as it brushed up against her leg. "Auburn, oh dear!" She spoke to the cat. "We gotta go, little kitty cat." She picked up the bowl of dry food, and the cat followed outside. "Go finish your food."

After finishing her second glass of wine, Delaney opened up and talked about her life. She would stop and inhale the salty evening air, letting out an ah and then resume. Justin's eyes could not leave her. His heart ached to find his lips on hers. He was eager for Hunter to leave the island. Keeping his eye on the patrons coming and going, he prayed Hunter was not one of them.

"Justin, thanks for asking me out tonight. Is this our second date?"

He leaned forward and reached for her hands. "Yes. Ice cream was our first. Or we can say that was our pre-date!"

Her face lit up. "Awesome! I have not been on a second date in." She counted her fingers. "Years!"

"I confess I have not either. Good things come to us who wait. Is that what they say?" His eyes landed on her lips as she spoke.

"Absolutely!" Raising her wineglass, she cheered. "To our second date." And she ordered another glass of wine.

"I should drive the golf cart on the way back. We do not want you running down pedestrians or us winding up in Silver Lake."

"Ha ha. You are such a gentleman. Are we still on for our fire pit party?"

"You bet." They sat back and chatted for a while when he waved the server over and asked for the bill. "And yes, I have the champagne in the fridge."

She placed her napkin on the table. "How long will you be staying at Miss Opal's place?"

He sat back, crossing his arms. "Fair question, since I'm here to help fix the place up. My parents insisted after I sold my company and the accident that devastated me and, as they put it, I was *moping, sad and bored.* And what they said was true. I was stuck."

"I see, so you are leaving Ocracoke when you are done with Miss Opal's place?" Her lips curled downward as she flashed her puppy-dog eyes.

"Not sure when or *if* I'll leave. If there is a reason to stay, then so be it." He placed his hand in hers. "I kept part of my company and still work daily, and I know that Aunt Opal left the cottage to my parents. I gotta a feeling that is why they wanted me here to fix it up! Free labor! They are paying for the repairs."

Delaney's heart both sank and leaped with hope at his words, especially when he reached for her hand, as if there was a reason to stay.

"How about we head over to your cottage, Delaney, and enjoy a fire? I know it's 80 degrees out, but it's all about the ambience."

Delaney was falling in love with him. How could this be? Just days ago, in her nightgown, he came close to running her over. And then she spilled carrot juice all over his car, and now they are sitting at a table enjoying drinks and each other's company.

"Let me text my friends and see what they are up to. It's supposed to be their relaxation night, and I think Margo is heading over to Miss Opal's — something about recipes."

The server came over with the bill. As he paid, Delaney texted Elisa.

Are you watching a movie?

Elisa texted: No, we are at Miss Opal's.

Delaney texted: I see.

Elisa texted: Miss Opal is sharing her recipes with her. And we are sipping brandy and eating those yummy cookies.

Delaney texted: Enjoy. Heading back. We are going to sit down by the water. Fire pit time.

Elisa texted: And sharing Milky Way kisses. Bye.✨🌙💋🔥

Delaney wore a star-studded smile. *Milky Way kisses*

24

Justin opened the back door and walked into Opal's cottage, where he could hear the women in the parlor chatting, adding laughs here and there. He reached into the refrigerator for the champagne. As he closed the door, he found Margo standing there.

"Hey Margo. I did not hear you enter the kitchen."

"Hey Justin." Her stare landed on the bottle in his hands. "Delaney told us you are having a private party! No worries, we will stay here." She giggled. "I love your aunt. She is the best and is willing to share your or her—" She hiccupped. "Family recipes with me!"

Justin could tell she had a little too much brandy and agreed. "She is amazing! Enjoy. Delaney is waiting, and I do not want the champagne to get warm."

"Before you go," she caught his arm. "Hunter is an asshole. I mean a complete one, and you have no competition. Elisa and I'll make sure he stays away — that creep." She added a double wink. "We, I, you got this! And you never hear this from me, but Delaney really likes you." She pressed her finger over her lips, then grabbed a bottle of brandy and left the room.

Justin was wondering, what does she mean, *no worries, they have it under control.* He needed to do some research on Hunter. Pushing those negative thoughts away, he met Delaney at the fire pit.

"Ugh, these sticks will not light, and the breeze is not helping. But I brought this old Coleman lantern I found in the garage. And it has oil in it!" She struck a match and lit it. "Ta da, we have light." She placed it on the ground.

Placing the champagne down, he got the fire lit.

"You are the man!" She giggled as she crossed her arms over her chest. As the fire flames flickered, the gleam in his eyes caught her attention, and her spirits soared like a butterfly taking flight.

Flexing his muscles under his tee shirt, he asked her to feel them.

She approached him and did so. "Wow, you're incredibly strong." She could not help but wonder what it would feel like to be held in his embrace, so she leaned closer. "I apologize." Taking a step back, she created some distance.

"Apologizing for what?" he advanced, placing his hand in hers. "Delaney, I'll never pressure you for anything. I like where we are now. If we go further, then we do so, but not without both of us feeling it."

What man says such a thing? This is surreal. Who sent him? Was this a setup by Hunter to trick her? No! She cleared that silly thought.

He moved closer and ran his index finger over the outline of her face. The fire burned behind her, mirroring the last rays of the sun on the water's surface.

She reached for his hand and traced her face with his finger. No words were exchanged, only the gentle meow of Lollie, the cat, who came to pay a visit.

Delaney looked down and spoke to it. "You nosy little lady, go find a mouse! Go now." The cat refused as it got comfortable in an Adirondack chair. "Would you look at that?"

"She must be a spirit guide."

"What?"

"Ask Aunt Opal. She believes that animals enter our lives to teach us lessons and that they are little angels or guides." Justin walked over to pet the cat and put his ear up to her snout. "She just told me that if you want me to, I'll kiss you!"

Delaney's face lit up. "You talk to cats too?"

"Sure, why not!" He met Delaney and brushed her hair past her shoulders. "Is it okay?"

"Okay?" She looked sideways at the cat and went back to Justin. "Oh—the kiss." Her voice trailed off. "Let me think about it." She tapped her temple.

"I can wait." He looked at his watch and back at Delaney only to find her soft, salty lips pressed into his. As their bodies came together, he pulled her in, and she longed for his lips to remain on hers.

He pulled away, gazing into her eyes as he placed his index finger on her lips. "Shush, do not say a word." Their lips met again until the cat began meowing, and Delaney broke away laughing.

Justin went over to a small table and picked up the lantern. "How about we take a walk? Maybe this nosy cat will wander off."

"Or she may join us, giving you subtle hints as to what to do next!" She felt giddy as she weaved her arm through his. "We can head to the left where this is a small beachy area."

"Lead the way." He held up the lantern as they ventured along the shoreline.

The tepid water of the sound tickled their feet as it met the shore.

Delaney pointed into the distance. "There is an old cypress that came down in a storm, and we can sit on it to watch the stars introduce the Milky Way, which will be in the western sky. I bet you are curious how I know."

"You could say that."

"My Uncle Bo was a big-time stargazer, and when I was small visiting, he would take me down to the beach and spend hours pointing out the constellations. It was fabulous and memorable."

Justin held her hand as they sat on the cypress tree. "You must have had a wonderful time here with your family. I came to the island a few times, but with my family there was always drama after a few bottles of wine." He dug his toes into the cool sand. "And not always paradise. My parents argue over everything, and Aunt Opal was the referee! They are long divorced, and I know they both will inherit the cottage, and not sure how that will go down."

She felt a tinge of sadness learning that his childhood memories of Ocracoke were tainted with anger. She knew it was time to change not only the subject but time for him to experience how beautiful Ocracoke is.

"Do you recall Dottie over on Hatteras?"

Justin placed the lantern on the sand. The small flicker illuminated Delaney's face. "How can I forget? Her husband is a hoot. Poor guy."

"She is my aunt. Uncle Bo was my dad's brother, and Dottie is his sister."

Justin placed his hands on the tree and leaned back. "I had not known that."

"Dottie is one storyteller, and my dad wears earplugs when he visits Hatteras, and my mom drags Dad to her shop and always returns with some sort of wild dress. My parents own a rental cottage over there, and guess who pays a visit?"

"Dottie!" Justin said. "I know Aunt Opal knows Dottie, but I'm not sure how they are connected. I think it's best I never learn!"

Delaney rested her head on his strong shoulder and spoke. "All kidding aside, Dottie loves to tell tall tales, and one of which is that there are women over on Hatteras who own a few homes, and one is a retreat. I stayed there, and that is how I found a father and his son, who fixed up my cottage. Beautiful retreat."

"Is that the couple you mentioned when I arrived at Dottie's store?"

"Yup, Dottie told us that—whoa—did you hear that?"

"I did. That sounds like an egret, or maybe it's your stray cat following us." He let out a short-lived laugh as he peered into the bushes behind him.

"Listen." She got up and walked over to the shoreline and into the ankle-deep water, cupping her ears. "There it is again." Splashing through the water, she dashed back to Justin.

"I assume someone at a rental cottage is having fun." He pulled her close and kissed her forehead.

Her eyes darted around, landing on Justin's. "Dottie told us that there is a sea siren that sings a delicate, angelic song at night looking for her sailor from the mid-1800s. The women who live over in Hatteras at the retreat celebrate her."

"Geeze that is a good tall tale. Delaney, there are no sea sirens frolicking around here or anywhere. You said Dottie tells stories. Hmm. Do you think Dottie hits the brandy at night?"

She inhaled and let it out, adding a chuckle. "Maybe she does, but I cannot help it. I let her get to me! She is funny and so expressive, full of life and laughter."

"Let me get to you."

Caught by surprise, Delaney looked away and back to Justin, needing the change the subject. "She said if you find a black whelk shell the morning after you heard the sea siren at night, it means she was nearby. And in the morning, one will see a school of dolphins playing in a circle." She fanned her face as tears tickled her eyelashes.

"Please do not cry. What Dottie told you is a fairy tale." The lantern's light revealed the tears streaming down her face. "It's okay. Do you want to go back to the cottage? We left a small fire behind."

"I apologize. My emotions get the best of me with such a story."

Justin gave a quick nod.

"We had better go since I do not want to burn the cottage down."

"Allow me." With his finger, he tenderly wiped away her tears.

She reached for his hand. "Thanks."

Hand in hand, they walked back to the fire pit to find it had burned out.

Delaney could not get the sound that she heard out of mind, no less Dottie's story. Rubbing her arms, she pressed her body into Justin, where they shared an endless kiss. She kept one eye on the water as the sweet echoes of gentle songs drifted to her.

25

Delaney was up bright and early for her morning jog. She had one of the best nights of slumber in months! Could it have been Justin's kiss?

As she was in the kitchen doing some stretches, the sun's rays from the eastern-facing window surrounded her. Glancing at the weather on her phone, she realized it was time to head out for a run before the island heat set in. Quietly, so as not to disturb her friends, she slipped out through the back porch door and made her way to the fire pit. Reflecting on the previous night and still feeling the warmth of Justin's kiss, she couldn't help but break into a bright smile as she approached the water to continue her stretches. Just as she was about to finish, something caught her attention.

"No way." She murmured to herself as she walked over to the object and stooped to run her hand over the shell. "Justin must have put it here." She stood up, and in her hands was a large black whelk shell. Water and sand dripped out as she held it up to the sun and gave it a wiggle. "Maybe Dottie is telling the truth and there is a mystical siren. Nope, this was planted here. I bet Elisa bought it over at a gift shop." Giving it one last shake, she heard splashes and looked out over the water. She dropped her shell as she watched a school of dolphins frolic near the shore.

With her mouth agape as she stooped, picked up the shell, and made her way back to the shore. She shielded her eyes with her hands, discovering that the water's surface was calm. Intrigued by Dottie's stories of the sea siren's enchanting song, she held the shell to her ear but pulled it away and looked at it.

"Okay, this must be what happens when one is losing their marbles. I heard her sing! No more champagne and listening to wild tales. I need to go for my run."

As she jogged past Miss Opal's place, she wore a brilliant smile.

Miss Opal was on her front porch sipping her tea when Justin walked out.

"Morning!"

"Morning Justin. You are up early. There is a fresh blueberry coffee cake on the counter that I made last night."

"Thanks, I already had a slice, and it's delicious." He sat down. "My buddy texted me late last night. Sally is ready to be picked up."

Miss Opal sat back and sipped her tea. "Are you heading over to Hatteras today?"

"Yes, I am. I gotta catch the 10:00 passenger ferry and bring Sally home where she belongs." He stretched his legs out and gave a wide stretch. "Soon we can get started on fixing your place up. I'm no electrician. We need to hire someone out for that. The flickering light in the dining room worries me."

Putting her teacup on the saucer, she faced him. "I can ask around, and I noticed you had a late-night?"

"Yes, and no. It was an enjoyable night." He knew she would pry at some point. "I heard you had fun with Elisa and Margo last night sharing recipes."

"Yes, we did! They are lovely young ladies, and I gave them my grandmother's handwritten cards. Not all, only the ones I thought were appropriate. And she will name them after our family."

He gave a slow nod. "That is terrific."

They were silent, glancing past the porch and waving to the nearby residents and visitors.

Delaney was on her way back to the cottage when she stopped to stretch. Her left leg was cramping, as were her ribs. She rarely drank, yet she understood her dehydration was from the wine that she had consumed the prior night. Waiting for the cramps to subside, she took out her phone, debating whether to text Justin about the whelk shell. Why not? After all, he believes that her stray cat talks to him!

Justin felt his phone buzz in his pocket and looked at it.

Delaney texted: Morning!

Justin texted: 🌅 ☺

Delaney texted: Just finished my jog. I gotta share what I found this morning by the water in my backyard. Kinda weird!

Justin texted: I like weird. I must catch the 10:00 passenger ferry over to Hatteras. The truck is ready.

Delaney texted: Terrific news. How about I see you later? I found something this morning I want to share with you.

Justin texted: I look forward to seeing you later. Last night was great. Psst. I cannot get your kisses out of my mind.

Her fingers hovered over the keyboard. This was happening so fast. Too fast. She hesitated for a moment.

Delaney texted: It was wonderful and I, uh.

Justin texted: And you, uh what?

Why do I play hard to get? She enjoyed being with him. Just say how you feel! *Say it*. She was talking out loud when a couple walked past her, expressing questionable stares.

Justin texted: Hello?

Delaney texted: Sorry, I had a foot cramp. I had a super time last night, and yes, your kisses are all I think about.

A schoolboy smile found his face, which did not go unnoticed by Opal. He texted her when he got back on Ocracoke, maybe they could take a ride in Sally and go out for ice cream.

Delaney responded with a few cheerful emoji smiles, tucked her phone into her pocket, and continued her run back to the cottage, where she found her friends lounging on the front porch. Suddenly, she felt her phone vibrate in her pocket and paused beneath the arbor to check her messages. Her eyes widened, and she gasped as she glanced at Miss Opal's place and then back at her phone. Justin had sent her a heart emoji, sending shivers through her body while her heart raced. With a newfound lightness in her step, she walked up onto the porch and settled onto the top step.

"Morning Delaney. Did you have a Milky Way night with Justin?" Elisa teased just before she sipped her coffee.

Delaney turned to face her. "I did! And FYI, his kisses are dreamy." She blew a tease of a kiss to Elisa.

Elisa caught it. "I think this belongs across the street." She blew it over to Miss Opal's place.

"What!" Margo cried out. "You did not—did you?"

"You bet we did. He is so sweet, and I'll see him later — that is, if it's okay with your girls. You are here on vacation to see me."

Elisa faced Margo and spoke. "We have to ask you something."

Delaney put her phone on the step beside her. "Are you pissed that I was out last night?"

"Gosh, no," Margo replied as she got up to sit next to Delaney. "Ewe, you are all sweaty. You need a shower, but before you do, we have to ask if we can stay another week?" She squeezed her face, then looked over her shoulder at Elisa and back to Delaney.

"Of course! I would love it. We have had splendid weather so far, and I promise to spend more time with both of you." Pulling Margo close, she rested her head on her shoulder. "I love you both."

Margo pushed Delaney away, pinching her nose. "A shower is most definitely needed. You are one sweaty hottie. And by the way, we saw Justin out on the porch watching you when you left earlier."

"You spied on him?"

"You bet we did!" Elisa said as she leaned forward. "I have to see if I can afford to take another week off. This new salon opens in six weeks, and I'm not sure if I can do this. If I cannot, Margo has to go with me, since I have no other way to get home."

"Quit your job and move here! I could use a roommate and company, plus I'm about to learn exactly what Hunter's mother left me, and if it's what I think it is and I use the patterns and designs, I'll need help."

Elisa's eyes perked open. "I love that idea, but my job is a stylist, and love working with hair."

"Just a thought, and Margo, you can open a restaurant here on the island. What if you baked and cooked what Miss Opal gave you? Maybe she could help you? How about a food truck with yummy cookies and cakes?" Delaney had a flurry of ideas, as if the creation fairy had sprinkled idea dust on her. "Guess I'm on a roll."

"I bet a certain Justin had something to do with it!" Margo said as she gave Delaney a slight nudge. "Hello, I'm getting married and work at David's family restaurant. But I love your idea. But I could entertain it later! First go shower.

We would like to go bike riding this morning and have lunch at the restaurant by the water."

"Love it. We can visit the lighthouse. And girls, check this out." Her face lit up as she held up her phone, showing off the heart emoji from Justin.

Elisa and Margo glanced at each other and knew their best friend was falling in love!

26

Justin pulled Sally into Miss Opal's driveway the following day, a little after three thirty in the afternoon. Delaney was on the phone with the lawyers regarding Hunter's mother's wishes. She had to get into town and find a notary public as soon as the official documents arrived. The lawyers were not eager to let her know what she was about to receive. She was fine with that since it led to more of an element of surprise.

There was a knock on the front door. Elisa opened it and let out a yelp. Delaney, still on the phone, rushed over to the door to find Justin with a little tan and white puppy in his arms.

"Come in, and who is this little angel?" Elisa cried out with pure excitement as she clapped her hands. "You are so cute!"

Delaney, smiling, gave a clear signal that she was on her phone as she stepped outside through the back door to have some privacy.

Justin put the puppy down. It sniffed and wagged its tail and then rolled onto its back.

Margo rushed over and cried out, "*Oh my gosh*!" as she got closer to the front door and knelt. "Look at this little baby. You are so adorable!" Talking silly baby talk as she petted the puppy's head. Looking up, she asked. "Who and where?"

Justin picked the puppy up with its nonstop wagging tail and wet kisses. "I hope this is all right to have a puppy in here?"

Elisa was petting the puppy's head. "Of course she can be here. She is a she?"

"She is, and her name is Katydid." He hugged the puppy and then turned it to face him. "Welcome home to Ocracoke."

Margo had her hands out. "Can I hold her? She is so tiny. What breed is she? Her blonde fur is so soft."

He handed the wiggle pup over. "Katydid is a little of this and that and medium-sized. She is about nine weeks old. My buddy, who fixed my truck, has a litter at his place. How could I say no? Plus, Aunt Opal will love having company as long as Katydid learns potty is outside!"

Delaney walked over. "Justin, who is this? You are so darned adorable. Look at the freckles on your little face." She petted the puppy's head.

"Her name is Katydid," Margo said as she held her. "Oh, she is like a little baby, and she has puppy breath!"

"She is a baby, silly?" Elisa reminded her.

"Justin, where did you get her?" Delaney's curious eyes remained on the puppy.

He confessed that the sight of the puppies running around in his friend's backyard was too much for him to resist. Being she is the runt, how could he leave her behind?

Delaney shut the front door and got on her knees. "Margo, can you put her down to let her run around?"

"You sure? I hope she will not have an accident." Margo said as she put her on the floor, and Katydid ran into Delaney's arms, giving her nonstop kisses.

"Justin, she is gorgeous, and anytime she wants to have a sleepover here, she is welcome." She hugged the puppy. "Welcome to my home, Katydid!"

"Delaney, I need to take her to Aunt Opal. I sure hope she accepts her."

Delaney got up with Katydid in her arms and met Justin. "If she says no, then bring her here! I would love to be her mommy!"

Justin took the wiggling puppy and spoke to Delaney. "You can be her mommy across the street! And sleepovers are a sure thing. Let me break the news to Aunt Opal, and if all goes well, you will not see me at your door." He glanced at the puppy and went back to Delaney. "With someone in my arms."

Elisa was petting Katydid's head. "Miss Opal will be fine with a new roommate! Look at her gentle Hershey Kiss eyes. You are one cute puppy." She turned to Delaney. "Maybe as she grows up, she can go on morning runs with you." She faced Justin. "If that is okay with her daddy."

"I have a better idea."

"What is that, Justin?" Delaney asked softly.

"I can run too! I once was a track star in college, and I would love to run again." He pressed Katydid up to his cheek and then kissed her wet snout.

His kind smile and the way he cared for the puppy had Delaney in a dreamy state. *Look at how he loves that little puppy.*

"I'll text you later, Delaney. I need to introduce someone to her grandmother across the street!"

Margo chuckled. "Miss Opal is a grandmother! Love it."

The women followed Justin out to the arbor, waving and blowing kisses at the puppy. He stopped and turned, and using her little paw, he waved at them.

Margo grabbed Delaney's hand and spoke quietly. "You had better not let him go. He is one heck of a catch! He will make a wonderful father."

"Stop it! He is just a neighborhood friend. Father? Really, Margo." She crossed her arms.

"Pretend you lack the hots for him."

Delaney rolled her lips in and out, ignoring her friend.

Elisa pulled Delaney close and spoke in her ear. "What is going on? I mean, is Justin for real? A puppy? He is helping his aunt fix her home. He is polite, kind and sexy. Whew… I get hot just mentioning that." With drama, she fanned her face.

Wearing a knowing smile. "That he is, and his kisses are surreal." Delaney waved her hands over Elisa's face. "Hot."

"Now that the excitement is over, how did the call go with the lawyers?" Elisa's curious eyes met Delaney's as they made their way out to the porch.

Delaney sat on the wooden swing. "It went well, and we will button it up in a few days. Just wondering what she left me. It must be a big deal since it requires this legality. Geeze." The swing rocked back and forth. "I know that Hunter has nothing to do with this. And I doubt he will bother me again."

Margo made an ugly face. "I never want to see him and his cocky face."

Elisa looked out over to Miss Opal's place. "How about we go have a glass of wine down by the water in the backyard and chill out?" She paid attention to the sign above the door. "Sea Gypsy." She tapped her upper lip. "If I moved in, you would need to change that sign to Two Sea Gypsies!"

Margo wasted no time adding. *"Three Sea Gypsies!"*

27

Delaney was getting dinner ready when her phone rang. She did not recognize the number.

"Hello?"

"I'm still here on Ocracoke."

Her heart sank to the floor as her face blushed rose red. "Hunter, go home. We are over and have been. You need to find someone else. And whose phone are you using?" She put the phone on speaker as she dumped the pot of pasta into a strainer.

Elisa entered the kitchen, staring at the phone and at Delaney. She whispered. "No way. Hang up."

Delaney shook her head, picked up the phone, and went out onto the back porch. "Hunter, what is going on with you?"

"I want you back in my life."

"That is not happening. You just cannot enter my life and think all is well and believe you will run off into the Ocracoke sunset with me. Goodbye."

"Wait!"

She let out a huff. "What?"

"Did you get the package from the attorney yet?"

"Tomorrow. Why?"

Silence ensued as Delaney paced. She then stopped to rearrange a few pillows on the porch loveseat.

"You will find out. My mother was generous."

Delaney sat down and pulled her hair forward, twirling it. "Generous?" she placed the phone on the table.

"Yes. There is a minor stipulation, and that is you have to marry me to get the inheritance. My mom was generous, my love?"

She squeezed her face. "Funny. Absolutely hysterical and time to go." She felt her heart pound with worry that he was telling the truth. If that is what is in the package, it will go back to where it came from. Better yet, burn it.

"I want to see you tonight. I miss you, baby. Come to the inn and we can talk and make love like we once did. You are the best."

"Ugh. Stop it. You are drunk. Talk about what? And who left whom? You put my heart on ice. Oh, how we forget?" She tilted her head back, staring at a water bug on the ceiling. She knew she had to cut him loose.

"Us. You can sell your cottage, and we can move up to my place in the Hamptons, and I'll get you an office in the city and a staff. We can build a new company."

She let out a loud laugh. "Enough. You have been drinking, and I'm not moving. If the contents of the package say I *am* to marry you, then I'll call the attorney, and it goes back. Goodbye." She hung up and sat back, rubbing her arms. Her gaze was out at the water.

Unknown to Delaney, Justin was on his way over to let Katydid run around the backyard. Holding the pup, he stopped when he heard most of their conversation and turned around.

Elisa stepped onto the porch. She hesitated, rubbing her hands together, and asked. "Hey, is everything okay?"

Delaney pulled her lips in, adding a slow nod.

Margo met them with Katydid in her arms. "Look what Justin just dropped off. He asked if we could puppy sit for an hour since he has errands to do and is getting puppy supplies, and Miss Opal loves her!" She kissed the sleepy pup's snout as she cuddled her in her arms. "I want to keep her."

Teary-eyed Delaney gave a fast smile and went inside.

"What's going on?"

"Hunter called, and Margo, it was not good. He refuses to leave Ocracoke." Elisa said, since she overheard most of the conversation and, not wanting to upset Delaney any further, spoke in a quiet tone. "Bring Katydid down to the water where I can talk and Delaney cannot hear us."

"Here," she handed the pup over to Elisa. "Oops, the garlic bread is in the oven. Let me take it out, and I can meet you down there." She went inside and dashed back out. "This is her leash."

Delaney was speaking with the attorney's office, making a concerted effort to remain composed. While they could not provide her with extensive information, they reassured her that no marriages were at stake and that they were quite busy dealing with Hunter, who was upset about the buyout he had to accept. She set the phone down on her desk and leaned her head into her hands, feeling the weight of the situation.

The sudden loud pop from Sally's engine grabbed her focus to the window in her office, where she watched Justin drive away.

Hunter opened the door to his room to find Justin. "What do you want?" He looked past Justin's shoulder to the parking lot. "Is Delaney with you?"

Justin stepped back. The smell of alcohol tainted Hunter's breath. "No, she is not with me. She is home, upset, no thanks to you."

Hunter cocked his head back. "Yeah, sure she is. She wants to leave this island and be with me. You want a beer?"

Justin found it hard to fathom the level of arrogance displayed by this man. He thrust his hands deep into his pockets, his neck and jaw tense as he shifted his head from side to side, then spoke. "No. I recommend you leave the island sooner rather than later."

Hunter's steely eyes burned into Justin's. "So what, are you her protector? Lover? I can do what I want and stay here as long as I like. I can buy the inn if I want." He laughed, adding a snort. "I guess her taste went downhill after we split. Surfer boy!"

Rage consumed Justin as his bunched fist flew out of his pocket. He launched himself forward and, the next thing he knew, Hunter was holding his nose as blood dribbled down onto his mint green polo shirt. Pulling his hand back, giving it a shake, he spoke through gritted teeth. "Get off the island and leave Delaney alone." Justin could not believe he had punched Hunter square in the nose! Elisa will be proud of him. Was Hunter going to retaliate? He stepped back. "Take that as a warning!"

Hunter was in disbelief, as he had never experienced being punched in his perfect nose. What to do? His hand covered in his blood; he watched Justin leave and went into his room, slamming the door behind him.

Justin parked in front of Miss Opal's and went inside to put ice on his sore hand. He reached into the freezer when Miss Opal walked in.

"What on earth happened to your hand?" She asked, noticing it was not only red but swollen.

A bag of frozen peas in his other hand. She closed the door of the freezer. "Nothing, Aunt Opal," Justin said as he sat down and placed the peas on his hand.

Miss Opal knew it was nothing as she reached for ice in the freezer and wrapped it in a dish towel. "This works much better."

He put it in his hand and hid his wince from her. He was still fuming, and Opal knew something was amiss. She did not want to push and prepared supper, humming a song as she did.

"I punched Delaney's ex in the nose." He sat back and chuckled, recalling the look on Hunter's face.

"Good Lord! What are ya doing in her business?" She turned around with a pot in her hand. "Does she know?"

"Nope, and I refuse to tell her. He is a pompous creep and refuses to leave her alone." He took the ice off his hand and flexed his fingers. "The arrogant ass deserved it."

Opal sat down at the table. "Justin, ya best not get involved with her ex. I heard he is a drinker and not all there in the head and makes trouble wherever he roams."

Justin put ice back on his injured hand. "Maybe so, but he may need a new nose."

"Good golly! I sure hope Sheriff Watkin does not show up at the door." She got up and opened the fridge, and reached for a pitcher of cold water. She placed it, along with a glass, on the table. "The sheriff and are old friends, and I would be upset to find out you are gonna have to be accused of assault of a tourist on the island." She fanned her face as she went over to the stove.

Justin let out a chuckle.

"And what is so funny? Seeing you in handcuffs?"

"No, Aunt Opal. Before he even got the chance to say that he was calling the Sheriff Watkins, I told Hunter he was my cousin and that it was unfortunate that he bumped into the door after too many cocktails."

She slapped her hand over her heart as she spun around. "Heavens, Justin, did you say that?"

"Yup." He realized his actions, although spontaneous, could have repercussions if Hunter challenged him.

Opal knew that Justin's heart was settling in with Delaney, but he had to remain in control. She knew they were developing a bond. A bond she prayed would last a lifetime.

28

"Where is the puppy?"

Justin looked up at Opal. "She is with Margo across the street."

Miss Opal went over and placed her hand on Justin's shoulder. "You go get that sweet pup. I made her a chicken dinner, and I fixed her a little welcome home bed in the living room." She could tell Justin was not hearing a word she said. "Take her for a walk and get that pesky ex off your mind. And do not let Delaney see that swollen hand!"

He removed the ice pack and wiggled his fingers. "It looks better." He got up. "Going over there now. Thanks for letting the puppy live here."

She ran her hand over his cheek as her face softened. "I love the company. Now go get Katydid. If ya need to tell Delaney how you feel about her, then do it. No sense missing out on the one who steals your heart, and for Pete's sake, never tell her that you punched that fella in the nose!"

Justin went to knock on Delaney's door when it opened.

Cuddled like a baby in Elisa's arms was Katydid. Her childlike smile met Justin. "I love her! She is so sweet and soft. And I love puppy breath! We played in the backyard. She loves to chase sticks." She kissed the pup's head. "And I'm going online puppy shopping." Her eyes met Justin's. "If okay with your daddy?"

"Absolutely! She is a sweetie."

Margo was at the door. "She sure is. We can puppy sit anytime until we leave."

He quickly nodded to her. "Sure, let me get her home. Aunt Opal made her a chicken dinner and a bed."

Elisa spoke with concern. "She should be on puppy chow."

"No worry I have a bag in the truck. Aunt Opal is a doggy grandma. Time to come home, Katydid." He glanced into the cottage and asked. "Is Delaney around?"

"Yes, she is down by the water on the phone talking to her mother. Her dad is in the hospital with the flu."

"Okay, let her know that I'll check back later." He held his hands out, forgetting all about the swollen knuckles.

Elisa's stare was on his hand and then moved to his eyes. "Did you get hurt? That looks very swollen."

Margo peeked. "You need ice."

"Oh, this is nothing."

Elisa held the puppy. "Hmmm. I know you left here in a flurry after Hunter and his crap. He enjoys upsetting Delaney."

He was silent as his eyes bounced around the porch and back to Elisa. "Listen, if I tell you both what happened, please never tell Delaney."

They looked at each other, adding anxious nods.

"I punched Hunter in the nose over at the inn. And just know the sheriff may pull up. All I recall was he said something arrogant, and the next thing I knew, my hand hurt, and blood was running down Hunter's chin onto his shirt."

Wide-eyed Margo squeezed past Elisa and started speaking. "No way! OMG, he got what was coming to him." She pressed her finger to Elisa's lips. "Hush, and not a word to Delaney," she removed her finger. "This is epic!"

Elisa dropped her shoulders as she cuddled the sleepy pup. "Are you kidding me? I wish I were there. Now he *will* need another nose job!" She had a devilish laugh, adding. "Thank you!" She leaned over and kissed his cheek. "Knowing Hunter, he will run home with his you know what between his legs."

They were on the porch sharing laughter when Delaney appeared. "Hey, who needs a nose job?"

Startled and in a fast search for an answer, Elisa responded. "I do! I never liked the tip." She tapped her nose.

Delaney waved her off. "Silly, you are gorgeous." She paid attention to Justin and then Katydid. "Hi! Katydid is a delight!"

Margo glanced at his hand, which he wasted no time hiding behind him.

"She is, and it's time to get her home and settle down before her next puppy outburst."

Elisa knew he could not hold his hand out without Delaney noticing how red, swollen and purple it was and since the pup was now asleep in her arms. She suggested walking to Miss Opal's with Justin.

Margo wasted no time agreeing as she turned to Delaney. "How about we head to the village and get a few things for dinner?"

Delaney stretched and then leaned against the door frame. "Perfect idea." She gave a slight wave to Justin. "See you later. Text me?"

He was already down the porch steps and called out. "Sure will."

Elisa at a fast pace met him and whispered. "Thank you for putting Hunter in his place, that buffoon!"

He maintained his stride, looking downward. Once on Opal's porch, she handed Katydid over to him and met Delaney over at the golf cart.

"Is Margo going to the village with us?"

"Nope. Her fiancé has restaurant menu drama unfolding and needs her." Delaney said as she got into the golf cart.

Elisa asked Delaney how her father was doing.

"He is being released tonight. Mom was afraid his pacemaker would fail. You know my mom, the worrywart."

Elisa held onto the seat as Delaney backed up the golf cart and drove down the street. She sensed Delaney's mood was down. They pulled up to the small grocery store, and Elisa went to get out when Delaney stopped her.

"What were you all laughing about on the porch?"

With a casual lift of her shoulders, Elisa told her it was all about her nose. Delaney questioned why they were talking about noses when Elisa froze.

"Ah ha! I knew it — you were talking about my lousy cooking skills since I burned this morning's omelet, and Miss Opal came over with her fire extinguisher since the house was full of smoke."

"No, but admit that was comical. I mean, even I have never burned an omelet and smoke out a house. Let Margo do the cooking. But in all seriousness, it was not about you. It was how cute the pup is, and since the pup licked my nose, I sneezed." *Whew, she thought fast on that one.*

Delaney found inward laughter as she got out of the golf cart. "Life is never dull with you around, Elisa, and yes, all the cooking is now in the hands of Margo."

"Yeah, and we need another dozen eggs." Elisa let out a silent breath, thankful the nose discussion was over.

Elisa was entering the store when she noticed Delaney was not behind her.

Delaney had stopped and was looking at her phone, shaking her head, then put it in her pocket and met Elisa.

"Delaney, what's going on? You have a weird look on your face?"

She took a deep inhale and, letting it out, she told Elisa she had a strange text from Hunter.

"Strange?" Elisa worried about the punch in the nose. She moved aside to let a couple go past her and enter the store.

"He texted goodbye, my love."

"Good!"

"Yes, but I went to text him back, and I was blocked."

"Even better."

"Elisa, do you think he finally got the message?" Delaney put her hair up in a clip she had on her belt.

"I think he did. Good riddance to evil juju."

Delaney's stare found Elisa. "You suck at lying?

"What? Time to go into the store." Elisa opened the door and went to step inside when Delaney stopped her.

"Could it be that Justin punched Hunter in the nose?"

29

Elisa held a bag of groceries on her lap as they headed back to the cottage. She had to say something since they had been silent in the store.

"Delaney, I love you, and you are my best friend, and I'm sorry we told you a fib. We avoided upsetting you since you were already dealing with your dad."

Keeping her eyes on the road, Delaney spoke. "Upset no. In fact, I'm overjoyed that *slick weasel* is gone for good. And I overheard your conversations. You need to talk in whispers in the future! Justin's swollen hand was a giveaway!" she pulled into the driveway and turned to Elisa. "We need to celebrate!"

"Agreed. And how about we invite Justin to our soiree? He sent the buffoon running with his tail — or you know what — between his legs and, as a bonus, a broken nose!"

Delaney pulled her lips in and out as she glanced across the street and went back to Elisa. "I had better go over there and privately thank him."

Elisa reached into the grocery bag. "You should take the bandages and creams you bought too!" She handed them over. "He needs your TLC and go take care of the man who saved you from Hunter!"

"I see you have been reading too many romance novels."

"If you only knew!"

Delaney, with her small first-aid kit in hand, went over to Miss Opal's place and knocked on the door. No one answered. She knocked once again. Still, no answer. After walking along the porch that went all the way around the house, she arrived in the backyard and saw Miss Opal in a chair while Justin was exiting the garage.

"Miss Opal!" she waved at her.

"Delaney, honey, come join me and have a glass of lemonade. I'm about to go inside and prepare supper and check on the puppy. She is a wild child. I moved her bed into the bathroom until Justin gets her into a tiny house of her own. Would ya like to join us?"

Standing next to Miss Opal, Delaney reminded her that the following afternoon was spa day.

"I'm so happy." She ran her hand through her gray hair. "Elisa is going to give me my youth back."

Delaney helped herself to a glass of lemonade as she kept a close eye on Justin as he backed Sally out of the garage. "I heard you are going to be a new woman. Sunset auburn is the hair color, and Elisa is the best!" she placed the bag of bandages on a side table.

"Honey, help me up. I need to get inside and out of this darned heat. I need to be in air conditioning." She fanned her face. "This air is thicker than a cheating man's lies."

Delaney chuckled at the comment, having heard that term before.

Miss Opal's focus was on the former back gardens. "When I was young, I sure had a beautiful garden abundant with fresh tomatoes, cucumbers, and peppers. Your Uncle Bo and I would have such enjoyment making tomato pudding."

Miss Opal's eyes lit up for a moment. "Maybe one day Justin could till those gardens and get that old water fountain running again. I bet both of you would grow a wonderful garden back here and share laughter as I once did."

Delaney held out her hand as her heartbeat faster. "Maybe one day."

Miss Opal went inside as Justin made his way over to Delaney. His work gloves concealed his bruised hand.

Squinting in the sun's glare, she asked. "Hi Justin, it sure is a hot day. Would you like a few sips of my lemonade?"

"Thanks. I appreciate it." He went to take the glass from her when her lemony lips met his.

Stepping back, she spoke into his eyes. "I have been busy at my cottage with my friends." She said as she pulled back and ran her finger over his cheek.

"Wow, I did not expect that. You sure are bursting with surprises."

She swayed from side to side and stopped. "Ya think? Give me your hands."

"Huh?" he instinctively held his sore hand back.

"Ah, both, please." She reached for his hands and removed the gloves.

"What do we have here? A boo-boo from punching a total asshole in his fake nose?" Her eyes were wide as she surveyed the damage.

He went to pull his hand back, but she kept a tight grip. "Shit, Delaney, I asked the girls not to tell you. I'm——so–"

She placed her index finger over his lips. "Hush, your nurse is here to bandage you up and help you heal. And I overheard the three of you chatting about the Hunter incident. Thank you. He ran home, and now he will leave me alone."

"Aw, shucks, Nurse Delaney, I had to save the damsel across the street from that dreadful, snobby tyrant."

"Sit down and let me put some antiseptic cream on that scrape, and then I can bandage you up." She went to work and with her gentle fingers she applied the cream to the swelling. When she finished, she found her stare was on Sally. "Surely you were not thinking of working on that truck with that open cut and your swollen hand?" She lifted her left eyebrow. "Were you?"

"What do you think? I'm a guy! What sore hand?" he pursed his lips as he looked at his newly bandaged hand. "Time to pull the front seat out, and if you would give me some ideas for new fabric coverings, I would enjoy that."

Tapping her fingers on her chin, she agreed.

With some effort and a few tugs, the rusted front bench seat came out. The seat or remains of it were a disaster, and Delaney was unsure of what she had signed up for.

"I sure am no mechanic, Delaney, but I can paint and clean this up. The seat is not my territory." Using his foot, he turned it over. "Wow, this is in rough shape. I can call my Buddy. He may know someone who works on truck seats. I may have to buy a new one."

Delaney wiped her forehead as she twisted her lips and then spoke. "Let me try, and if I fail, then give your friend a call. Deal?"

"Deal. I want to open the glove box in hopes that there is the original owner's manual in it." Justin went back to the truck and fought to open it. After several attempts with various tools, Delaney came up behind him.

"Maybe this will help." She handed him a pitted key.

He looked at it. "Where did you find that?"

She directed her finger towards the back seat. "On the floor under a bunch of ancient newspapers. And, uh, that back seat is as bad as the front one."

"I know. How about a two for one deal?" His lips curled.

How could she say no? "Deal."

"Okay, how about I try this key? Watch me!" he did, and the glove box popped open. He waved his hand around as silty dust escaped. "Geeze this is in rough shape and stuffed with papers."

Delaney was beside him. "My place was not nearly as bad as this when I walked through the door three years ago. Before we begin, I know a little backstory as to why my Uncle Bo's truck is here at Opal's."

He leaned against the truck. "You do? Aunt Opal keeps that to herself, and I feel uncomfortable asking her. Hey, let's look for the owner's manual."

Pursing her lips, Delaney knew eventually she would fill him in on why the truck was in Opal's garage. Noting his body language, she knew this was not the time.

Justin reached into the truck's glove box. "Back to work." He pulled out papers, handing them to Delaney while reaching the far back, found a small white velvet box and handed it to Delaney.

She turned it from side to side and set it on the grass. He then handed her a few more papers and called out. "I found the owner's manual!"

"And I found an envelope with Opal's name handwritten on it." She brushed the dust off the delicate find. "This looks very similar to my Uncle Bo's handwriting." Turning the envelope over, she realized it was sealed. She picked up the white velvet box. "I wonder what this is all about?" She blew some dust off it. "The velvet, once white, is so dirty. Should we open it?" With the envelope in her other hand, she fanned her face.

Justin brushed the grime off his shirt as he stared at the box and envelope. "We should open it. I bet it's another key."

"Yeah, but this envelope, I think, is a card. Maybe we need to give this to Opal?"

Justin scratched his day-old beard. "What if this is something that was not meant to be opened?"

Delaney was peeling the back of it, hoping that it

would open without damage. "Not meant to be. And this box? We gotta open it."

Making sure Opal was not watching, Justin stole a look at the kitchen window and went back to Delaney. "How about we open both of them in the garage?"

They went inside the garage and over to the large window.

"Open the box." Delaney's eager eyes were on the object. "It was once a lovely box. It must be special."

With care, he lifted the top. Delaney gasped and placed her hand over her mouth as the play of colors danced on the white, round stone surrounded by diamonds.

Delaney pushed her hair behind her ears as she leaned in. "Oh my gosh, this is an opal ring." Her eyes found Justin's. "This is beautiful." She wiggled her toes. "Open the envelope?"

He pulled it closer to get a better look. "Delaney, this must belong to Opal?"

"Yeah, but why was it in the glove box of an old truck that has sat for years in the garage? Not to forget the truck that is falling apart that belonged to my uncle."

"Not a clue, but here." He handed the box to Delaney. "I'm going to open the envelope." He pried it open and pulled out a card decorated with a heart and cupids surrounded by cloth lace. "This is a Valentine's Day card, and an old one."

Delaney stood next to him. "Open it!" She took a quick look over her shoulder. "No sign of Opal."

As he did, a folded piece of paper slid out and fell onto the floor. Delaney went to pick it up, and as she did, she could hear Opal saying something. Suddenly, the puppy appeared and began running in circles in the garage, almost trampling the paper.

Delaney snatched the puppy before it could misbehave or tear up the paper, and then she looked up to see Opal coming down the back porch stairs. In a loud whisper, she told Justin to hide everything since Opal is on her way over.

"Shit," he picked up the paper. With the card and ring in its box in hand, he went over to the workbench and put it in an empty, rusty Charlie Chips can and met Delaney, who handed the squirming pup over to him.

Opal, out of breath, stood at the open garage door and firmly reminded Justin that he needed to get a puppy pen and or gate. "That little rascal slipped past me as I was about to come out to get some fresh basil from my porch pots. That little firecracker slid past my legs, nearly tripping me, looking for you. She is gonna need some training if she wants to live here." She fanned her flustered face.

"I know Aunt Opal, and it will not happen again. Sorry. Later I'll get a gate." He put the Katydid inside the truck and shut the door. "Be a good girl." He tapped her nose.

Delaney had never seen Opal so upset and walked over to her. "Come on, you need to go inside and get yourself some cold water and sit down."

Justin watched them go inside the house. His mind was swirling. What did the card and letter say? Never mind, what was the opal ring doing in the glove box?

30

Justin reached inside the Charlie Chips can. His fingers tickled the ring box, and he removed it. He walked over to the window and unlatched it. Dazzling beams of color met him as the brilliant opal mirrored every color imaginable.

"Psst…" Delaney tapped his shoulder. "Opal is fine, and she is making dinner. Can I see the ring again?"

He handed it to her.

She looked up at Justin and back at the ring. "Wow, this is stunning. It must have cost a small fortune." She held it up to the sunbeams that streamed into the window. "What do we do with it? Give it to Opal?"

As he spoke, he raised his shoulders. "Why was it in the truck? What if he gave it to her, and she rejected it, and out of his broken heart he stuffed it in the glove box?"

Delaney placed the ring in the box and closed it. She folded her arms across her waist. Shaking her head as she spoke. "That is a possibility."

His stare landed on the can. "How about we read the letter and card and then we can decide?" He felt like an intruder, but wanted to know. "Here goes." Reaching into the chip can, he pulled out the card and then handed it to Delaney.

With care, she opened it. "There is nothing written on the card. Huh?" She turned it over. "Nada."

"Wait! I forgot the letter that was inside the card that slid out when Katydid came running in here." He removed it from the can and gave it to Delaney. "You may have the honor."

She glanced over her shoulder at Miss Opal's house and back to Justin and then the letter.

"Well, read it!" He rubbed his anxious hands together.

"Give me a moment to read it." Her eyes volleyed over to Justin. "This is a love letter from Uncle Bo to Opal, dated years after my uncle passed away. In fact, Uncle Bo died the day before Valentine's Day."

Katydid barked as she pawed at the open window of the truck door.

"Okay. Hold on, Katydid," Justin found a small rope on the workbench and latched it onto her collar. "Be back in a minute." He dashed off and placed a bowl of water in a shaded area under a yaupon tree and tied the rope to it. "You have plenty of room to roam for the next few minutes and stay out from under Aunt Opal's feet!" He kissed her head and went back to Delaney. "I need to get her some obedience, or she and I'll be living in the garage."

Delaney shook her head. "Yeah, I noticed she had piddled in the hallway. I cleaned it before Miss Opal saw it. She is a baby." She blew a kiss to Katydid. "You be a good girl and if okay with Justin, I can take you for a beach walk later."

"She sure can, and I would like to go as well." Rubbing his hands together, he suggested they take Katydid for a walk, but first they headed over to Delaney's cottage and read the letter.

He untied Katydid, and they crossed the street to Delaney's place, where they found Elisa and Margo down by the water's edge, laughing and screaming as they paddled around on stand-up boards.

"Good, they are busy out there," Delaney said with a twinkle in her eyes. "Do you mind if I read it?"

Justin muttered a laugh. "Go ahead."

Pulling her lips in and out, she looked out over the water. "Time to let the imprisoned words free!"

Justin held onto the ring as he handed the letter over to Delaney.

She sat down on the sandy shore with Justin and Katydid beside her. "Ready? Can I have the ring?"

"Sure." He took the box out of his shirt pocket, and Delaney opened it and removed the ring.

She held the ring as she read the letter to Justin.

Opal Mae-

You are the sunrise and sunset in my heart and soul. Without you, my life would have no meaning. When we were fishing on the beach that day and our lines became twisted, I realized you would be a part of my life. We laughed until sunset.

Your laughter, sunny smile, and enchanting eyes called to me. I waited a long time, and when you became free, my heart leaped at the chance that you and I would be one.

Though I may struggle to express my emotions, I'm trying to show you how important you are to my life's story. This opal ring is a symbol of my love for you. The way it gleams reminds me of your eyes. You are my Opal!

It's Valentine's Day! Please accept this ring as our bond for a lifetime together. Be my wife.

Love, Beuford (Bo) McCormac

Delaney let the letter slide into her lap as she faced Justin. "This was an engagement ring." She looked at it and frowned. "I think?"

"Whoa. That is so bittersweet." He rubbed his forehead as his eyes found the letter.

Delaney gave the ring to Justin and leaned back on her elbows. "What is sad, it was on Valentine's Day he was going to give this to her. My mom told me he crafted the heart on my porch swing for Miss Opal from a piece of wood they had found washed up near my place. He passed away on February 13th that same year. I bet he was going to propose on Valentine's Day and give her the ring. That leaves me guessing he kept it in his truck, and they were going on a Valentine's Day date, and he passed away before he could give it to her."

Justin leaned back and looked up at the sky, then faced Delaney. "She had no idea did she?"

"I doubt it. So, what do we do? I mean, if we give the ring and letter to her, it could break her heart and stir up painful memories."

Justin sat up, plucking at the grass. "I think for now we need to keep a lid on this and not say a word to anyone.

"I agree, and I can keep them here inside my desk drawer. If that is good with you?" Delaney could feel the heartbreak if Miss Opal found out. Do they tell her, or should they keep it a secret? No, she shook her head. What to do? She moaned as she ran her hands through her hair. "How about we put them back in the truck?"

"The truck is going to be cleaned and painted in the next few days. Then it will be flat bedded on a trailer out of here and up to Virginia Beach."

"Got it. So, it remains here. But not for too long, you know one of us might slip and mention it."

Justin agreed with a slight smile as he caressed her arm. "That was a beautiful letter your uncle wrote. I can only imagine how hurt Aunt Opal must have been when he passed away."

"Yup. She mentioned to me several times that she is a retired nurse and that she took care of him after his first heart attack. They must have been so in love. Did you know Uncle

Bo made, painted, and put the pink heart on my porch swing? It was out of the piece of wood I mentioned earlier that they found on the shore."

Justin pulled her closer and studied her lips. "Bittersweet love story."

"I discovered the swing in my garage when I moved in and fixed it up. Miss Opal told me that they would spend countless days and nights on that swing."

Justin ran his index finger over Delaney's lips. "I have decided to call it a *sweetheart swing*. Because you have the sweetest heart!"

31

Elisa and Margo set the table for dinner, wondering why Delaney had been so silent. Elisa could no longer take it. She had to ask and stepped inside the room that hosted the dollhouse.

"What is going on? You have not said a word since we got inside. And why are you hanging out at the dollhouse?"

Delaney was at her dollhouse, moving furniture around. "Nothing. I'm doing fabulously." She tapped her cheek, adding. "Do you think I should add a porch swing to the dollhouse?"

"A porch swing?" Elisa walked over to the dollhouse, narrowing her stare on it, then to Delaney. "Where?"

Margo entered the room. "I think that is a terrific idea. But first, you need a porch."

Delaney went over to the front of the dollhouse and tapped on the façade. "I can put one on. They have kits. And I'm adding a swing just like the one out on my front porch."

"If that makes you happy, then do it. And by the way, Margo and I can stay another week, and I'm considering backing out of the salon deal." Elisa was behind Delaney as she continued. "Or you could ask Justin to build one!" She let out a teasing giggle. "You know that."

Margo joined them. "Did you say you are backing out of the salon offer?" her phone rang. "Gotta get this." She left the room.

Delaney was overthinking the front porch addition and the swing. After reading the letter and seeing the ring, she knew how much love had been shared on her front porch. "I think I'll put it right there." She tapped her index finger left of the front door and turned to Elisa. "Sorry. I was lost in my dollhouse world. You said you are not taking the salon deal. That is huge. Will you regret it down the road?"

Elisa picked up a tiny chair from the dollhouse. "It's way too much money, and I do not have it. Nor do I want the stress. The potential partner can be aggressive. I love my little salon and interesting, gossipy customers. They will not follow me if a haircut will cost them triple." She folded her arms across her chest. "Done deal. And with that, I'll stay where I am for now with no regrets!

Delaney paid attention to Elisa and gave her a hug. "If your heart tells you to back out, then do so. I love your salon. And tomorrow is Miss Opal's spa day. She is looking forward to it."

"I'm ready. She is going to love it. Listen, Margo made a Greek dish, and it smells too yummy. Before we eat, I must ask."

"I know what you are going to ask. And yes, Justin and I are having a wonderful time. Nothing serious, and it's best that way. But I have to tell you something. Better yet, show you." She curled her index finger to follow her to the office and opened the top drawer. She put the white box and the envelope on the desktop. "Can you keep a secret?"

Elisa studied them. Her eyes rolled up to Delaney's. "Secret? Sure, but what is this?"

"Justin and I found them in the glove box of Sally, my Uncle Bo's old truck. We are not sure what to do with them."

Elisa picked up the box, turning it from side to side. "Did you open it? This looks as if it has been hanging around for a while."

"We opened it, and it had been idle, locked in the glove box for years. There is a ring in there and a love letter or proposal to go with it. We think Uncle Bo was going to propose since he died the day before he was going to give this to her."

Elisa scrunched her face. "Back up. Who is the woman he was going to ask?"

"Miss Opal," Delaney said as she handed the envelope over. "Read the card, the date, and the letter. He was going to give this to her on Valentine's Day, but he died the day before."

Elisa's mouth fell open as she read the letter. "This is so sad. He was proposing to her. I want to cry."

Delaney tapped her nails on the desktop. "If you think that makes you sad, open the box."

She did. "Wow." Her surprised eyes met Delaney's and journeyed back to the ring. "This is an opal with diamonds." She held it to her heart. "This is a tragic romance. What will you do with it?"

Delaney sat down. "Justin and I are not sure. I mean, did she know? Would she have said yes, or no? Did she love him? Would giving the ring and letter to her at this stage of her life be upsetting?"

Elisa removed the ring and held it up to the window. "This is gorgeous. Look how it sparkles in the light." She went over to Delaney and placed it in her hand. "This is a huge decision. But to be honest, it's up to Justin since she is his aunt."

"I know, and for now it will remain here in a safe space."

Margo marched into the room. "Dinner is ready." And she stomped out.

"What the heck?" Elisa said as she shrugged. "I think she was on the phone with her fiancé, and we had better not be late for dinner."

Delaney put the ring, card, and letter back into the drawer. "We had better go find out what got Margo so sour."

Margo was huffing and puffing as she put the dinner on the table. Muttering unkind words under her breath, she sat down, flagging her napkin around and onto her lap. She mouthed. "Idiot. Moron."

Delaney glanced at Elisa as she picked up her fork. "This looks so good."

Margo tossed her napkin onto the table. She got up, went into the kitchen and returned with the pepper grinder, and sat down, letting out a huff.

Elisa couldn't take the huffing and muttering any longer and spoke up. "Spill the beans. Now Margo."

Margo took a long sip of her wine and was silent.

Outside, raindrops tapped on the windows as the wind picked up, breaking the silence.

"I can stay another week. And for your information, it did not go well with my fiancé. So be it. Enjoy dinner." Margo said as she refilled her wineglass.

Elisa and Delaney knew there was more to the story and let it go for another day.

32

Delaney came back from her morning run and headed straight to her office, where she opened the desk drawer. She retrieved the ring, letter, and card, then settled into her desk chair, reading each word over again. She realized that she and Justin needed to decide: should they keep this a secret from Miss Opal or reveal the truth? Regretting ever opening that glove box.

Justin came back from the village with donuts and coffee for everyone. Stepping onto Delaney's front porch, he tapped on the front door.

Delaney met him and wasted no time planting a tender kiss on his lips.

With coffee and donuts in hand, he spoke. "Wow, I'm finding you like to give daily surprise kisses! How about I stop by every morning?"

She swayed as her cheeks flushed rosy pink. "How can I help myself? You are kissable! And as a bonus, you bring us the best treats from Ocracoke Coffee!" She motioned for him to step inside. "Follow me to my office."

He placed the coffee and donuts down on the table by the front window, lined with plants. She handed her a cup.

"Thank you!" She lifted the lid and inhaled the aroma of the brew. "Delicious. I usually opt for carrot juice after my morning run, but it's nice to indulge now and then. Plus, I have a lot on my plate today, so this will keep my energy up." Taking a sip, she glanced around the room and at Justin. "My friends are staying for another week, and I'm absolutely thrilled," she whispered. "I have a mountain of work and a few deadlines looming, so they'll need to manage without me for a bit."

Justin sat down on a soft chair. "There are plenty for them to do! I could use some help in Aunt Opal's garden of they are they are looking to get their hands dirty."

She offered a slight shrug. "It won't hurt to ask. And later this afternoon is Miss Opal's spa day. No men allowed!"

He took a sip of his coffee. "She told me and has been turning the dining room into a pink palace! Besides, Sally and I have a date, which reminds me."

"I know you want to look at upholstery fabric?"

"Wow, you can read minds too." He winked, adding his sexy smile. A smile that made her legs weak. "If you help me pick something out. FYI, I'm keeping the truck the original blue paint color."

Delaney picked up a thick donut coated in luscious chocolate and spoke to it with a smile. "You look absolutely irresistible, but indulging means I must add an extra mile to my morning run." With a decisive bite, she savored the flavor. "Completely worth the extra mile."

"That is one delicious donut!" Justin said as he got up and reached for a cinnamon roll. They enjoyed their treats in silence.

Delaney finished hers and suggested later in the day that if he comes back, she will help him pick out fabric. Something close to what the truck had, or go in a new direction.

He finished the last of his coffee and had to ask. "I was up most of the night thinking about the ring and letter." He scratched his chin. "What do we do?"

"Not sure. We need to think about it. And I was up too! If I had known you were up, I would have tossed a rock at your window, and you could have slid down the gutter and met me!"

He burst into laughter. "Well, the gutter will most likely break because it has been there since 1959! And guaranteed a fractured bone or two as I land on my ass on the thorny rose bushes."

Delaney studied him in the morning light. "Ha ha. Yup, that is a very unromantic scenario. How about we have a code with the front porch light like I have with Miss Opal? We flash the porch lights."

He went up to her and pushed her past her shoulders. "I like that. A secret code. One means I'm going to bed, twice for maybe meet me on the porch, and three times meet me in my bed!"

She pulled him into her body. "Well, now, you are being very naughty, and I admit I like the latter suggestion."

He tapped the tip of her nose. "I hope we do not break the light switches with these codes."

Delaney tilted her head back. "Honestly, I think we need to wait on the three flicks of the switch, and for now, two is good for me." She had to say something, feeling they may be getting too close too soon. She needed time to decide if they were even ready for the three front porch light flicks.

"Agreed. I like you a lot and no need to rush anything, although—"

She placed her index finger on his lips. "Ah, no number three."

"Shucks. But I understand." He looked at his watch. "Time to get back home. I have work to do on my laptop. I sold my company, but I still have a vested interest, and they pay me well for my freelance input."

With a subtle frown, Delaney guided him toward the front door. "Text me after one and if you are free, I can bring over some ideas for the truck's seats. I can recreate anything you want, even the old pattern, and have it made. You will need someone to install it on the seat."

"Working on that. I may have found a guy up in Virginia Beach." He kissed her cheek. His hand slid out of hers. He went down the porch steps and home.

Around eleven, Delaney and her friends went out to the village to pick up a few appetizers for Miss Opal's spa day. Miss Opal was busy getting ready when there was a knock on her front door. She called out to Justin. He did not answer and looked out the kitchen window, noticing his red car was gone. She heard another knock on the door.

A grin spread across her face as she looked out the side window. She opened the door to find a familiar courier with a large overnight envelope.

"Afternoon, Miss Opal."

"Hi Pete!" Her stare fell on the envelope in his hand. "I have not ordered anything. This must be for my nephew." Her eyes remained on the envelope.

Pete looked at it. "The envelope is addressed to Delaney across the street. I knocked over there, but she is not answering, and I felt it was important, so can I leave it with you?"

"You know you can trust me. I once babysat you!"

Red-faced, he replied. "I know. Please give this to her." He handed it over. "Thanks. I'll be leaving for vacation tomorrow and would hate to leave it back in the truck and the sub makes an error."

"No problem. I'll take it and enjoy your vacation. Bye now." She waved as he turned and made his way out to his delivery truck.

Miss Opal realized that Delaney's golf cart was missing. Holding the envelope, she crossed the street, passed under the arbor, and approached the porch. She knocked on the front door and called out for Delaney. Concerned about leaving the envelope on the side table, she checked to see if the front door was locked. To her surprise, it was not!

She stepped inside. Looking from side to side, she called out one more time. With no answer, she headed for the office and went to place it on the desk when she spotted a Valentine's Day card, envelope, and a note with her name on it. Next to it was a white box. She looked closer. Without question, the handwriting belonged to Bo.

"What is this?" Wondering if it was something Delaney found in the walls or while renovating, she toyed with reading it or walking out the door. Biting her bottom lip, she moved in closer. Temptation got the best of her as she picked up the card. Her heart fell to her feet and back up as she covered her mouth. The handwriting on the card envelope looking back at her was Bo's. It slipped out as her hands shook.

She picked it up when she noticed the small white box that had rested near it. Curious, she picked up the box and turned it from side to side. Guilt settled in. This was none of her business or was it? Her name is on the envelope and the note. She went to place them back when a chill found her, and in her mind's eye she could see Bo standing next to her. Something brushed across her cheek to her lips. Taking it as a sign that Bo wanted her to read the letter and open the box, she settled onto the sofa by the window.

She read the letter twice, examining the card. As her fingers glided over the delicate lace, memories flooded back—

a time filled with love and innocence, where joy occupied every moment and her nights with Bo felt endless. Days passed as swiftly as her heartbeat. With a deep sigh, she placed the box on her lap and opened it. Seeing the round-cut opal and its vibrant hues, her shoulders slumped, and a tear rolled down her soft cheek. He wanted to marry her; this was her engagement ring. But where had Delaney found it? Just as she reached for the ring, a commotion in the hallway startled her, and she could faintly hear Elisa speaking nearby.

"We are going to have so much fun at Miss Opal's today. I bet she is gonna love her new look. And I'm bringing my nail polishes too!"

Realizing they had returned from the village, she went to get up and put everything back when Delaney walked into the room. Her eyes landed on what was in Miss Opal's hand and lap as a lump grew in her throat.

Delaney, at a slow pace, walked over to her. "I know you are wondering where I got those items." She was so annoyed with herself. How could she have been so careless and left them out? She promised Justin that she would keep them safe.

Miss Opal looked at what was in hand. She inhaled and let it out as she met Delaney's alarmed stare. "That would be one question." Her face tensed as she closed the lid of the box.

Elisa and Margo were standing at the doorway to the room.

"Please try not to be upset. We—" Delaney twisted her lips as she struggled for words.

Miss Opal shook her head. "We?"

Delaney pushed her hair behind her ears as she mustered the courage to speak. "Justin and I found them in Sally's glove box yesterday and were unsure when to tell you."

Miss Opal's voice was tired. "There is no time like the present."

Elisa walked over. "Miss Opal. Delaney was trying to protect you from being hurt. She meant no harm. Can you forgive fer?"

"Yes, I can. She did this out of love for me, as did Justin." She lifted the card and stared at it as she spoke. "Bo had wonderful taste. Did you look at the card he picked out? It has real lace around the heart, and the tiny cupid on top has glitter on its wings. He always gave me a heart-shaped box of candy on Valentine's Day, and he ate most of it!" Her laughter faded into tears as she traced the lace with her finger. "He was a man with a heart of gold. I miss him. He is here in your cottage, Delaney. I can feel him beside me."

Margo dashed in with a handful of tissues and rubbed Miss Opal's arm. "What Bo left you is so beautiful." She shot a stare at Delaney, who walked over to them.

Elisa rubbed her arms, alarmed that Uncle Bo was roaming the cottage, and that it chilled her.

"Girls, I need to go home and spend time alone. Before I forget, I came here with this overnight letter for you, Delaney. Pete, our delivery guy, did not want to leave it on the porch. It looks important."

Delaney glanced at her desk at the overnight letter from the New York law firm, realizing that is how Miss Opal found everything. She was being kindhearted and caring only to enter Delaney's cottage and have her heart shattered. That was not neighborly!

Elisa, in a cheerful tone, spoke. "I know what will give you a smile. How about we have our spa day in an hour?"

Margo added in a cheerful tone. "I think that is a wonderful idea."

Miss Opal opened the box and took the ring out. Turning it from side to side, she then pulled it close. "This is from my beautiful Bo. He always said my smile shined like an opal." She kissed the stone and put it back in the box and looked at the girls. "I say we have our spa day and toast my Bo to his spectacular taste and humor!"

"Humor?" Delaney asked.

"Yes, he had to go and die the day before he was going to ask me to marry him."

Confused by the comment, Delaney helped Miss Opal off the sofa. "We will be over in an hour!"

"Delaney. Thank you for wanting to protect my heart. I never had children, and you are a daughter to me." She brushed her hand over Delaney's cheek. She then picked up the letter, card, and ring box.

As Miss Opal made her way down the walkway, she encountered Justin, who was approaching her. Noticing the items in her hands, he halted in surprise. His concerned gaze turned toward Delaney, who stood on her porch. With her arms crossed over her chest, she tilted her head before turning and heading inside.

33

Delaney went over to her desk and picked up the overnight envelope, opened the top desk drawer, and reached for a letter opener.

Margo walked in with Elisa behind her. "Wow, that was very tense. I was concerned that you might have lost Miss Opal as a friend, but it seems she handled it well."

Delaney sat down. "I feel horrible. Justin trusted me to keep it safe, and I failed."

Elisa walked over to her. "Miss Opal will be fine. As they say, things happen for a reason. And I believe it was time for her to find out that he wanted to marry her. But it's all in the past now, and she seemed to be okay with it."

Regardless of how Elisa and Margo tried to cheer her up, she still harbored terrible guilt. She looked out the window at Miss Opal's house. In her hand was the envelope from the attorneys in New York.

"It's time to find out just what Hunter's mother left me." She opened the envelope to find a letter with the attorney's address on it and a set of keys. She held the keys in her hand as she read the letter.

"The suspense is too much." Elisa said as she got herself comfortable on the sofa.

"These are the keys to three storage units in of all places." Her gaze fell on Elisa. "In Long Island."

Elisa shot up off the sofa. "No way. Where?"

Delaney handed the letter over.

"I know where this place is. And three units? What did she leave you?"

Margo walked over to Delaney. "Looks like you have a road trip. I bet there are all sorts of goodies in those units. Fabrics, beads, sequins, mannequins, patterns. Wow!"

Delaney rubbed her forehead. "Wow, is an understatement. First the letter and ring incident with Miss Opal, and now this. Geeze it was so serene, and you two show up, and it has gotten a little zany around here!" She laughed out loud. "I love it! I admit I miss a small part of my former life."

Elisa reached for Delaney's hands and gave her a tug. "Put the keys in a safe place. We have a spa day across the street! Come on."

Delaney, adding smiles and agreeable nods, got up and placed the keys in her top drawer and locked it.

Opal's heart was full when she saw the girls standing at her front door. "Step into Miss Opal's Spa. We have treats and drinks!" She kissed the girls as they entered. As Delaney passed by, she stopped her. "Thank you for today."

"I hope this has not fractured our relationship. I was unsure what to do."

"No, honey, it bonded us closer. Now let us have some fun!"

Delaney held a pitcher filled with lemonade. She asked if she could put it in the refrigerator, where she bumped into Justin.

He pulled her aside, and before he could speak, she placed her index finger over his lips. "I know I messed up, and I'm beyond sorry."

He moved her finger away. "Aunt Opal is fine, and we had a pleasant conversation. She really needed to read that letter and see the ring. This has helped her, believe it or not. But in the future, I gotta remember not to give you anything that has to be hidden!" he teased, then kissed her lips. "Heading out to get Sally ready for the flatbed, which will be here in an hour. Have fun." He turned and, with Katydid by his side, he walked out the back door, leaving Delaney relieved that she had not ruined her new friendship.

Taking a deep and needed breath, she fanned her face as she walked into the dining room to enjoy food and drinks before the spa day began.

As Miss Opal settled into a chair at the kitchen table, with a towel draped over her shoulders and hair dye worked its colorful magic, she told the story of the ring and the letter. Her captive listeners leaned in, intrigued by the romantic tale of Bo and Opal. Clearing her throat, she placed her hands in her lap as her eyes drifted to a polaroid photograph on the refrigerator of her and Bo at the beach. "We were in our late teens. Silly, awkward kids who did not understand what love was. Or at least we thought we did." She had a tissue in her hand, which she twisted as she continued. "We paddled kayaks on Silver Lake to Bo's parent's cottage. Your place Delaney. Once on the shore, we sat on the sandy beach where he asked me to marry him and offered me a ring he had made of copper wire with a tiny shell entwined on the top of it. Imagine that? I was seventeen, and he was twenty-one. We were so naïve. *Youth can do that!* I said no and broke his heart. I wanted to go to school to be a nurse, and I did."

"I know you were one of the best nurses out in Raleigh," Delaney said as she pointed to the certificates on a side table in the dining room. "Impressive!"

Miss Opal's face wore a smooth smile as she continued. "Bo never recovered and refused to marry anyone else. We lost touch as our lives moved on." She stopped needing to gather her thoughts.

"Miss Opal, would you like some water?" Margo asked.

"Yes, thank you." She took a sip and continued in a tender voice. "My late husband had passed away years and years ago, and it was time for me to retire and head back to Ocracoke into my childhood home. That was when I fell in love all over again with Bo. I mean love deeper than the ocean out there."

Delaney asked her to tell the story about the wooden heart on the swing.

Her face became softer, as if time had erased thirty years. "We found a piece of wood after a storm at the back of your place, Delaney. Days later, he had made a heart out of it and nailed it to the porch swing." She folded her hands in her lap. "What hurts is that he had a heart attack not long after. He left the hospital and came home to Ocracoke to heal. He was a man never to sit still and would *not* listen to me or his doctors. I took care of him until he passed away months later." She moved her hands to her chest and showed the women a gold heart that was on a chain. "Inside this locket is my Bo. His smile, his hearty laugh, and my heart with his."

A timer went off. They jumped.

"Miss Opal, it's time to rinse your hair," Elisa said, holding back her tears. *What a beautiful love story*, she thought to herself, wishing she could have known them when they were together.

Delaney felt reflective. Despite not knowing the truth, she felt a mix of happiness and sadness. After all those years of waiting, Bo had Opal back in his life for a few months, then he left her. As if he had known to wait. How ironic. She left him, and then he left her.

Margo had nothing to say. Her romance with her fiancé was boring compared to Miss Opal's life. Leaving her to wonder, would her fiancé wait for her? Would she wait for him? She wanted to call him.

Elisa finished rinsing Miss Opal's hair and gave her a fresh cut and a blow dry.

"Close your eyes!" Elisa said as she handed her a mirror. "Open!"

Miss Opal's face lit up as she turned her head from side to side. "Look at me! I'm twenty years younger!" She reached for Elisa's hand and pulled her close. "Thank you, honey! Now feel like going out dancing, but I doubt my hip will let me."

They laughed as they enjoyed each other's company.

34

Several days had gone by when there was a knock on the front door of Delaney's cottage.

Margo answered it. Her eyes grew large as she said hello.

A sunburned, good-looking man was standing there. "I hope I have the correct cottage. Is Elisa here?"

"You have the correct place. Hold on. Have a seat on the porch and let me get her." She shut the door and dashed to the back porch.

"What has got you so excited?"

"Not what, it's who!" She met Elisa, who was about to take a nap on the cozy outdoor sofa.

Elisa elevated her head, adding a tight squint. "Who?"

Margo stood over her. "Get up. The hot guy on the ferry is here, sitting on the front porch!"

"No!" Elisa, wide eyed popped up. "Seriously?"

"Yes. And go brush your hair and put on some lip gloss. Hurry! I can make small talk."

They dashed into the cottage, leaving Delaney to chuckle when Justin texted her. He wants to know if she would like to head over to the beach for a walk.

She wasted no time grabbing her beach bag. Stepping onto her front porch, she noticed the man from the ferry and Margo chatting.

"Hi!" Delaney said as she stopped on the porch.

Margo introduced the stranger. "This is Sam. His family has a cottage here on Ocracoke, and they will be here most of the summer. And Sam, this is Delaney, who owns this cottage."

Delaney said hello again and asked where his place was.

He walked to the edge of the porch and pointed up the street. "Close to the village, and the one next door to you that needs work. My parents are debating whether to sell it as is or knock it down and sell the lot."

"Wow," Delaney pushed her beach bag over her shoulder. "My place was just like the one next door, and I fixed it up." She wore a proud grin.

"Hard to believe, since your place is nice. The cottage next to yours was a rental. But after the last hurricane, my parents let it go."

Delaney glanced across the street and turned to Sam. "Have your parents stop over and I can show them what my place was like. I consider the cottage next door a twin to mine."

He gave a slow, consistent nod. "I'll tell them. Your name again?"

"Delaney! The only person with that name on the island. I gotta run! Bye." She made her way across the street to meet Justin.

Elisa could not believe the man from the ferry and his sunburned face were on the front porch. Her full lips shaded in soft pink gloss, her long hair down wearing a flirty floral summer dress, her face blushed crimson as she greeted Sam with a welcoming smile.

Not aspiring to be involved in a budding romance, Margo went inside to give them privacy and picked up one of Elisa's romance novels to settle down on the back porch. She had plenty of fun in the sun and salty water for a while.

Delaney got out of Justin's car and put her floppy sun hat on. "Wow, a little different riding in vintage Sally!"

"Smarty pants!" he said, wearing a broad smile.

"Let me think. The painful springs of the seats and the musty smell are what I miss the most!"

He came around to her side of the car. "This is what I miss." His eager lips met hers, and she did not resist or wish to halt the moment. In her mind, she could hear Miss Opal's romantic tale unfolding—how she had patiently awaited her true love, only to find it was too late. Needing a moment to regain her breath, she gradually pulled away.

He traced her outline of her lips as she spoke into them. "We are not alone!"

"I know!" She embraced him by wrapping her arms around his neck and tilted her head back.

"We had better behave. There are tourists here with kids, and that lady over by the garbage can is giving me the stink eye!" he said as he took her hand. "Time to head to the beach!"

She stopped him. "Before we do, I want to tell you something."

"Huh?" he put his sunglasses on.

"It's about your Aunt Opal and what we found in the glove box. Her love life. It's been stuck on rewind in my head. The bittersweetness of their story, and that ring. They were so in love."

"Hey, that was then. They had a beautiful yet sad story. I mean, he waited for her only to leave. Most men are not like that."

She peered into his eyes. "Are you like most men?"

He removed his sunglasses and looked around the parking lot and back at her. "Wow, that is loaded with answers. This is the place or time to talk about it."

A frown found her. "I guess not, but can you give me a tiny answer?" She held her hand up, pinching her thumb and index finger together. "Tiny."

"Would I wait for you? Is that what you want to know?"

She swayed, now embarrassed that she had asked such a dizzy question, since they had only known each other for a few weeks. She answered. "Yes. Would you wait for me?"

He drew her close until his warm breath found her ear. "The more I discover about you, the more eager I'm to learn. I truly like you—more than I can express. You have restored balance to my heart and rekindled my laughter, which I have not experienced in quite some time. You bring a smile to my face and inspire me to rise each morning. Your wit, creativity, and intelligence are truly captivating my heart."

Delaney could not believe he said, *she captivates his heart.* Although his reply was giving her a warm fuzzy feeling, she pulled her shoulder to her ear and spoke. "Would you wait for the woman you love?"

He was feeling pressured and kept tiptoeing around it. "Delaney, would I wait for the woman that I loved deeply like your Uncle Bo did? Yes. Now, can we go to the beach?" He was breaking into a sweat as the sun beat down on him.

"Yes." She put on her sunglasses as he grabbed the beach chairs and umbrella.

They walked on the wooden walkway and onto the sandy path through the dunes when Justin stopped and faced Delaney. "I would wait for you!"

35

In just two days, Elisa and Margo would be departing. Their enjoyable summer getaway in Ocracoke was drawing to a close, making way for them to return to their work lives. They vowed to come back the next summer, as it had been one of their most memorable vacations. They admitted they would miss Delaney's cozy cottage and Miss Opal's delightful Southern charm. Miss Opal even resolved to have her hair styled more frequently. Additionally, she had stored away the opal ring and letter, choosing never to mention them again.

Elisa had struck up a potential romance with Sam; the tourist whose family owned the cottage next door. She was in Sam la-la land and feverishly read her romance novels when alone, to Delaney's teasing.

Margo was in her room packing when she heard a knock on the front door. She called out for Delaney and Elisa and forgot that they had gone out to the gift shops.

She opened the door to find Sam standing there with an older couple behind him.

"Hi, Margo, is it?" His smile was brighter than the sun, but his sunburn still gave him a glow!

"Yes, and Elisa should be back shortly." Margo glanced past him, smiled at the couple, and went back to Sam and asked. "Do you have her number? You can text her." She wanted to finish packing.

"That is all right." He turned to the couple. "My parents wanted to see Delaney's place. They own the dilapidated cottage next door."

"Yes, I heard. Hmmm. Let me text Delaney. Hold on. Have a seat. Back in a sec." She returned. "Delaney will return in about 20 minutes. She said that if you want to walk around the yard and down to the water, go ahead."

The older man stepped forward. "Thanks! Our place has the same view, but it's so overgrown you cannot see much." He turned to his wife, who agreed.

"Go ahead. She will be back soon. I'm packing to head back home in two days, and it's hard to leave Ocracoke."

Sam thanked her as they went to the back of the cottage.

Margo was about to shut the door when a flatbed pulled up with Sally parked on it. She was going to miss island life and the new friends she had made. Her fiancé had been difficult since she had been away, and going back to him and her life left her to question so many things.

Justin came out of Miss Opal's place and spent time with the driver of the flatbed. She watched as they unloaded Sally, all shiny with fresh blue paint. She waved at Justin and went inside to finish packing.

Delaney and Elisa came back a little while later, carrying many shopping bags.

Margo met them. "Sam and his family are out back. They seem nice." Her stare landed on Elisa's bags. "Guess you had some fun!"

"I did, and I no way do I want to go home." She hugged Delaney. "Thanks again for letting me stay at your cottage. It has been a blast! How about?" she turned to Margo. "We come down for the holidays! I know it's not beach weather, but heck, it would be fun if we bundled up and went out for blustery beach walks and then sat by the fireplace sipping hot cocoa."

"I knew you had a Hallmark fantasy in you!" Margo laughed at her friend. "I'm in if I can escape the restaurant during our busy season."

Delaney put her arms around her friends. "You are welcome anytime. Honestly, I'll miss you both."

Margo perked up. "Sally is back in town! They just delivered it to Justin. It looks better with fresh paint!"

Delaney went over to the window. "Awesome. Oh crap, I have people roaming around my yard. Let me go meet with them." She dashed out the back door.

Elisa faced Margo with a sigh. "Ugh, I dread going home."

Margo agreed, adding a frown. "Yup. And what is up with you and Sam?"

"He is nice, but he lives in Ohio, and that is a little too far for me. But he has been fun to hang out with, and we are going to stay in touch."

"Too bad. He seems like a nice guy." She put her hair in a ponytail. "I gotta go pack and do some laundry."

"Me too. I almost forgot, Delaney said, Miss Opal would like us to stop by later. She wants to say goodbye." Elisa plopped down onto the sofa and threw her hands in the air. "I hate goodbyes!"

Margo was heading to her room when Delaney and the couple stepped inside the cottage.

"This is my place. I believe it's about the same size and built the same year as yours was." Delaney talked about her renovations and who to call as she led Sam's family around.

Elisa went to meet Sam out on the front porch when Justin walked up the steps.

"Hi Elisa." He turned to Sam and said hello and then asked where Delaney was. Elisa explained and paid attention to Sam.

"Excuse me, Elisa, can you tell her I can stop by later?"

"Sure."

Justin went back to Miss Opal's and not long after returned with her by his side just as Delaney and the couple were walking outside.

Delaney stopped and greeted them.

Miss Opal stepped forward with a warm smile. "Hi, I'm Opal and live across the street. I heard you own the cottage next door to Delaney's."

The man went over to introduce himself.

His wife spoke. "Yes, we have owned it for?"

He turned to his wife and back to Opal. "About twelve years. We used to rent it out, but after the last storm, we need to decide to sell it as is or tear it down and sell the lot."

Delaney wore a tight smile, not happy with the thought of the magical cottage being destroyed.

"Well now, that cottage goes back to the 1960s when my sister and her husband built it and lived in it for most of their lives. They are no longer with us," Miss Opal said. "It was a beautiful cottage at one time, blooming with canas and cosmos. Every Friday night we had a fish fry out back, come rain or shine."

The woman walked over to Miss Opal. "Those must have been wonderful times, and surely your sister would be happy with whatever we do with it."

Miss Opal tensed as she looked around and back at the woman. "Whatever you do with it, you have my blessings. It has been quite a few years since I last visited that place. Does it still have the wallpaper with the tiny red and blue fish on it?

I helped my sister hang it." A reflection of the past settled into her eyes as she continued. "We picked it out of the Sears catalog and drove up to Virginia Beach to pick it up. That day she found the perfect red and blue stained-glass light to go over the kitchen table. You had to see her husband fuss as he installed it."

The woman's smile was kind as she replied. "Most of the wallpaper has fallen, and the last time I was in there, the light was still hanging. We are concerned about kids going in there and getting hurt."

The man faced Delaney. "Or it collapses."

"That, too." The woman added. "The place has become a liability at this point."

The man spoke to Delaney. "Your cottage is beautiful. I find it hard to imagine it was in the same shape as ours. If possible, I would like to call the people you had work on your place and see what it would cost to bring mine back to the current day." He looked at his wife. "Maybe we should fix it up and rent it out. The view of the sound from the backyard is hard to deny."

His wife gave a slow nod and spoke to her husband. "Honey, we have a lot to think over."

The man drummed his fingers on the railing of the front porch. "That we do, honey. That we do."

They thanked Delaney and left, with Sam not far behind.

Miss Opal was fanning her face. "I need to sit down." Justin led her to a chair. She waited until they drove off and spoke. "Imagine they want to tear down the happy memories in that place. My sister must be rolling in her grave. Lord knows that I had to bite my tongue."

Elisa said with bright eyes. "What if we go over and check it out?" She went over to Miss Opal. "And if you like, I can take a piece of that wallpaper and have it framed for you! A keepsake." Her face lit up. "What do you say?"

"I say yes!" Miss Opal cheered.

Justin burst into laughter. "You will need a helmet, boots, and a respirator. It most likely has mold."

Miss Opal reached for Elisa's hand. "Justin is correct. I have the past in my heart. I know you meant well. This is not for us to decide what happens to that place."

Everyone settled on the fact that it was not wise to go in there when Delaney told Justin she heard Sally was back on Ocracoke.

"She looks fantastic with fresh paint, and the inside is clean. Now with your help, I would like to get fabric and send the seat off to the upholsterer."

"Tomorrow, I can help you out."

Miss Opal got up from the chair. "See you girls later for our goodbye soiree. And come empty-handed! I'm hosting." She insisted as she made her way down the steps and went home.

"I need to finish packing." Margo said with a clap of her hands.

Elisa moaned. "Me too. This sucks!" She dropped her shoulders and followed Margo into the cottage.

Justin wrapped his arms around Delaney. "We're all by ourselves now. Before long, it will be wonderfully quiet as your friends make their way home."

She let out a sigh as their eyes met. "I wish they could stay. I love having them here, and we have shared so many laughs."

"I know. I have enjoyed them as well. And I see Elisa found a love interest."

"I have no idea what's going on with that." She laughed to herself.

His phone buzzed in his pocket. He looked at it. "Huh, I gotta take this. See you tonight? How about a beach stroll?"

"Not sure, since this is the last full night with my friends. How about we go for a *late-night* beach stroll under the stars?"

"Sure!" he said, then placed his phone to his ear as he walked across the street.

36

Delaney was up just as the sun rose. Postponing her morning run, she was busy preparing a pot of coffee when Margo and Elisa walked into the kitchen wearing frowns.

Elisa headed to the coffeepot and poured a full cup, and sat down at the kitchen table. "I dread leaving." She tapped her cup. "Maybe I can get a job down here helping you with your windfall."

Delaney went over and put her hands on Elisa's shoulders. "If you moved here, it would be awesome. But first, let me see what is in those storage units. You told me earlier that you love being a hairstylist. I know I'll miss both of you. It has been such a blast being together again. How about we plan the holidays here?"

A frown creased Margo's face as she crossed her arms and then spoke. "Not if my fiancé has his say. He has been complaining nonstop since I left." She reached for a mug, filling it with coffee.

Elisa spoke in a flat tone. "The heck with him."

Margo settled into a chair. "There is so much I want to tell you, girls, but I cannot go there now. He is not the person I said I would marry. I'm considering my options."

Delaney could not believe what she had just heard. "You are still on vacation time. Surely it will be fine once you are back in a routine. And I need to get back to work too!"

Elisa added sugar to her coffee and spoke as she stirred it. "You have dreamy Justin across the street. I mean, he is totally in love with you! And you know how we will miss his morning donut run."

Delaney's face warmed as she walked over to Elisa. "Stop it. We are friends. But he has a knack for picking out the best donuts!"

Elisa laughed. "Friends with sweet benefits?"

Margo gave a shake of her head as she sat back, looking out the window at Miss Opal's place and to Delaney. "You are too much. Leave them alone, but I admit he looks at you with those dreamy eyes. He is in love for sure, but the burning question is, are you in love with him?"

Shrugging her shoulders and adding a schoolgirl smile, she said yes.

"I knew it!" Margo cried out. "He is a keeper."

Elisa leaned back. "As usual, I find myself single."

"Get out the violins!" Margo teased her as she tapped Elisa's arm. "You will find the perfect soulmate soon. What is your rush?"

"No rush, and speaking of rush, we better get going to avoid the traffic and catch the ferry. We have a long journey home."

Margo finished her coffee and put the mug in the sink. "We are staying at a hotel in Maryland. A long two days ahead of us." She walked over to Delaney and gave her what felt like an endless hug. "I'm gonna miss you. Thank you so much for letting me stay here. And I'll return for the holidays! I love you." She kissed her cheek.

Elisa joined them in their goodbyes.

Delaney walked them out to the car when Justin jogged over.

"I wanted to say goodbye and thanks for being so kind to my aunt. She is sitting in the kitchen with tears in her eyes and told me she had not had that much fun in years! Thanks so much." He kissed Elisa and Margo on their cheeks. "Safe travels." He faced Delaney. "If you are up for it, Katydid and I would enjoy joining you for your morning jog!"

Delaney threw her hands up in the air. "Why not!"

"Great. I'll be over in a few minutes. Let me get Katydid," he sprinted to Miss Opal's place.

Elisa spoke in a low voice. "I told you he is in love, and so are you!" She blew a kiss to Delaney. "I love you too." She got into the car.

Margo embraced Delaney. "Thank you once more; I adore you and your charming dollhouse gypsy cottage and make sure to visit me when you are in New York. Lunch and dinner are my treat. I'm also eager to try Miss Opal's cookie recipes!" She planted a kiss on Delaney's cheek. "Goodbye." With that, she climbed into the driver's seat and shut the door.

The car backed out and vanished down the street. Delaney held her hand over her heart and let a few tears trickle down her cheeks. Inhaling the morning sea mist, she wiped her cheeks and went inside to put her hair up when Justin called out.

"I'm here!"

"Be there in a sec."

Katydid darted into the cottage and up to Delaney, covering her with puppy kisses, with Justin not far behind.

"Do you think I should stop over at Miss Opal's to make sure she is okay?"

Justin glanced across the street and at Delaney. "Maybe later. She loves you, your friends, and entertaining them. I feel she needs some alone time. She was up most of the night going through photo albums."

Delaney pulled her lips in and out.

"What's wrong?" He asked as he moved closer to her.

"The reality is sinking in how much I'll miss my friends. But they live up north, and I live here. And I need to get back to work. I nearly forgot. I'm leaving in three days for New York to check out the storage units I inherited."

"Huh?"

"Come on, time for our jog, and I'll tell you all about it."

Justin tried to keep up with Delaney. She knew he was having a difficult time, and after the first half-mile, they slowed the pace to a walk. Katydid had no problem keeping pace. They found a coffee shop by the water and sat outside.

"How about an iced coffee?" Justin asked as he wiped the sweat off his brow. "I need something cool."

Delaney was petting Katydid. "Sure, and can you get some water for your puppy! She looks like she is gonna pass out."

He glanced around and pointed at a tree. "Over there is a water bowl under the tree."

Delaney spotted the bowl and took Katydid over to it. In no time, she emptied it.

Justin returned with two iced coffees and a cup of ice for Katydid.

Sipping her iced coffee, Delaney sat back and watched a stray cat run across the road.

Justin could tell she was in a somber mood and asked if she was okay.

She faced him, adding a pout while fiddling with her straw and ice cubes. "I miss my friends. We grew up together, and they are sisters to me."

He took her hand in his. "Aunt Opal misses them also, and I get it. I miss my friends too. But I would rather be here than back home. I gotta ask you, where did you learn to run like you do?"

She placed her cup on the table. "I ran track in high school and college and loved it."

Katydid settled down at Delaney's feet.

Justin watched a group of people pull up in a golf cart and go inside the coffee shop. "Nice day ahead. I have work to do inside, and then I plan to spend a few hours kayaking. If you are free, I would enjoy it if you could go with me."

How could she say no to that smile? "Sure would love to."

"Great. I'll text you."

"We can launch from my backyard. But I have work to do first as well. And book my flight to New York to find out what is in the storage units." She tipped her cup over her mouth and crunched on the last of her ice cubes. "Going up to New York is not something I care to do. I have orders to fill and clients to talk to."

Justin stood up and touched his toes. "Ouch. Wow, I thought I was I better shape!" He stood up with his hands behind his head, twisting his body from side to side, then suggested. "Why not have one of your friends open the storage units, film it for you, and then you can decide? Where are you going to put three storage units of stuff down here?"

She took a breath and released it. "That is a perfect idea. I was not in the mindset to head up there." The actual reason was that she did not want Hunter to find out she was in New York. Although he said he was heading to Europe to heal, she knew him all too well. He loved to bloat with fake news.

"Just a thought." He extended his hand to her. "I need to head back and get to work. Calls to make." He questioned if Hunter had anything to do with her not wanting to head to New York.

She got up and reached for Katydid's leash. "I'll ask Elisa if she could run over to the units. They are in the town next to where she lives. I can send her the keys." With a perky smile, she kissed his cheek. "Love your idea!"

Her use of the word *"love"* surprised him. Or is that what women say when they love an idea or when they love someone?

37

Elisa was more than happy to open the storage units and film it live. For sure, it would be an arduous task, and she was up for it. Delaney wanted to pay her, but she declined and instead insisted on visiting Ocracoke for the holidays.

Delaney was getting into her golf cart to head into the village for groceries when she spotted a truck with a real estate logo on it parked next door. She noticed a man digging a hole in front of the neighboring cottage. She approached the dilapidated fence, garlanded with blooming pink tea roses, and moved closer to the man to say hello.

He stopped digging as his stare met hers. "Afternoon, ma'am."

"Hi, are you selling the cottage?"

"Nope, but this here real estate company is." He reached into his truck and removed a large white sign. Her heart sunk. They were selling the cottage. At least they were not tearing it down. What if a new buyer did? Her peace and quiet would be gone and filled with the harsh sounds of hammers and workers.

With a frown, she thanked the man and at a quick pace went across the street to Miss Opal's and knocked on the side door.

It opened.

"Delaney, I have my shopping list." Miss Opal had a piece of paper in hand.

She had forgotten that earlier she had told Miss Opal she would do a little grocery shopping for her. Being busy for well over an hour with Elisa as she toured the storage units, her mind was elsewhere.

"Oh, geez, yes, the shopping list."

"Step in." Miss Opal gestured as she moved aside. "Now I need 1% milk, not whole, and the bread. I need whole grain, not white." She was rambling on when Delaney stopped her.

"Miss Opal, the cottage next to me. Your sister's place is going on the market! It's for sale!" she reached for Miss Opal's hand. "Follow me." She led her onto the side porch and pointed at the man who was attaching the sign to the post.

Miss Opal squinted. "Well, darn it. Those two-faced people are selling my past!" In a loud, hurried voice, she called out for Justin, who was upstairs working.

He came downstairs and onto the side porch. Alarmed, he asked. "What is wrong?" His face calmed when he saw Delaney and moved over to her side.

"Look across the street!" Miss Opal was red in the face, and she aimed her chin toward the man and the real estate sign.

He walked to the edge of the porch and watched the man get into his truck and drive off. "That is too bad. Sorry, Aunt Opal." He checked his watch and spoke to Delaney. "In about two hours, I'll be ready for kayaking."

Her face flooded with frustration as she met him. "Does it bother you that the cottage is being sold?" She pushed her hair behind her ears. "That was your aunt and uncle's place at one time."

He shook his head as he glanced at Miss Opal and back across the street. "*At one time* are keywords. The property has been out of our family for decades, and look at it. Looks as if it's about to collapse."

Delaney huffed as she looked over at the *for-sale* sign. "Ugh. Well, it's still sad for me. I know the overgrown yard is a mess, but so was my place at one time."

With no emotion, Justin suggested she buy it.

"With what? Seashells? Honestly." She moved away from him and rested her back against the house.

Miss Opal sensed the high emotions that were going nowhere and handed Delaney her grocery list. "

"How about you go to the village and get some shopping done?" She went into the kitchen while Justin and Delaney were silent. She returned to the porch. "Here you go. A ten-dollar bill and get yourself a cool smoothie and calm down. Honey, it's just a cottage that gave me wonderful memories. Maybe a new family will fix it up and bring fresh memories and life to it." She said as she ran her hand over Delaney's cheek.

"Or they tear it down and build an ugly house!"

Justin tapped the porch rails, and he turned to Delaney. "How about I join you for that smoothie?" His eyes calmed her. "I can put my work off until later."

With her lips twisted and arms crossed, she agreed.

As they drove to the village, Justin asked Delaney to pull over.

"I apologize if I sounded insensitive earlier."

"I get it." She said as she dropped her head.

"No, you do not *get it*. I was incorrect in being callous. Yes, it's unfortunate that the cottage next to yours is being sold. I bet it was once a beautiful place, filled with life and love."

She moved her eyes toward him. "This has been a tough day for me. Seeing the man putting the sign up was my tipping point."

Justin placed his comforting hand in hers. "How did it go with Elisa and the storage units?"

After laughing, she leaned over and rested her head on his shoulder, letting out a long moan. "There are years and years of patterns and fabrics she never used. I'm not sure what to do with them since, as per the attorney's phone call last night, I *will* have to pay for those storage units beginning next month!"

"That sounds expensive. What will you do?" Justin ran his hand through her hair. "I certainly don't know about the fashion industry, but if this were my decision, I would consider auctioning some of it off. Notify the competition and sell. Keep what you want."

She lifted her head. "Wow, I like that idea. It would take me three lifetimes to use what she left me, and I know what is in there is most likely worth a pretty penny."

"I'm here for you, neighbor!" he winked.

"Thank you, and how about we get the ten-dollar smoothie?"

They drove off. Justin had news to break to her. Now was not the time.

Justin brought Miss Opal's groceries inside her home, and then he went over to help Delaney bring hers into her kitchen.

Delaney placed a few groceries on the kitchen counter. "How about you share dinner with me? Chicken burgers on the grill and an arugula salad with watermelon are on the menu."

He rubbed his chin.

"I bet you want juicy beef burgers and thick fries!" She walked up to him and wrapped her arms around his waist.

"You are getting to know me, and whatever you make is fine with me." He pulled her closer, gazing into her eyes. "I'm not a man of words like your Uncle Bo had. His Valentine's letter to my aunt is magical. I mean, how did he do it?"

Delaney ran her finger over his bottom lip, and then she tapped the tip of his nose. "He was in love. That is how."

Justin swept her hair past her shoulders. "Wow, do I need to write a letter like that to let you know how I feel?" He felt his face flush.

"A letter?" She tilted her head, realizing what he was trying to say. "You mean a *love* letter?"

"Geez, I stink at this."

"Stink at what?" She knew what he wanted to say and waited.

Feeling his face warm, he needed to escape what he wanted to say. He lifted his wrist. "Hey look, it's four, and I need to get back to work on my laptop. What time is dinner? I'll bring the wine and beer."

Delaney sensed he was nervous and let it go. "How about stopping over around seven? And you can start the grill. The charcoal is in the garage if you wouldn't mind bringing it with you?"

He felt a lump grow in his throat, feeling like a fool. Standing in front of him was Delaney, and he was falling in love. How could he express how he felt since they have only known each other for a few weeks, but in his heart, it was a lifetime? She is the one. But of all times, this was not good.

He took her hand in his. "Delaney—"

"Yes?"

"See you at seven with charcoal in hand." He stepped back and left her cottage.

She watched him cross the street, wondering what was going on when her phone rang.

"Hey Elisa,"

"Are you sitting down?"

Delaney began unpacking her groceries. "I'm in the kitchen."

"David broke off the engagement to Margo. This is on the hush, and I'm not supposed to tell you, but I had to."

"What?" She looked at her phone and put it on speaker. "Are you serious?"

"Yes, remember when we suggested that he find an intern to cover for Margo when we added a week to our vacation?"

"Ah, huh?"

"Well. Guess what?"

Delaney was rolling the watermelon around on the countertop and stopped. "No, he fell in love with her?" She put her hand on her cheek. "Is Margo okay? I should call her."

"Not just yet. But here is the kicker. He had been seeing her for months, the sneaky rat!"

"Holy crap!"

"Yup. I just learned this, so please not a word. I just got off the phone with her. And she's not upset, and I got a sense of relief. I knew he was no good and never trusted him with those wandering hands. He hit on me twice."

"Wow, well, I guess the wedding's off. And what about the restaurant? His father owns it. She will need our support." Delaney always knew her fiancé was not the one. He was a player and a flirt. Even though she knew it was hurtful for her friend, she too was glad they broke it off.

"I have a client coming in. I'll call you tonight."

Delaney paced. "Wait. Justin is coming over for a cookout. Can we talk late tonight or tomorrow when you are free?"

"A cookout. I miss you and Ocracoke." She let out a long sigh. "The ocean, the sun, the fun, and Miss Opal, and I cannot forget Justin's morning coffee and donuts. One more thing. The way he looks at you!"

Delaney was silent as a smile lit her face.

"Hello?"

"I'm here."

"I sent Miss Opal a thank-you card the other day. I love her!"

Delaney agreed. "She is one of a kind."

"My client just walked in for a total hair and face makeover. Gotta run and do not reveal a word and let Margo tell you."

"Got it, and I love you!"

"Love you too." Delaney hung up. Her mind was swirling as she opened the fridge to put away a few groceries. They seemed to have bad luck with relationships. First she, and Hunter and his drama, and now Margo. Then Elisa finds a guy who lives too far away. Maybe they are destined to live as three spinsters together! She laughed to herself at the thought of changing the welcome sign from *Sea Gypsy* to *The Three Sea Spinsters*!

38

Justin lit the charcoal in the grill and stared out over the water. Delaney met him wearing the sunniest smile as she handed him the burgers.

"These look so good!"

"I hope you like them since they are chicken."

He placed them on the grill when Delaney's phone rang.

"Ut—oh." She muttered and told Justin it was Margo and she had to take it. With her back to him, she walked down to the sandy shore.

"Delaney, my fiancé is an ass. The wedding is off, and I know Elisa told you. She confessed to me, and that is why I had to call you."

"Are you all right?"

"Yes. I caught the idiot in the back office of the restaurant. He was well—taking care of her. I knew it, but I had no proof."

Delaney turned to wave at Justin and spoke in a quiet voice. "There are no words for me to say. My concern is how you are handling this?"

Justin glanced over at Delaney and then reached for his mug of beer.

"His father is livid, and the intern — or his little *slutlet* was fired. His father wants me to run the bakery and loves my Miss Opal cookies. I can do that until I can land on my feet elsewhere. As for the idiot, his father has him far from me."

"Margo, this is for the best. I hate to say it, but what if you married him and he behaved this way?"

"I know. Hey, enough of my drama. How are Ocracoke and Justin? I miss you and Miss Opal. And kayaking and, mostly, the golf cart rides to the village. The humidity and heat here in the city, with no relief, are unbearable."

Delaney wanted to share how much fun she was having and that Justin was over. How could she when her best friend had just broken off her engagement? She skirted around the subject and spoke about what Elisa had filmed in the storage units until Justin let her know the burgers were done.

She hung up and made her way to Justin.

"Is everything okay? You look tense."

Waving her hands around, she told him all was good, and they went inside to enjoy dinner. After they ate, he took her hand and led her onto the front porch.

"What a gorgeous night, and I thought we could sit out here on the swing for a little while," Justin said as he gave the swing a gentle push. "It's in excellent shape, and you did one bang out job getting it cleaned up. Aunt Opal told me a love story about her, Bo, and this swing. They planned their life and dreams on it."

Delaney went over to it and ran her finger over the heart. "Uncle Bo made this for Miss Opal from a piece of wood they found out back that had washed up onto the shore. Miss Opal told me it was once pink, so I had to bring it back to its original color. Pink is the color of inner power, affection, romance, and innocence."

"Let's sit and enjoy it." Justin let Delaney settle in first, and then he joined her."

Delaney sat close to him and added. "Pink is a soft color that carries a calming aspect, and I love it!"

Facing her, he put his hand under her chin. "You know what I love?"

"Pink?" she poked his chest.

"You!"

Delaney pulled away and could not believe what she had heard. Did he say what she thought he said? He did. Her words fell from her lips. "Justin." She held his hand firmly. Her gaze was unwavering and remained locked on his.

"This is too soon. Is that what you are thinking?" He felt a twinge in his stomach. Did he just blow it with the best woman he had ever met?

Delaney's kind eyes sought his as she spoke. "I wanted to tell you earlier today that I, too, am falling in love with you."

He caressed her neck and played with her hair, and stopped. "I too have been falling in love with you. Love is a word I take to heart and rarely, if ever, say."

Dusk had descended, and a flurry of fireflies danced around the porch. Delaney told Justin it was a sign of good luck. As the swing swayed and the fireflies danced, Delaney suggested they go inside.

Delaney awoke to find her bed empty. Sitting up, she pondered Justin's whereabouts. After stretching, she glanced at her phone and saw his message: he had gone out for donuts and coffee, inviting her to join him on the swing once she was awake. Wrapping her arms around the pillow he had used, she embraced it, feeling a bliss she had not experienced in years. He filled her heart with joy. Setting the pillow back on the bed, she got up and got dressed, and went outside to find Justin on the porch swing. His smile was brighter than the morning sun as he got up to meet her.

"Breakfast is served!" he aimed his hand at the side table.

"Wow, thanks."

"And I got your carrot juice. Well, I found it in the fridge." He picked up the glass on the porch railing. "And I almost forgot." He kissed her lips. "Hello sunshine!"

Gazing around, still sleepy, she thanked him as they sat on the swing.

"Delaney, I have something to tell you. There is no perfect time, so I need to mention it now." His face tensed as he continued. "I have to leave the country for work."

She stopped the swing. Her eyes widened. "What? Leave the country?"

He let out a sigh. "I'm a freelancer for my former company and stayed on for a decent salary if I consult. And they need me in London."

She pushed her head back and squeaked out. "London?"

"Yeah. It will be for a few months to help them get the new offices set up. Then I'll come back. Aunt Opal is not too happy since I was about to start the work on her place."

Delaney wanted to cry. How could this be happening? London? Long-distance relationships never work. Why bother telling her he loves her, then he leaves? Was it to get her into bed? Ewe, she was upset. Yup, the spinster sign is going up over the front door.

"Why not tell me before I invited you into my bed?" Her mood switched from melancholy to angry. "You need to leave now." She went to get up when he pulled her down.

"Please, you are being irrational. This is only for a few months, and it's no big deal. We can chat every day. This is not forever, and I'll be back in late January when my contract with them is over."

"Katydid, you naughty dog! Get back here!" Miss Opal called out.

The puppy dashed across the street and flew onto Justin's lap, knocking over his coffee. He shot up off the swing, as did Delaney.

Miss Opal was across the street clapping her hands for the puppy when Justin picked her up and turned to Delaney. "Let me take her home. Can we talk about this?"

Delaney's lips were tight as she shook her head.

"Is that a yes or no?"

She got up and went inside, slamming the door behind her.

Cradling Katydid in his arms and feeling a wave of sadness, he made his way to Miss Opal's house. She, too, was disheartened by the news, as she had been looking forward to the start of the repairs on her home and enjoyed his presence.

39

Justin sent Delaney several text messages, which she ignored. How could he do that to her? Why was he not honest earlier that evening?

There was a knock on the door. Then a few taps on her front window. With her arms crossed, she walked over to the window.

"Delaney, I cannot leave Ocracoke until we talk."

She looked away, pulled her lips in and out, then walked over to the front door and opened it.

"I guess you will not leave me alone, so tell me what is there to talk about? You need to go to London."

He let out a loud sigh as he ran his hands through his hair. Glancing over his shoulder and back to Delaney, he explained that he had just learned about the trip and was not sure when to tell her.

With her arms still crossed, standing at the threshold, she looked away and then back at him. "Why wait. I trusted you were not like the others."

"Shit, Delaney, I'm not like these others you knew or know. I have to work. This is temporary. I love you!"

She let her arms drop to her sides as she twisted her lips. Her eyes landed on his once swollen hand. Which did not go unnoticed by him.

"I still have a sore hand! If you recall what happened when I went to defend you! I doubt your ex will return."

Delaney's mood was sliding to a calmer demeanor. "I guess not." She stepped back. "Come on inside."

He did.

"We need to go out on the back porch to talk," Delaney led the way.

They settled on the outdoor sofa as the cicadas' chitchat filled the warm air.

Delaney waited a moment in silence and then faced him. "I'm still upset and not sure why, since we have only known each other a short time. I mean, we rushed into something that is most likely nothing." She pulled her knees to her chest. "Am I wrong?"

"Absolutely wrong. One hundred percent wrong. I came here to heal my heart and help my aunt, having no intention of meeting a terrific, talented woman and fall in love." He leaned toward her, pulling a few strands of her hair forward. "I'll return in a few months, and we can pick up where we left off."

Taken aback by what he said, she knew she was acting foolishly. *He punched Hunter in the nose*. How many men would do that for her? She dropped her head onto her knees and then looked up at him. "I have a lot going on, and I do not have the best track record with love and men. You are different, and I'm scared you are not who I think you are."

He reached for her fingers. "I'm who you see. No one else. There is not much I can do or say, but I must go to London. Aunt Opal is upset with me as well. So much so that she did not leave me any dinner last night!"

Delaney found a minor smile and teased. "No dinner, huh? That is bad!"

"Yeah, it was. She sent me to bed with no dinner!" He moved closer to her.

She leaned her head on his shoulder. "You better not find a hot English woman over there!"

"Ah no. I'll be working non-stop and anxious to get back home to you and Ocracoke."

"What about Katydid?"

"I was gonna ask you if you could take care of her. I'll pay for her food and whatever you need."

She ran her hand over his thigh. "Sure."

"Aunt Opal agreed to take her at night if you could take her during the day. She is a good pup."

"Deal." She kissed his lips. Lips she could not live without.

♥

Later that evening, they shared dinner. Justin had to be at the airport early in the morning. Delaney had to fight with herself to keep a smile on her face and in her heart. Miss Opal and Katydid stopped over for dessert.

Miss Opal's mood and facial expressions could not be ignored as Delaney tried to smooth over the tension. Justin could not stop apologizing.

Justin glanced at his watch and said it was time he headed back to Miss Opal's and pack his bags. He had to be at the Raleigh airport by ten, and a long drive was ahead of him.

Miss Opal took the lead and left first with Katydid, whom she had become fond of, and spoke to the pup as if she were a child. Not forgetting all the treats, she fed her!

Holding hands, Justin and Delaney stood on her front porch.

"When I get to Raleigh, I'll text you."

Delaney turned away, not wanting him to see her watery eyes.

"Hey,"

She faced him as she wiped her tears. "You had better go now so I can go cry on my pillow."

He pulled her into an endless embrace and whispered in her ear. "I love you. Wait for me."

She traced his face and lips with her finger. "I love you too, and text or call me."

He let her go and walked across the street. She leaned against a column on the porch and watched him fade into the night.

Her phone buzzed. She took it out of her pocket to find a text from Margo.

40

Delaney kept busy with her work and moving many of the items from storage in New York to her place. The guest bedroom housed bolts of fabric, piles of patterns, and a few mannequins. She took Justin's advice and, after much research, was entertaining selling the contents she left behind to up-and-coming design houses. All the interest in the items was surprising to her.

Knowing she would have the extra funds coming in from the sale enabled her to get estimates on a new roof for the back porch. It was very uplifting since she had to keep her mind off Justin. She had placed a large calendar on the wall behind her desk and crossed off days as they ended. Justin, as promised, video chatted and texted daily. In her heart, Delaney knew she could trust him, and he loves her. And the funny thing is, after the breakup with Hunter, she promised never to love again, and here she was head over heels.

Whispers in social circles were that Hunter had moved to France, preparing to marry into a family that had managed a vineyard for three generations. She also learned that his mother had left him with minimal assets, compelling him to sell the beach house in the Hamptons. The understanding that he was now permanently out of her life filled her with relief. From time to time, the thought of Justin landing a punch on Hunter's nose would bring a smile to her face.

Mid-November had arrived, bringing with it a chill that lingered in the Ocracoke air. The summer crowds were long gone, and the streets were quiet once again. Thanksgiving was not far away, and Delaney planned on heading to Florida to spend time with her parents.

Margo and Elisa made plans to come down to Ocracoke for Christmas into the New Year. Why not? Margo had left the restaurant and was selling Miss Opal's cookies online with enormous success. She was so thrilled to see Miss Opal and tell her!

Elisa was busy at her salon and stayed in touch with Sam from Ohio. Even better was that his family was planning on staying on Ocracoke for the holidays.

Every morning around seven, Miss Opal walked Katydid across the street to spend the day with Delaney. She was growing into a sweet, loving and now semi-obedient dog thanks to Delaney's daily training class. She loved Katydid and her sloppy puppy kisses! Even her stray Lollie Cat liked to rub up against Katydid and follow her around the yard.

Miss Opal showed up at Delaney's cottage one morning with Katydid. In her hand was a basket of homemade dog cookies.

"Hi Miss Opal," Delaney said as Katydid squeezed past her to greet Opal and sniff the basket.

"Here you go." She handed Katydid a cookie and looked at Delaney. "I made her peanut butter cookies. She loves them, and I thought that you may want a basket of them! The human version!" She handed it to Delaney.

"Thanks!" She placed the basket on a side table and stepped out onto the porch. "Do you want to sit down? It's so nice outside!"

"Sure, my feet are sore today!" Miss Opal said as she made her way to the swing. "Do you mind if I sit here?"

"Nope," Delaney sat down next to her. "Would you like a blanket for your lap?"

"Yes."

Delaney reached into a basket and grabbed one. She placed it on Miss Opal's lap.

"Ah, this brings back memories, and lovely ones at that. I miss Bo."

Delaney ran her hand over Miss Opal's arm. "I understand. And I admit, I miss Justin. Seven weeks to go and I worry about him being so far from home. It has been difficult for me to focus on my work. I cannot believe how much I think about him, and I wonder if he feels the same."

Miss Opal tenderly patted Delaney's hand. "Honey, worrying is like a rocking chair. It gives you something to do, but you ain't going anywhere. You gotta get up and keep moving, or the mind wanders." She stopped as her lips curled and she spoke with fondness. "I returned to Ocracoke after my husband passed away to find myself alone in the empty house, only to hear the halls echo with my footsteps and remembrances. I too was sitting in that rocking chair, and then I realized I needed to get up and feel alive again. Not long after my heart was back with Bo, I realized I had made a big mistake. I should have married Bo, but I waited too long over a career and someone I thought I loved."

Delaney wore a warm smile at her, knowing she had never spoken of her uncle this way and the deep love they had shared.

Miss Opal ran her hand over the warn wood of the swing and continued. "My heart is at home now with Bo, and it always will be. I spent several beautiful years with the man I love. And I wanted you to know that life is short. I sat in that rocking chair far too long. I do not want to see you repeat what I did. We are here for a brief time, and we must find joy and comfort. To find your soul love is to be treasured."

Delaney took every word to heart. "Thank you for sharing this with me. I know my Uncle Bo loved you. The card and letter he left you are beautiful. And the opal ring. It breaks my heart that he never gave it to you."

Miss Opal's eyes were teary, and she turned to Delaney. "Once you find the one, do not let him go! And for heaven's sake, please do not wear one of Dottie's ruffle dresses for him!" She burst into laughter, as did Delaney.

"Ah, thanks for the warning."

"I best get back home to put another batch of cookies in the oven for Katydid. I love that little rascal. She keeps me company at night and has eaten two pairs of old shoes."

"Oh, no! Speaking of her, I left her in the cottage!" Delaney got off the swing and dashed inside to find Katydid had helped herself to the bag of cookies and was licking up the crumbs.

Miss Opal met Delaney. "Good Lord she had gone gobbled all the cookies and chewed part of the basket, that little varmint!"

After they cleaned up the mess, Miss Opal went home, leaving Delaney with the dog and her bloated belly! She took her out for a walk down the street when the same man who had put up the for-sale sign next door was taking it down. Curious, she walked up to him and asked if it was sold.

He tossed the post into his pickup truck. "Sure was. I guess ya got new neighbors coming soon."

Her face fell as her heart added a few beats. She looked around and back at the man. "Too bad. I hope they fix it up and not tear it down."

"No idea, miss, but you have a nice day." He got into his truck and drove off, leaving Delaney deflated. Trying to find positivity in the sale, she resumed her walk deep in thought when she found herself back home. With two new clients, she needed to get back to work. She was getting anxious since her afternoon calls to Justin and texts were going unanswered.

At last, just after midnight, he informed her that he had a hectic day ahead. He was also counting down the weeks until he could return to Ocracoke and be by her side.

The following morning Delaney woke up to a slight wind and cool air. She realized she had left her windows open since the day before it had been so warm. Sliding into her slippers and robe. She headed downstairs. It was too cold for carrot juice. Aside from that, it reminded her of the day she spilled it on Justin's car. But first, she walked into her office and marked off another day on the calendar. She needed something warm and opened the coffee can when she heard Katydid barking at the front door. Worried that something had happened to Miss Opal, she sprinted to the door and opened it to find Katydid and Lollie Cat looking up at her. She said good morning to Katydid and knelt to pet the cat when she heard a sharp whistle and turned around to see Katydid dash off the porch.

There, standing under the arbor, was Justin! In disbelief and heart beating, she ran down the front porch stairs and jumped into his arms. With her legs wrapped around his waist and her lips found his.

"You brat! You are home two months early!" She cried out. "Is this why you were not answering me yesterday?"

He spun her around. "Yup. I was on the flight home. The job is over early."

"I missed you!"

"It feels good to be back on Ocracoke and with you. And I left something for you on your porch."

He embraced her and suggested they go up on the porch and have their coffee and donuts that he hid behind a side table. "I had a hard time finding carrot juice." He teased.

"Coffee goes better with donuts." She slid off his body and, hand in hand, they went onto the front porch with Katydid trotting behind them.

Lollie Cat was sitting on the swing with a small red box near her.

Justin picked up a coffee cup as his curious eyes narrowed onto the box. "Hmm, I wonder what that is?"

Delaney had a puzzled look on her face as she tapped her cheek. "Should I open it? Did Santa arrive early? English tea?"

"I think you should open it and stop guessing." His smile was brighter than the Ocracoke sun. "Let's sit on the swing."

Lollie Cat jumped off as they sat together as the swing swayed. With the box in hand, she gave it a shake. "Is it fragile?"

"Depends," he sipped his coffee. "I know my heart is."

"Hmmm." She opened it and gasped. Gazing up at her was the opal ring that Uncle Bo had given to Miss Opal. "Justin, I—wow. Are you?"

He put his coffee down, removed the ring from the familiar white box, and held it up to the rising sun as he stood up. "Yes, Delaney, will you marry me? I have known you for a short time, but it feels like a lifetime. You have been all I have thought about since the day you spilled carrot juice on my car."

She slapped her hands over her heart and got off the swing to face him.

Katydid barked and pawed at her leg.

"Oh, my gosh." Her body trembled as she covered her mouth with her hand.

"Will you?" Justin asked as his eyes shone brighter than the opal ring. "Be my forever neighbor and wife?" His brilliant smile echoed his love for her. "I mean, we can be forever together, but not as neighbors. You know what I mean."

"Yes!" She curled her toes in her slippers. "Yes!"

She extended her trembling finger as he gently placed it on. He kissed her hand. "I love you, Delaney, and your cozy cottage."

Her voice was shaky. "I'm so in love with you, Justin."

He walked over and reached into a basket and draped a blanket over her shoulders.

"Is this a dream?" She kept her eyes fixed on the ring, mesmerized by its shifting colors. Pulling him close, she asked. "Is Miss Opal aware that you are giving me her ring? I mean, it's special." She realized that was why Miss Opal had stopped over the day before and told her about her love for Uncle Bo. She was letting go of the ring and recalled what she had said. *Once you find the one, never let him go!*

"No dream, and Aunt Opal is over the moon with joy. And I know you need more space, so heck, I thought you may need this." He reached into his coat pocket and handed her a set of keys.

"Huh?" she squinted at them.

"I know how distraught you were about the cottage next door being for sale, so I'm the new owner. It needs a heck of a lot of work, but we can do it together, and you can grow your business. I know you need a workroom and some help sooner than later, so bought it! Plus, Aunt Opal is happy since it was her sister's place!"

"Miss Opal is so good at keeping secrets. Thank you, Justin." Overjoyed by the ring and cottage next door, she burst into tears as she wrapped her arms around his neck while Katydid barked.

Justin swooped her into his arms and walked over to the edge of the porch by the stairs.

Delaney's eyes widened as they landed across the street. "You did not? How? When?"

"I did, and never you mind." He kissed the tip of her nose.

To her surprise, Miss Opal, Elisa, and Margo were standing on Miss Opal's front porch, waving when he called out, "She said yes!"

The End

About the Author

Diana loved telling stories even in childhood (much to my parents' disapproval) A few years back, she came upon an abandoned antebellum mansion in North Carolina and began writing. The walls begged me to tell their twisted tale. The Eastport series (previously known as DuBois Manor) received five stars. It will be re-released.

You will find a pinch of the paranormal, mystery, and romance in her stories

Living on the eastern shores of North Carolina, what better place to create beachside romance with a little humor? Diana is also an accomplished, trained artist and former owner of an interior design retail store. She has taught art and volunteered for the annual Labor Day Parade and the Holiday Festival committees in Connecticut for many years.

"Stories are everywhere, and using my vivid imagination, I can weave them into my stories. I hope you enjoy this book and all the others I'm writing. It's my passion to take you away with my characters and settings."

DianaBaxternovels.com for more information and new releases

Available books:

Beach Heart Cottage – Book 1
Sea Glass Retreat – Book 2
A Hatteras Kiss – Book 3
The Mosaic Mermaid
You Left Me Once
Sapphire Moon

www.ingramcontent.com/pod-product-compliance
Lightning Source LLC
Chambersburg PA
CBHW070241130726
48053CB00023B/213

* 9 7 9 8 9 8 8 8 5 0 0 8 3 *